THE COURTSHIP OF
UTOPIA MINER

GOLD RUSH SERIES

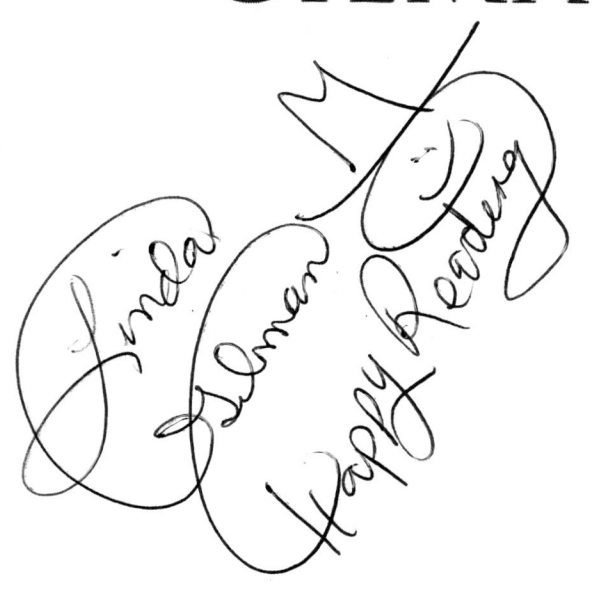

LINDA GILMAN

Linda Gilman
Happy Reading

Copyright © 2015 Linda Gilman

ISBN No. 978-151-7538941
ISBN No. 1517538947

All rights reserved under International and Pan-American Copyright Conventions

By payment of required fees, you have been granted the *non*-exclusive, *non*-transferable right to access and read the text of this book. No part of this text may be reproduced, transmitted, downloaded, decompiled, reverse engineered, or stored in or introduced into any information storage and retrieval system, in any form or by any means, whether electronic or mechanical, now known or hereinafter invented without the express written permission of copyright owner.

Please Note

The reverse engineering, uploading, and/or distributing of this book via the internet or via any other means without the permission of the copyright owner is illegal and punishable by law. Please purchase only authorized electronic editions, and do not participate in or encourage electronic piracy of copyrighted materials. Your support of the author's rights is appreciated.

No part of this book may be reproduced or transmitted in any form or by any electronic or mechanical means, including photocopying, recording or by any information storage and retrieval system, without the written permission of the publisher, except where permitted by law.

Cover Design and Interior format by The Killion Group http://thekilliongroupinc.com

DEDICATION

It isn't often one gets to publically thank some great friends for all their support. I wish to acknowledge my three great critique partners; Claudia Shelton, Suzie T. Roos and Michelle Sharp. Their weekly comments helped to bring this book to print. A writer couldn't wish for anything more helpful than this trio of fun and brilliantly talented gals.

Many thanks go out to my dear friends at Missouri Romance Writers of America (MORWA). This organization's support has nurtured my career for over twenty years, keeping me writing even in my darkest days when I had many doubts about ever completing a manuscript.

I also wish to dedicate this book to my parents. They instilled in me a love of the west, taking me on wonderful summer vacations westward to Wyoming and beyond, vivid adventures that I remember to this day. Although both mother and father are gone from me now, the memories of them are cherished forever.

THE COURTSHIP OF UTOPIA MINER by Linda Gilman is a humorous, sexy, playful, and slightly suspenseful story about chasing your dreams, falling in love, and taking risks to find true happiness. What happens when a spunky young woman in a gold rush town wants to learn how to be a saloon girl? You teach her how to kiss and hope to God one of her three fathers doesn't kill you for it!

CHAPTER ONE

Bound to Be Lucky Mining Camp
Rocky Mountains of Colorado
April 30, 1875

Lancelot Jones adjusted the brown felt derby on his head. He inhaled a deep breath and gave the door of the rustic cabin three solid knocks. The door opened and a deluge of water flooded him from head to toe. "For the love of . . ." He swiped soap suds off his face and pulled together a civil response for the person who'd tossed the unexpected shower.

A lady wearing damp long underwear and dripping red hair stood before him. Her wash-bucket dropped to the porch with a loud clank. She gasped. "Oh, my stars. I wasn't expecting a body would be standing in the way of tossing out my wash water."

"That's all right, miss." His head tipped downward. Water poured off his hat brim in a long stream, drenching the tips of his boots. "I'd been pondering a good cooling off after riding most of the morning. I'd say that you've quickly dispatched a cure for such thoughts."

Her emerald green eyes squinted at him.

"You're one of them long-winded sorts, aren't you?"

"I beg your pardon?"

"What's your business in these parts, mister?"

"Well I . . ." Lance rubbed his fists at the burn of lye soap in his eyes. When the sting dissipated enough to see, a second unexpected event confronted him. The lady's breasts were displayed in fine, round proportions through her soaked garment. "Well, I . . . I . . ."

Any red-blooded male would naturally be tongue-tied by such a sight. He couldn't help that his gaze hovered in the wrong place far too long while the gal twisted water from her lengthy hair. Suddenly, she noticed where his interest lingered.

Another gasp escaped her lips. "Oh, my stars."

Lance watched her tawny freckled complexion turn a shy pink. Her arms folded over her upper torso, and she scuttled backwards into the cabin and slammed the door.

"If you're one of them medicine peddlers, you best move on. We don't need any," she yelled through the closed barrier.

He leaned toward the door. "I can assure you, miss—I'm not a peddler."

Lance had to admit this newspaper assignment was off to a unique start. He removed his doused frock coat and draped it over his arm. Could the indecently clad redhead be the bride-to-be offered in the courtship contest he was to report on?

Based on what he'd seen so far, she was certainly worth further investigation.

He cautiously knocked a second time.

The latch raised and the door opened a crack. The barrel of a shotgun slipped out.

"Are you certain you're not selling something?"

Lance plopped his derby back on his head and quickly raised his hands high. He retreated back a step from the weapon. "No, ma'am. I'm not selling anything."

The shotgun disappeared. The gal peeked through the small gap of the doorway. Her untamed hair hung like a crinkled curtain across her face. She parted her veiled locks and smiled. "Don't you run off. You hear? I'll be out directly."

Before he could voice a reply, the lass slammed the door a second time.

Lance retrieved a small notebook from his vest pocket and flipped through several damp pages of notes. "Miss . . . I'm looking for a Jargus Knudsen. Is he around?"

"Who wants to know?" she hollered back in a distracted voice.

"I'm Lancelot Jones. I'm a repor—" He halted midsentence.

Mr. Knudsen, the father, had instructed the editor of the *Rocky Mountain Gazette* newspaper, Barris Baines, that the contest details should not be discussed with the daughter. If this girl was the young lady in question, then her father gave specific instructions to use the secret code to gain admittance to the mining camp. "Miss, this Mr.

Knudsen will want to see me. I'm here about some . . ." He checked his reporter notes for the code word. "Whiskey."

Several tin cups clanked against the interior walls before the cabin fell silent.

"Miss, is everything all right in there? Oh, miss?"

Lance put his ear to the door. He thought about using his shoulder to gain entry into the cabin when he heard a scraping noise. What on earth was she doing in there?

"I'll be out in a minute," she yelled. "Where in blazes are those dang ribbons?"

"Did you say something, miss?" He continued to press his ear to the door when he heard a tapping on glass. Shifting his body toward the sound, he glanced at the window to the right of the door. There she was grinning and vigorously rubbing a towel on her damp hair.

"I'm hurrying fast as I can. I'll be out directly." The lass flashed him a pretty smile before she vanished behind a gingham curtain hanging across the window.

This gal was a most strange creature. Never in his short journalism career, which spanned only a month, had he encountered such an intriguing girl. In fact, the visual of her damply clad chest wouldn't clear from his mind. If he'd known covering the news was so surprisingly interesting, he would have considered giving up his marshal's badge much sooner.

Lance turned his back on the cabin and walked to the edge of the porch to size up the rest of the mining camp.

Sixty yards of sparse grass separated her cabin from the other structures. Three similar shacks and a false-fronted building, all in varied stages of decay dotted the area. In truth, the entire place appeared on the verge of being a ghost town.

Toward the north, the snowy Rockies walled off the blue skyline. Aspen trees dotted the hillsides like a soft green canvas. The rushing water of a spring thaw could be heard in a creek behind the gal's cabin.

His attention drew back to the latch as it lifted. Out she stepped. The lass now wore buckskin pants, mid-calf muck boots, and a threadbare, snug fitting shirt. She finished tying a ribbon on the end of her braid then tucked her shirttail in the back of her pants. She smiled. "Sorry I made you wait. I hope you don't hold hard feelings against me for getting you all wet."

"No. Not at all."

Her hand quickly jutted out for a handshake. "Howdy. I'm Utopia Miner."

Lance returned her greeting. He recognized her name from the contest information his editor printed in the newspaper. Her grip was strong, and she cranked his arm up and down as if working a pump handle. It took him a bit of pulling to get his fingers out of her calloused hold. A quick glance gave him notice of her short nails. This girl must do a fair amount of hard work. He'd make a note of that. It could be a fact relevant to this event he'd come to cover.

If he were to guess Miss Utopia's age, based on her mannerisms, sixteen suited her. But then again, such splendid curves were of a more mature woman. He revised his assessment, aging her more toward nineteen.

"So, you mentioned you want to talk with my Pa Jargus?"

The gal's face took on an expression of what seemed to be acute worry as her fingers blindly fumbled down her shirt placard, checking that she'd secured each button. She gave a relieved sigh. He could barely compile his answer with such a distraction. "Uh . . . yes, ma'am. I need to speak with Mr. Knudsen. It's very important."

"We'll have to go looking for him. Follow me." She headed down the stairs but on the last step turned back to him. Her eyebrows arched in queried concern. "You say you only want to talk with Pa Jargus but not my other fathers?"

"I'm sorry. I don't believe I heard you correctly." Could the gal have him any more confused? He needed to have these strange facts straight for his articles. "How many . . . let me rephrase my question. Mr. Knudsen is your father, isn't he?"

Her green eyes squinted in the morning sunlight. She shielded her stare with her hand. "I don't rightly know how you come by that information, mister, but yes, Jargus Knudsen is my pa. But I also have two others. That's three fathers in all. How many you got?"

He smirked at her odd question. "Oh, I have the usual number. One."

"How about that? I guess I'm right lucky to have so many." Utopia spun around and with an elongated step she left the last porch step. Her arm waved at him. "Are you coming or not?"

Lance followed her with a million questions circling in his brain, mostly regarding the possibility of someone–anyone–claiming to have three fathers. The gal's long strides across the grassy divide drew his eyes to the sway of her buckskinned hips. Any further inquiries were consolidated down to one. "Where are we going?"

She called over her shoulder, "I have a pretty good idea where to look for my Pa."

Utopia's insides were all giddy as she walked her dandy stranger toward the whiskey barn. That was what her Fathers called the false-fronted building. In her nightly prayers, she'd all but given up on her dream of getting off this mountain. But she had to hand it to the good Lord Almighty. He'd come through in a grand way this time.

This Lance sure was a fancy dresser in his silky brown vest and tan coat. Why, the man even had a chained pocket watch to keep folks from stealing his timepiece. He had puppy dog brown eyes with feathery dark lashes. And unlike her fathers, the man had no whiskers on his tanned face. He wore his dark brown hair neatly trimmed around his ears, which were nicely sized to his head. She liked seeing a fella scrubbed clean and smelling fine as a new leather saddle.

Adding up all his handsomeness and citified trappings, she gathered this Lance was a man who'd seen places and done things. Done things she'd never been privy to. Including seeing the inside of a saloon. Lance was of real interest to her for one big reason.

He'd be her ticket to get on with her plans of learning to be a saloon girl. Once she had herself dancehall refined, she'd move her fathers and herself off this mountain once and for all.

It had taken nineteen years of waiting, but the day finally had come. Now she had a way to learn a few singing, dancing and kissing skills to move along her plans.

Utopia rolled her eyes toward heaven. *Lord, he's handsomer than a shiny new nugget. And he's just what I've been praying for. I promise. I'll take real good care of him.*

"Did you say something, miss?"

"Never no mind. I mumble sometimes." Her eyes locked with his, and for a moment the question on the tip of her tongue seemed stuck. "Uh, do you mind if I call you by your first name?"

"No. Not if you'll allow me to call you by your first name."

"It's a deal. Say Lance, why don't you tell me what brings you up this way?"

She knew full well that miracles couldn't explain themselves no matter how hard they tried. But she asked the question anyways because she liked to hear his voice and fancy talking.

"Like I said before, I have business to discuss with Jargus Knudsen."

"What might that be?" Heaven sent or not, a miracle man wanting a visit with her Pa Jargus that wasn't a smart thing for him to be doing.

"I'm afraid I can only discuss my affairs with Mr. Knudsen."

"I was afraid you'd say that." She bit on one of her fingernails. Whatever could possess a smart looking man to have such a foolish notion? "Umm . . . I don't suppose I could talk you out of meeting up with my Pa Jargus?"

"I'm afraid not. I must have a word with him. It's rather important." Lance paused. "I mean no offense, Miss Utopia, but can I ask you something?"

"I don't see why not. Go ahead and ask."

"How is it that you have three fathers?"

"My mama passed on shortly after I was born. Fergus, Jargus and Henry decided since they'd helped bring me into this world, they'd keep me a spell. I'll have you know my mama was a beautiful saloon girl. I have her dress in my trunk."

She didn't really want to talk about her fathers. She needed to know what city Lance came from and what saloons would be best to work in. He needed to know her interest was in saloons. "Did you hear what I said about my mama?"

"That explains everything. These men aren't related. They adopted you."

"Adopted? I don't know about that. They're my fathers, that's all there is to it. Did I tell ya about my mama? She was a saloon girl."

They both reached the false-fronted building. Utopia climbed the steps and spun on her heels. She'd never seen a person so busy at scribbling in that little tablet of his. "If you plan on writing down my every word, I'll talk slower. I reckon I've plumb talked your ears off as it is."

"Not at all. I've enjoyed our chat. You're a very interesting creature."

"Do you really think so?"

"Most definitely," he said. "Now, if you don't mind, I'd like to meet your father."

Her hand went to the door's latch and paused. It was time she let the city man know what he was up against if he insisted on talking to her Pa Jargus. "Now, whatever you do, don't let Jargus get the best of you. Stand your ground."

"Stand my ground? What do you mean?"

"You'll know soon enough."

CHAPTER TWO

Lance's eyes adjusted to the darkness of the room. Out the opened rear doorway, he spotted three men tending to a homemade still. The odor of sour mash carried on a breeze throughout the entire room. His senses reeled, and he swiped his fingers across his watering eyes.

Utopia shielded a hand alongside her mouth. "Jargus, there's a fella here says he needs a word with ya."

Judging by the plentiful wrinkles on his face, the fellow appeared to be the oldest of the trio. This Jargus entered the room. Lance watched the hobbled gent stop short inside the doorway. He grabbed a shotgun from a nearby whiskey barrel. "Girl, you're in my line of fire, move away from that feller." The hammers on the double barrels cocked and the weapon aimed. "Who are ya, mister? And what do ya want?"

This was the second time this morning he'd been threatened with a weapon, and he didn't care for that much. This Jargus carried some kind of chip on his shoulder or a pain that made him extremely irritable. No wonder the girl had warned him about the man. *Stand your ground.* He'd do that. Pausing only long enough to raise his hands, Lance remembered that he needed to use the code word. "Name's Lancelot Jones. I've come about *whiskey*."

"Whiskey?" The grizzled gent's gray bushy eyebrows shot up in surprise. He immediately stepped to the doorway. "Henry. Fergus. Git yourselves in here. We got ourselves one of them visitors we been expectin'

"A visitor? Already?"

"You heard me. We got us a visitor." Jargus waved his arm. "Now git in here."

Utopia's hands shot to her hips. "Pa, what are you getting yourself all worked up about?"

The old man eased the hammers down on his shotgun and laid it on a nearby table. Jargus grabbed hold of his daughter's arm with both his hands. As fast as his crippled gait could muster, the elder tugged his offspring toward the front porch entrance. "Girl, go fetch me coffee."

She twisted and turned, trying to free herself from her father's grasp. "Coffee? But Pa, this time of day you drink whiskey for your pains."

"My rheumatiz is fine. I want coffee. And don't be none too quick about fetching it."

Lance watched the old man finally get his girl out on the porch, but the lass put up a bit of resistance on having the door closed on her.

Utopia forced her way back inside. "Pa, what in blazes is going on here?"

"Look here, girl. Get that coffee like I done told you." Jargus' face turned red. His chest puffed up. "Me, Fergus and Henry have business with this fella that don't concern you none."

"Okay. I'll fetch your dang coffee. But I warn you, Pa." She thrust an angry finger in her pa's face. "You best not hurt him." She spun on her heels, and her swinging braid slapped the old man's cheek. She stormed out the door.

Jargus watched out the window a minute or two, making sure his daughter was long gone before he turned around and picked up his shotgun and aimed it at Lance. "You listen here, sonny. If you've mentioned one word of a contest to our daughter I'll plug you so full of holes we'll be sifting our corn mash through ya. Git over to this table and sit yerself down."

The other two whiskey makers stepped inside the room.

Lance took a seat. He removed his hat and placed it on the round, wobbly table. "Gentlemen, I'm here regarding the contest. I assure you that I've not mentioned the matter to your lovely daughter."

The lanky gent, with a body so skeletal it required the wearing of suspenders, took a seat beside Jargus. He sat in his chair and stroked his wispy twelve inch length of gray beard. "I'm Henry Mengas. You've probably gathered by now my cousin doesn't take kindly to strangers."

The other fellow was a twin match of Jargus in respects that he had the same gray-blue eyes and bushy, mangy looking hair. However, he was minus the severe hunched form and bad attitude. He grabbed Lance's hand in eager greeting. "I-I'm Fergus. Jargus and me, we're brothers."

Like Utopia, this fellow did a lot of hand pumping. He was a happy sort, with a simpleminded look about him. A nest of bristly salt and pepper whiskers surrounded his gaping wide smile. Lance winced at Fergus' crushing handshake. "I'm pleased to meet you."

Henry patted his cousin's shoulder. "You're cutting off the man's circulation."

Overzealous Fergus ceased his greeting and took a seat. "H-hope I didn't hurt you none."

Henry tugged his suspenders to the middle of his chest and leaned back in his chair, lifting the two front legs off the floor. "Don't mean to be short on hospitality, but what do you want to talk about, mister?"

Lance decided it would be prudent to avoid small talk and get right to the purpose of his visit. "Gentlemen, I'm a reporter with the *Gazette* newspaper. One of you talked to my editor about your contest. I've been assigned to write about your daughter's engagement proceedings."

"G-golly. Are y-you a newspaperman?" Fergus asked.

"Yes, I am." Lance felt relieved that one of the men was impressed with his credentials.

"That tears it," Jargus said. "There's no way to keep the contest a secret with a nosey reporter around. They're nothing but blabbermouths. The way I see it, we got to get rid of him."

Lance raised his hands up in anxious concern. "Whoa, gentlemen, let's talk about this. I am aware you wish to keep this contest a secret from your daughter, although I do not comprehend how you'll succeed at such an endeavor. I assure you that during my coverage of your contest, I will be totally discreet."

"Discreet," Jargus yelled. "We don't need any of your discreet. You've come snooping for trouble, Mr. Newspaperman, and you've found it." He grabbed for his shotgun again.

Fergus swiped the weapon out of his brother's reach. "Y-you can't shoot him."

"Sure, I can." Jargus struggled to gain his feet. "Give me my gun. I'll show ya."

There was little time to convince the men to let him cover this story. Lance thought a timely bribe might persuade the men. "Gentlemen, I have a proposition for you. If you don't like what I have to offer, I'll take my leave, and your secret will safely go with me. No harm done."

"You got one thing right, sonny," Jargus said. "Yer leaving. Fergus, give me my gun."

Henry slapped his cousin upside his head. "Shut up, you old coot. Let him talk."

Lance cleared his throat. "I totally understand your dilemma. I believe I have a solution."

"W-what's a solution? Fergus asked.

Jargus glared at his brother. "Shut up. Let him git on with what he's saying so I can git on with gitting rid of him."

Utopia's warning of standing his ground with Jargus repeated over and over in his brain. Lance took a breath and pressed on with his plan. "Gentlemen, my editor authorized me to offer you a slight sum of compensation in exchange for the coverage of your daughter's courtship."

Jargus' eyes instantly widened in greedy interest. "You mean to say you'll pay money?"

"Indeed I will." Lance released a relived sigh at this small breakthrough. Finally, the obstinate father seemed to have a change of his stubborn mind. He hoped.

"How much money are we talking?" Henry asked.

Lance's total savings didn't amount to much. Whatever he offered the fathers would need to be conservative in order to retain enough funds to purchase the newspaper business from Barris after the contest ended. "I'll pay twenty-five cents per article that I'm allowed to write."

Fergus' face lit up. "G-golly. Twenty-five cents is a lot."

"That ain't much," Jargus said. "A reporter like him wouldn't drag himself all this way for any old story. We must have something real special if'n he wants to write about it. I say that our price is three dollars."

Lance drummed his fingers on the table. *Blast it all.* The men had him over one of their whiskey barrels and they darn well knew it. He couldn't possibly go as high as three dollars though. "Perhaps my initial offer was a bit low." He held up one finger and gave a stern look. "I'll pay one dollar. However, my editor must have some assurance your daughter actually intends to marry. Gentleman, one dollar is my final offer."

He crossed his arms over his chest and waited with baited breath for a reply, hoping this offer didn't bankrupt him or get him riddled with bullets.

"There's something else needs to be added to this deal," Henry stated. His fingers wrapped around his suspenders and stretched the bands outward. "We sort of jumped the gun a bit with our contest."

Had the Gazette *prematurely printed the contest ad?* Lance felt sweat roll down his back at the possibility of some journalism liability looming overhead. "What do you mean you jumped the gun?"

"I think we're gonna have a heap of trouble when all those beaus show up for our contest." Henry stroked his beard in sly pause. "I think we need ourselves a protector in case our girl's suitors forget their courting manners."

"What?" Had he heard Cousin Henry correctly? "Are you asking me to be your daughter's chaperone?" Henry nodded and Lance shook his head. "That's not possible. I can't be your daughter's *protector*. My reporter ethics state I must not be bias to the story I cover."

"Bias? Bias—who gives a crap about bias," Jargus growled. "Give me my shotgun. I'll plug his bias ass right now."

Henry stretched a restraining arm across his riled cousin's chest. "Well, what will it be? You get yourself a story and agree to be our daughter's protector, or should I let Jargus make you into a whiskey sieve?"

Henry turned the restrained father loose, and Jargus immediately took up the shotgun.

Lance looked down its double barrels and pondered how hard it would be to keep the gal safe during courtship. He envisioned Utopia's tight fitting shirt, her well rounded bottom in snug buckskins, and her green eyes that could make any man, including him, lose their soul.

Blast it all. Trying to keep a bunch of lusty men in line around an innocent girl like Utopia could very well get him killed protecting her. Considering the dangers he would face if he remained a lawman, this would definitely be the more interesting way to die.

Lance drummed his fingers on the table. "How long do I have to think on your offer?"

"Until Utopia gets back with Jargus' coffee," Henry stated.

In the past, he'd defended less virginal women for far less reward than a fresh start in life. "Very well, gentlemen, you have yourselves a deal."

Jargus spit in his hand and extended it to Lance. "Once we shake on the deal, there's no turning back. You got that, sonny?"

"I understand." Lance gave his hand a similar spit. "I'll not renege on our agreement."

Henry eagerly rubbed his hands together. "Now all we have to do is come up with a good reason you'll be hanging around in camp. Otherwise, Utopia will get suspicious."

Fergus waved his hand in the air. "W-what if he's here and wants to buy our whiskey."

"No, gentlemen." Lance sternly objected by waving his hands back and forth. "That's not a plausible idea. I'm not much of a drinker. Nor do I care to be." He fidgeted with his derby lying on the table and waited for another suggestion. None came. "Isn't there some other plan you can come up with? You'll have to explain the contest suitors to your daughter. Why can't you tell Utopia I'm here for the same reason those men are?"

Jargus' fist pounded on the table.

Lance jumped a foot off his chair at the man's sudden fit of rage.

"We haven't started our gold rush," Jargus said. "We can't explain you the same way we intend to fib about all them others."

"You're here too early," Henry calmly offered. "Our contest won't start for another week. And we haven't got our gold rush ready. So for now, Fergus's whiskey buying idea is best."

Lance didn't know the reason these fathers were so anxious to get their girl wedded. The only thing he was concerned with was the price to do his job. Judging by the looks on the three men's faces there's no way he'd be able to persuade them away from using Fergus's idea.

"You're our new whiskey buyer. That settles it." Jargus scooted his chair back and slowly got to a hunched stand. He pointed the weapon in Lance's direction. "Now get yerself up, Mister Whiskey Buyer. We'll show you where you'll be bunking."

CHAPTER THREE

Morning, Day Two

Utopia held up the tiny mirror and closely examined her facial features. She glanced at the tin-typed photo in her other hand. It was like looking at identical ducks, not one feather of difference between the two redheads. Only a few freckles and a fancy saloon dress kept her from being the spitting image of her deceased mother.

Overnight, yet another miracle had occurred. Pa Jargus had actually let city fella Lance stay in camp. This was even more proof that her lucky stars were lining up. She always knew she was meant to follow the dancehall path of her mother.

With her dream so near to happening, Utopia felt a tingly buzz of hallelujah clear down in her bones. All the isolation, boredom, and drudgery on this mountain were soon to be over.

In fact, *the dream fulfiller* slept in his bunk across the way. With no time to waste, she put her mother's photo back on the shelf above the cook stove, and returned to her primping. Swiping a finger back and forth across her front teeth, she grinned in the looking glass to examine her polishing. Her reflective smile drooped into a frown.

Other than brushing a shine to her hair and tying bows on her braids, there wasn't much more to be done to pretty up. Even with all her gussying, it was hard not to look plain in comparison to the fancy man in camp. That brought up a worry.

Lance happened to be the first fella to show up in these hills in a coon's age who weren't creaky with rheumatism or smellier than sweaty socks. He was a pleasure to look at, for sure, especially for a gal weary of mountains and digging. But she wondered the reason a city fella like him would want to hang around their drab little mining camp.

Two possibilities came to her mind. It could be that he was a claim jumper after her gold. That didn't seem likely, though. Lance hadn't brought any mining tools with him that she could see. And mentally recalling his handshake of yesterday, his hands were callous-free. The man probably never dug a shovel of dirt in his life.

The more believable reason was that he was part of another marrying scheme. That was likely it. Boy, this time her fathers must be offering something really special. Something the city fella wanted badly enough he was willing to take a homely daughter off three miners' hands.

Well, hold onto your shovels, boys.

Her fathers best know they were beaten at this game right from the start. She'd not go to any altar, not willingly. Hell would have to make snowflakes first. Any man that tried to wed her, why she'd scratch his eyes out, kick him in his hurt spot, pummel him to a pulp, and for toppers, she'd drop him off a cliff. And, by golly, she knew all the highest cliffs in these mountains.

Saloon girls don't get married. No man was interfering with her glamorous job plans. There'd be no way in blazes wedding bells would ring on this mountain. Not for this gal.

The only solution to this newest marrying scheme of her fathers', if that's what this was, was to come up with a better scheme of her own. She'd bested her fathers at marriage arranging a time or two before. There was no reason she couldn't do it again.

She'd have to somehow finagle Lance into educating her on saloon and city ways without alerting her fathers that she was onto them. And she'd better be quick about learning her dancehall skills before the fathers rounded up a circuit preacher to do a wedding.

Too many of her years had been wasted away on this mountain. A twentieth birthday loomed in six weeks and her youth would be gone. She figured she'd be past prime saloon girl hiring age if she waited much longer.

She gave herself a stern look in the glass and etched her plans in mental stone. "Sometimes a gal's got to take her dream and run with it. By gosh, by golly, I'm singing and dancing myself all the way to a city, and no dang husband's tagging along."

Fergus, Henry and Jargus walked along Coon Creek each carrying empty wooden buckets, nibbling on the remnants of the charred breakfast Utopia had brought them.

"W-where'd all our nuggets go?" Fergus asked.

"Why don't ya yell it all over the dang mountain?" Jargus complained.

Henry scratched his head, wondering that himself. "I don't see how the gold we planted yesterday could vanish into thin air."

"M-m-maybe it all washed away," Fergus said.

Jargus tossed his bucket to the ground, giving it a good hard kick. "Ouch. *Dang-nabbit.*" He hobbled around with the pain inflicted on an ingrown toenail. "No, numbskull. If our gold washed this far, we'd have found it by now. Besides, the creek's barely floatin' leaves. I say someone's took our nuggets."

"There you go again, accusing me and Fergus of stealing." Henry raged.

"Not you two. It's that newsman. I should of plugged him and been done with it."

"U-Utopia digs," Fergus said. "Cu-could be she found our gold."

Henry pulled on his wispy beard and contemplated his cousin's comment. "Fergus, you may be on to something there. It'd be like our girl to squirrel away whatever she finds."

"That tears it," Jargus said. "How we gonna start a gold rush without any gold?"

Henry paced, giving the problem more thought.

Fergus fell into matched steps behind Cousin Henry and followed in a circle formation. "M-m-maybe Lance could help us think up a plan?"

Henry turned and slapped his hands down on Fergus' shoulders. "That's it. You've come up with the perfect solution."

"W-what's a solution?"

Jargus ripped off his hat and slapped it on his thigh. "That's a dumb idea."

"No, it's not. Yesterday, you said you'd tell Utopia about Lance being our new whiskey buyer. Did she believe the story?"

"Uh . . ." Jargus looked at his feet. "I didn't exactly get a chance to mention that to her."

"No matter," Henry said. "We'll make Lance tell her if he wants to write his articles, eat vittles and have a bed. He'll agree to our terms."

"Don't like it. Don't trust him," Jargus stated.

"You got a better plan? Well, mister big mouth. Let's hear it." Henry braced his stance and waited for Jargus to come around, as he knew he would.

"Give me a minute. I'm thinkin'."

"Either Lance distracts Utopia from her prospecting, or our little gold rush idea is a bust. Never mind. I've had all I can stand of you for one morning." Henry turned and headed the direction of camp.

"H-he's right." Fergus marched off in a huff like his cousin.

"You can do the explaining," Henry yelled over his shoulder. "All those suitors will expect a gold mine dowry. I don't reckon they'll take kindly to learning they're getting a worthless shaft along with their stubborn bride."

"*All right.* Have it your way." Jargus hurriedly grabbed his bucket off the ground and hobbled to catch up to Henry and Fergus. "But I'm keeping my eye on that news fella. If I catch him stealing even one nugget—why, he'll be sifting corn mash through buckshot holes before he can even put the rock in his pocket."

CHAPTER FOUR

Same Day Two

A poke of a shotgun awoke Lance from a dead sleep. He opened one eye a sliver to find the three fathers towered over his bed. "Is it morning already?" His voice felt gravelly.

Jargus ripped the blanket off. "Get up, you lazy newsman. We're adding something else to this article-writing deal."

"I don't understand. We shook hands. *Didn't we?*" Lance slowly sat up. A molasses-like sludge coated his tongue. Ah, yes, the fathers and their little sampling party last night. He smacked his lips, wishing for a drink of water. "Gentlemen, forget whatever I said last night. I was way into my cups."

"Our agreement ain't changed none, only yours is different," Jargus growled.

"What?" Lance blinked a couple times to clear his head. The all too familiar weapon poked his ribs.

"Listen up, sonny. Something's come up and you're in charge of fixing it."

"You have about as much tact as a snapping turtle." Henry shoved his cousin aside. "It's like this. We've saved up some gold—only thing is, it's disappearing."

"Don't look at me," Lance protested in now wide-awake self-defense. "I'm not taking it."

"N-not you," Fergus said.

Lance gave the fathers a quizzical look. "You suspect somebody else is stealing it?"

"Yes, and then again, not exactly," Henry said. "It's Utopia. She's taking it."

"That's good. At least it's staying in the family."

"You don't understand. Our gold mine hasn't exactly been a mother lode over the years, but we managed to save up just enough for Utopia's dowry."

Lance's head was pounding something fierce. He just wanted to go back to bed and sleep off this hangover. "It's nice she has a dowry, but what does this have to do with me?"

Henry took a seat next to Lance on the cot. "You see, we've planted gold about our camp so the suitors won't think Utopia's poor as a church mouse. That's our problem."

It could be the whiskey fog in his head making this hard to grasp. "Gentlemen, somehow I seem to be missing your problem."

"We ain't caring how you do it," Jargus said. "But you'll stop Utopia from her digging."

"*What*? Wait." Lance closed his eyes and hoped this would miraculously erase this conversation. He opened his eyes. Damn. The fathers were still there. "Let me get this straight.

You want me to distract your daughter from digging?"

The fathers all nodded a big yes.

"And just how am I supposed to do that?"

Henry put a hand under Lance's arm and helped him to his feet. "A smart city fella like you, I'm sure you'll think of something."

"And, sonny, no matter how you distract her, our girl is to remain unsullied. Understood?" The double barrels of Jargus' shotgun locked into firing mode.

Lance nodded. "I don't know your girl very well, but it seems to me things would be much easier if you tell her all about the contest and her dowry."

"You don't know the whole of it," Henry said. "Utopia is determined to be a . . . What I'm saying is she plans on becoming a . . ."

Lance was tired and wanted, no needed, to go back to bed and sleep. "Becoming a what?"

"*A whore*," the fathers shouted in unison.

Lance's mouth dropped open like the trap door on a gallows. "No! Why? How?"

"She got herself a peek of some of them dancehall girls through the saloon window when she was a little tyke," Henry said. "Right then she took up the notion of being like them. Utopia thinks singing and dancing is all those saloon girls have to do. We tried to tell her different."

"It's like talking to a stump," Jargus said. "We told her exactly what those girls do. She just shrugged it off. Says she won't give men-pokes. She'll just sing and dance."

Lance rubbed the back of his neck. This revelation sure shed new light on why the fathers decided to run a contest to wed her off. "I wish I could help you, but I have no ideas to offer."

"W-we'd be real beholden if you could think up something," Fergus said.

To Lance's ears this sounded every bit like a chance to negotiate. "How beholden?"

Henry's face lit up. "We might reduce our price on article-writing if you'll help us."

"How much will my article-writing price drop?"

Jargus turned his ire on Henry. "I ain't agreed to dropping nothin'. You said he's got to do what we tell him. There weren't nothin' mentioned 'bout giving him free article-writing privileges."

"He helps change Utopia's mind, I think he'd be entitled to a cheaper deal. Don't you?"

"I'll *try*–and I emphasize the word *try*–to talk your daughter into changing her choice of a job *if* you'll allow me to write my articles at no cost."

Jargus aimed his shotgun. "I've heard enough. It's time I make us a whiskey sieve."

Lance folded his arms, more than ready to call the old man's bluff. "Go ahead. Plug me. It won't solve anything. You'll still have a saloon girl problem on your hands."

Henry gave Jargus one of those cooperate-or-else shoves. "Get on with it. Tell him yes."

Jargus stood obstinate as ever, with the stock of the shotgun tucked under his armpit.

"Go ahead. Tell him you want his help and his writing will be free."

"What if'n he don't change her mind? Then what? He'll have cheated us out of paying for his privilege of living."

"So be it," Henry stated.

Lance could tell Jargus was mad by the red-hot-poker color on face. The father's mulish temperament wouldn't quite stand for giving in to a city fellow. Mute as stone and his jaw vice-tight, if the old coot passed wind right now his ass would shoot out flames.

"Tell him," Henry screamed.

Jargus mumbled in a barely audible tone, "If'n you help us, we'll not charge you."

"I don't think he heard you," Henry prodded. "Say it louder."

Lance found it hard to contain a smirk of satisfaction at Jargus' struggle to relent.

The shotgun jerked downward. "Your articles can be free. See if I care."

"That's more like it." Henry spit in his hand and offered a handshake. "Is it a deal?"

"Deal." Lance spit in his palm and put the seal of approval to his new terms.

CHAPTER FIVE

Lance walked along the path leading to Coon Creek where he'd been told Utopia did her panning. He practiced some plausible distracting ploys. "Pardon me, Miss Utopia. A pretty girl like you shouldn't be playing in cold creeks and mud. I'd like to interest you in a . . ." *Kiss.*

Blast it all. He'd never been any good at distracting women. It usually was the other way around. Besides, Utopia wasn't the type of girl he'd normally be attracted to. He'd classify her as a wholesome, down-to-earth sort of pretty gal with a quirky personality that bordered on . . . on . . . enjoyably appealing.

Who was he kidding? He found her totally distracting.

He wouldn't get any of his articles written if he didn't make some realistic adjustments about this attraction he seemed to have for the lady. For Pete's sake, the girl was engaged to a yet-to-be-determined male. The contest officially took her off the market, or she soon would be unavailable. So, knowing all this, and since he considered himself a practical man, why couldn't he drop this infatuation?

Maybe it had something to do with that ridiculous saloon girl notion of hers.

It was very unreasonable of the men to throw another task on him. Distracting Utopia would be very difficult now that his brain had been implanted with enticing images of her wearing a bosom-displaying dress.

They shouldn't expect him to chaperone her—especially when every potential groom that heard about her career choice will have thoughts of bedding down with her on his mind.

How unreasonable is that?

He had three things on his agenda; write unbiased articles, become owner of the *Gazette* and live a peaceful, non-dangerous life. But no. The fathers keep conjuring up these bizarre writing deals. As if their daughter wasn't a difficult enough problem for him to contend with.

Right now, his mind was his worst enemy. He didn't understand this strange attraction he had for this girl. *She's not even my type, for Pete's sake.* These constant thoughts of kissing Utopia were driving him crazy.

Why the hell couldn't she be an ugly bride-to-be?

Lance put some brisk into his steps and charged up the hill, determined to face this distracting problem with a bit of commonsense. He needed clearheaded focus at a time like this. He was dealing with one quite simple reality here. To give up his law badge once and for all, he had to protect and distract the lovely Utopia.

So what was the problem? Those heart-shaped lips of hers, and her perfect breasts, and her curvy hips. All that stuff needed to be wiped out of his mind. He needed focus.

Focus. Focus. Focus.

He rounded the bend and the tall Ponderosa pine trees off to his right thinned away, revealing a clearing. Off to his left, the creek quietly trickled. And directly ahead, in his line of sight—her.

Lance skidded to a stop. Utopia continued her work, undistracted by his approach.

She stood muck-boot deep in the water. Her curvy backside faced him. Her hips swished side-to-side as she worked the pan in her hands. That hip motion held his undivided attention.

Focus, he told himself.

When she bent at the waist and scooped up more water, lusty musings rushed through him like a hot geyser. He quickly spun around and aimed himself for camp. Damn. He'd tell the fathers, "I couldn't find her." No. They'd just send him out to look some more. Or they could end his article-writing privileges and send him packing.

His newspaper ownership happened to be on the line here. No articles meant that Barris wouldn't sell him the *Gazette*. He'd be stuck being a lawman. A dead-ending job if ever there was one. He needed to be a professional journalist and stick to what he'd come to this camp to do, write a good courtship story.

Lance faced his lovely gold-digger and cleared his throat. "Having any luck?"

Utopia startled at his sudden greeting and creek sediment splashed on her shirt. She turned and faced him with a soaked garment plastered to her chest, again. She swiped at the grit on her front. "Hell's bells. You shouldn't sneak up on a person like that. Look what you've done."

There was no keeping his eyes off the endowments that once again presented themselves in wet, molded fashion. He purged his rising interest in her figure by looking away. "I'm sorry."

"What are you doing wandering around in the woods anyways? If you don't know your way around these hills, you could find yourself lost."

He kept his head turned away from her and wiped his sweaty palms on his pant legs. *For Pete's sake, focus.* "Uh, your fathers and I haven't settled our business yet. I think Jargus wanted me out of his hair for a while. He sent me to look for you."

"You don't say." Utopia gave him a curious stare. No denying she'd been mad when he'd snuck up on her, mainly because whenever he was around she was always wearing a wet shirt. She couldn't help but notice his brown eyes darkened whenever he gazed on her chest.

Utopia quickly folded her arms over her breasts. When Lance looked at her like that, her insides got all fluttery and tingly. She didn't mind him looking. In fact, it was foolish to hide what he seemed real interested in. She dropped her arms to her sides. "What are you doing here?"

"Whoa. Well . . . I . . . I wanted to take in some of the beautiful–umm–scenery. You know the trees and all." He shielded his eyes against the glaring sunlight and looked toward the stand of pines. "I like trees. Trees are good."

"Trees? Yeah. We got lots of trees around here." Lance seemed to be acting very strange. Why? Her eyes scanned the graveled path he'd walked up. She perused the nearby bushes looking for her meddling fathers. The coast seemed clear enough. Could she be so lucky? She and Lance appeared to be all to their lonesome.

The fathers were likely busy with their whiskey making and would be at it for several hours. What could be more perfect? Nothing. She'd use this time alone with her handsome city fella to get down to some serious saloon learning. But bringing up a dancehall discussion would take some easing into the subject.

She rinsed her pan out in the water then sloshed herself toward the creek's bank. "I was just fixing to have me a bite of breakfast. Would you care to join me?"

Finally, he looked at her.

"That's the best invitation I've had all morning. I'd be delighted."

His eyes didn't focus on her face, but stared lower which filled her with this intense strange heat, like the pinpoint of light through one of them magnifier glasses, burning right near her heart. If he didn't stop staring at her like that, by gosh, by golly, she'd have to jump in the creek for some cooling off.

Utopia grabbed a flour sack off the creek's bank and pointed across the clearing. "Let's eat over yonder by those pines. There's a nice log to sit on and plenty of shade to cool us off."

"I could use cooling off." Lance swiped his shirtsleeve across his brow.

They walked over to the shady area, and danged if she couldn't feel his eyes staring on her rump. She stopped by a fallen timber and turned to Lance. He came to an abrupt stop and stood stock-still, like he'd suddenly gotten himself glued to the dirt.

He just stood there saying nothing. Maybe he was being polite, waiting for her to sit. Utopia dropped her rump down on the log and gave the spot next to her a pat. "Don't look so all fired worried. I ain't gonna bite you."

Lance took a seat on the ground with a good leg's distance put between them. He patted the bladed-green carpet around him. "This nice soft grass suits me better."

Utopia scowled, quiet disappointed Lance was being so standoffish. How could she bring up talking about saloons if they were sitting so far from each other? She slid herself to the ground and crawled closer to Lance. "You're right. Grass is much better for sitting."

He scooted over another foot. "Umm . . . I'm not sure the whiskey your fathers gave me last night will stay settled in my stomach. You may want to sit away from me a bit."

So that was why he was skittish. He drank a little too much shine. "Believe me. I know just how you feel."

"I don't think so," Lance said. He stroked his hand across the back of his neck. "The day's warming up quick. Isn't it?"

He swung his outstretched arms back and forth in front of him, working out a crick in the middle of his back. Utopia studied how the blue chambray shirt tightened around his chest and biceps as he stretched. "If you're too hot in that shirt of yours, you can take it off. You'd be cooler that way." And she'd get a gander at his muscles.

"No. I mean . . . boy, I'm tired. The sun barely cleared the horizon this morning when your fathers woke me up. I bet the rooster was still asleep when they came by."

"We don't have a rooster," she said. "But you're right. We're early risers around here. I like to be up early so I can enjoy the—*scenery*."

"Scenery?" His eyes shot to her slow drying shirt then quickly darted toward the cloth bag beside her. "Say, what's in that flour sack of yours?"

"Silly me. I done offered you a meal and here I sit yapping. Let's eat." She reached in the bag and pulled out something wrapped in a napkin and handed it to him.

"Thanks." Lance removed the cloth covering. He took a bite of the sandwich. "This is very good. When I was a boy my mother made apple butter just like this. My brother, Chance, and I would sit under the big apple tree eating a dozen of these sandwiches on a summer's day."

"I can't take credit for the making of anything but the bread. My fathers brought the apple butter back with them after one of their whiskey delivering city trips. Speaking of my fathers, they sell whiskey to all the saloons down in Tin Cup. I like saloons, don't you?"

All of a sudden, Lance lent out a gurgled sound and lurched forward. He pounded a fist on his chest then pointed to his throat, unable to utter the problem.

"*Oh, my stars.* You must be choking." Immediately, Utopia gave the area between his shoulder-blades a couple of good solid whacks. "How's that?"

He shook his head, wheezing.

"Your lips are turning blue. I best give you another whack or two." With the third pound to his back, Lance fell backwards and rolled from side-to-side on the ground, unable to catch his breath. Her whacks were making the problem worse. She'd never ever forgive herself if she killed her handsome saloon teacher with an apple butter sandwich.

Utopia didn't know what else to do. Somehow the blockage had to be popped out of him. She quickly stood up and straddled over his middle. "Now this might hurt a bit, but I'm pretty sure this will get that glob out of you." Her bottom came down on his midsection in a hard sit.

A loud grunt expelled from Lance the moment her rear-end crushed on top of his gut.

The obstruction ejected out of his mouth like a spent bullet, and she nabbed the flying dough-ball with her left hand when it whizzed by her head. She held the marble sized particle between her finger and thumb. "Good thing I thought of a way to loosen up this big clod."

Utopia tossed the dough into the bushes. The feel of him underneath her bottom made her blood warm, her insides near melting. She kept herself perched on his abdomen, enjoying the feel of him beneath her just a bit longer.

Their eyes met and for a minute, she feared Lance might still be choking for he seemed not to be breathing. She wiggled her rump back and forth on his stomach and pelvis to get him to draw some air. "What's the matter? Didn't I get it all out?" Utopia wiggled her bottom more and in an instant Lance bucked like a wild mustang touched with a hot branding iron. He bucked her right off of him and scrambled up off the ground.

He nervously brushed grass off his clothes. "Umm. I'm fine. Now."

She knew for the rest of her days, she'd never forget the exciting sizzle that'd gone through her insides with the fit of him between her legs. His body was so warm, she'd like to sit atop the man that way all day long. There weren't no denying she wished he'd choke again so the rescuing could be repeated.

But judging by the way he'd reacted to her sitting on him, Lance didn't seem too interested in her in exactly the same way she was interested in him. What had she expected? He was a city fella that had been around beautiful city women, not a plain Jane like her.

It didn't matter what kind of girl Lance liked to be with. She couldn't let herself like him for anything other than being her saloon teacher. Thinking about him in a marrying kind of way would ruin all her plans. She needed to remember saloon girls don't get married.

Utopia studied the man's shaking hands. He was probably thinking of something nice to say after he so rudely bucked her off him. Her plainness wasn't his fault. "If you want something to wash the rest of that sandwich down, I have some sweet tea."

"Tea would be good."

She quickly reached in her sack, pulled out a mason jar, nervously unscrewed the tin cap and handed him the drink. "You can have all you want. And while you're drinking, we can talk about that saloon you're opening."

Lance's sip of tea sprayed the air. He swiped his shirtsleeve across the dribble on his mouth. "Who said I was opening a saloon?"

"I'm not stupid. The only business you could possibly have with my fathers has to be about whiskey. You even said that's what you came to our camp for when you were at my door yesterday. I figure you must own a saloon. I'm real interested in hearing more about your place."

"Well, don't be. The whiskey and my business are things I don't talk about."

"So, it's true? You are opening a saloon. By gosh, by golly, I knew it. So, after you have your whiskey supply, and your place decorated, you'll need some saloon girls. Won't you?"

"Well . . . I . . ." Lance took another sip of tea, and another, and another, until the jar emptied. "Umm . . ." He wiped his brow with his shirtsleeve. "A nice girl like you shouldn't be troubling yourself about saloons."

"The hell you say. I've thought on saloons my whole life. In fact, you come on over here." Utopia grabbed Lance by the arm and pulled him over to the log. She put her hands to his shoulders and forced him to sit down. "You park yerself right there and watch this. Now don't judge me too harshly, I only know me one song right now. I heard it when this family came by camp a long time ago. If I'm off key a hair, it's because I don't have a pi-any playing along. Here goes."

Utopia inhaled a deep breath and let it out. "*A-mmaaa-zin' grace–how sweet you a-r-r-re, t'a-a-ah find a-a-a-a-a–*" Her mind went blank. "I forget what the Grace person in this song was looking for. I was only ten or so when I first heard the tune."

"That's a church song, not a saloon song," Lance informed her.

The burn of a hot blush crept to her cheeks. How could she be so knuckleheaded? She shrugged her shoulder. "Sure. I know that. I'm just showing you I can sing. I was hoping you'd be able to teach me a few dancehall tunes."

"I don't really know any songs," he said.

"Oh, well, that's okay. I can do other saloon girl things. Watch this."

Utopia stood in front of Lance as he sat on the log. She took in a good long breath before starting her next talent. She first kicked her right leg up, when it came back down she then kicked her left leg up. She repeated her high-kicking, alternating back and forth from one leg to the other, getting her leg kicks higher each time. On each kick, she gave a little grunt, for her performance had her getting a mite winded. "I saw real saloon girls doing this kicking stuff when I was little. Ever since, I've practiced my leg kicking whenever I have me time."

On the fifth left leg kick, her oversized muckboot flew off her foot. Lance ducked as the muddy footwear sailed over his head and thumped against a tree behind him.

She scrambled after her boot then scurried back around to face her lone audience. Utopia bent over and braced her hands on her knees, huffing and puffing for air. "I'm a tad winded right now because I've not practiced much lately." Her lungs took in a second wind. "Don't you worry none about your customers' heads. I'll be able to dance without throwing a shoe once I have me some real dancehall slippers instead of these big old boots."

Sitting down on the log next to Lance, she slipped her foot back into her boot. "Well, what do you think? Am I saloon girl material?"

Lance gave her comments about saloons some thought. The girl had evidently had her heart set on being a dancehall girl for a long time. Squelching her career without damping her spirits wouldn't be easy. *Unless.* Unless he could get her to give up the interest all on her own.

"Yes. With a bit of practice and the right apparel, I guess you'd be suitable. But then–" He folded his arms over his chest. "You do know about the other part of the job that you'd have to be willing to do, don't you?"

"Oh, you're meaning that poking part?"

"Yes. Being a saloon girl isn't just about entertaining the men with singing and dancing. Those fancy low-cut dresses are worn to entice a man to pay money for a poke, as you called it. In fact, if I hired a pretty girl like you, I guarantee you wouldn't have much time for singing and dancing." He knew that wasn't an over-exaggerated statement.

She gnawed on her fingernail with a puzzled look on her face. "Do I have to poke?"

Lance nodded. "Poking's the biggest money-maker in a saloon. That's what keeps the business going. Since I'm the owner of the place, I get most of the money that you take in selling drinks, and doing all that dancing and singing. I especially get a cut of your poking."

Utopia jabbed her hands to her hips. "That don't rightly seem fair now, does it?"

He could tell by her nail biting and the irritation in her voice, the subject of splitting her poke money bothered her. "The saloon owner's the one that provides a roof over your head. I feed you and buy those fancy dresses, feathers and such. All that stuff isn't free, you know."

"Oh. I never thought about that. I reckon when you put it that way, it doesn't sound like too bad a deal." She stuffed her hands in the back pockets of her britches. "I guess I'll have to think on that. How much money do you think I could make singing, dancing and if I were to do poking?"

How much could she earn lying on her back poking? What a loaded question.

Like a stick of dynamite, shards of images exploded in his brain, picturing her in a skimpy undergarment, panting beneath a man in the throes of passion. What would her poking earnings be? *Hell.* She'd own the damn saloon and every patron inside within a week. "Now hold on there. You're way ahead of things here. You're nowhere near ready to perform saloon girl duties. That's all there is to it. Now I'm tired of talking about saloons. Let's change the subject. Tell me what you folks do around here for excitement."

"Excitement? Hmm. Let me think." She paused with an I'm-thinking-hard look on her face. Her fingers snapped. "I know what we do. We watch pine trees grow. Does it look like there's anything exciting to do around here? There's no pi-a-ny music playing. No dancing and singing going on. No card playing. There are only these mountains, bugs, snakes, bears, chores and the sun setting and rising on a ton of boring days. Welp . . ." Utopia started packing up her food wrappers. "I best be getting back to my prospecting if we aren't gonna talk about saloons. Hand me my tea jar."

"What? Why?" Lance handed her the jar, realizing his gold distracting efforts were ended if saloon talk ended. What to do? "Now you disappoint me. I was hoping you'd show me around this beautiful mountain. We can talk about saloons while we stroll, can't we?"

She shielded her hand over her eyes, blocking the angle of the midmorning sun. "I can see you aren't interested in more talking. Besides, daylight's wasting, and it's too hot for digging in the afternoons. I have to do my gold hunting early."

"I'd be interested in seeing how you gold hunt. Maybe we could look around, talk and gold hunt all at the same time." Right now he wasn't worried about long term gold diversions. He just wanted to get her away from the fathers' gold planting creek. "What do you say?"

Utopia's boot kicked at a couple of dirt clumps. "I guess I could do that. You know, I have me a place in mind I think you should really see."

"Terrific." Lance breathed a sigh of relief. "You lead the way."

CHAPTER SIX

Lance followed his little mining instructor and designated tour guide up the hillside. Accustomed to the graveled path they were set upon, Utopia scaled the rocky grade with ease. Her legs reached from one foothold to the next in lithe strides. Her buckskins stretched tight around her enticing behind. So far, he'd not been able to tear his eyes off the physically fine feature above him. *Have mercy.* Focus. Focus. Focus.

"We only have a bit farther to the rocker," she informed.

"I'm glad of that." He was so winded his sides pained him. "How long are we going to be at prospecting? I hope it's not too long."

"It's early. I figure we'll dig two hours. That should be long enough."

"That's good." It would be long enough to grow plenty of blisters.

At the top of the grade, she halted and dropped her tools to the ground. "This is it."

He came alongside her, adding his shovel and pan to her pile. Glad for the stop, he bent over with stiffened arms on his knees and filled his lungs with crisp clean air. He straightened, taking in the surroundings.

They stood in a small valley nestled between twin peaks with summits hovering on either side of them. Imposing Ponderosa pines had matured over the centuries into a stately forest. To his left sat a wooden box he figured to be the rocker contraption she'd described. It wasn't until he looked ahead that he found one word expressive enough for the view.

"Spectacular."

"Oh, there's a better sight. You want to see?"

"Sure, why not?" He followed her farther into the stand of pines.

"I come here to get away from my fathers at times." She grabbed a rope hanging from the stocky lower branch of a solid pine and gave the cord a tug. "I built me a tree floor."

"A tree floor?"

"It's a high up space to sit and have peace and quiet. And it's all mine."

To his amazement her tug unrolled a rope ladder from the branches above their heads.

"Come on. Up we go." She grabbed a secure hold on both sides of the flexible staircase and shimmied up the tree.

He looked up the ladder and wondered how he'd muster up the energy to climb. "Do we really have to do this?" By the time he'd spoken, she'd disappeared from his view by the obstruction of a wooden platform resting between several of the lowest boughs of the tree. Well, if she could get up there, so could he. Lance made his way up the unstable rope rungs.

It wasn't until he settled his feet on this lofty perch that he noticed the broader vista that had been unseen from the view on the ground. It was sheer paradise.

Up here, standing on Utopia's tree floor, he could look out and see the midday sunrays reflecting off the stark white snowcaps of the distant Rocky peaks. To the right of their towering tree, a waterfall cascaded in glimmered crystals over cragged cliffs. The audible sound of the water roared in his ears as the sparkling liquid plunged into an aqua pool below, spraying a mist of airborne particles into a reflected crescent rainbow.

"This is one of the most beautiful things I've ever seen," he remarked.

"Yeah. Ain't it heaven?" The wooden floor became her perch. She pulled off her boots and dangled her bare feet over the side of the platform. "Nobody knows about my little hideaway."

"It's certainly a worthy secret." Lance sat down next to her and removed his boots and socks. He dangled his feet over the edge and wiggled his toes. The freedom from shoes, and also the quiet away from civilization, washed a peaceful calmness through his senses. He had rarely enjoyed such a feeling being a lawman.

"If you tell anyone, I'll have to cut your tongue out." She smirked and looked away.

Lance regarded her profile. This was the first time he'd really noticed the many tawny freckles dotted across her cheeks and pert nose. She was a perfect fit for this little tree floor of hers. Just as these mountains weren't seen in all their grandeur until viewed from up high, he realized a person had to look from a different perspective to see the true magnitude of Utopia's inner beauty.

All of a sudden his responsibility of guarding became two-fold. He needed to protect Utopia and now this place from greedy treasure seekers. "I'll not tell a soul," he promised.

There ensued a long pause while they both enjoyed the moment.

She turned her head his way and tilted it to one side. "Lance, do you have a girl?"

"You mean am I married or engaged?"

"Yeah. Someone special you have to get home to."

She kicked her legs and pulled one braid to the front. He watched her nervously toy with her hair. "No. I haven't found the right gal yet."

"What kind of gal would you want if you felt like marrying?"

If he had such a foolish notion of giving up his carefree lifestyle, he'd guess a respectable lady would be what he'd want for a wife. A genuine, respectable lady would fit nicely with his new respectable newspaper business. "Marriage isn't something I've given much thought to."

"Well . . . if you were to give thought to it, what would your gal be like?"

Again, a lady with genteel manners and interests in things he cared about came to his mind. "Oh, we'd have some common interests."

Utopia bent one leg up onto the platform. Her palms and chin rested on her kneecap. "Like what?"

The intensity of her green eyes upon him caused his brain to scramble for words. "First off, I'd like her to be a good cook."

"What else?"

"I don't know. I'd have to be attracted to her."

A scowl crossed her face. "You're meaning she'd need to be pretty?"

"Not really. I'd want her to be someone I can respect because she has moral values."

He watched Utopia chew at her fingernails then tuck her hands under her bottom.

"What about pollinating?" she asked with down-turned eyes.

"Pollinating?" What did plants have to do with anything?

He watched her fidget with the end of her braid.

"That poking you mentioned I'd have to do. Exactly how many pokes would it take before I'd get . . ." She paused. "Before I'd be pollinated?"

The change of subject confused Lance a minute until it dawned on him the girl was talking about sex. Her nervousness about the subject said she didn't exactly know the details. "Utopia, have your fathers ever explained the birds-and-the-bees to you?"

A pert smile spread across her face. "Hah, I should say they have. But I haven't exactly had too many chances to practice. If you know what I mean."

"No, I don't think I do." He was beginning to get the picture of just how virgin this girl was. "Utopia, have you ever seen animals poke?"

Her eyes darted to the floorboards. "Sure, I've seen—*that*."

Lance watched Utopia's cheeks turn a rosy hue, a telltale sign. He needed to know how much of a virgin. "Have you ever been kissed by a boy?"

"Are you counting the kisses I got when my fathers tucked me in bed when I was little?"

"No, you can't count those."

"Then I guess I haven't been what you're calling kissed." Her arms wrapped around her knees, and she rocked back and forth on her bottom.

The full ramifications of her innocence rolled over Lance like a snowballing avalanche. The lass sat on the catastrophic brink of being sullied once the contest started.

What self-respecting reporter would sit on the sidelines and watch a woman risk giving up her virginity and do nothing to try and make sure it didn't come down to rape?

This ordeal wouldn't be on his chaperoning conscience. It'd be in his journalistic best interest to familiarize the girl on some basics of courting, nothing too enticing, just enough husband-finding skills to get her safely through the contest. Give her a bit of feminine ammunition. But he'd have to make it very clear that she was to put a limit on how far she experimented. "Would you like a kiss?"

Utopia's head shot up with a bright smile on her pink face. "Are you meaning . . .?"

"Yes. Yes. That's what I'm meaning." He rubbed his hands through his hair. Focus. Focus.

Focus. This poor girl was on the brink of disaster. "If you pay attention and promise to do everything exactly like I tell you . . . then yes, I'll give you a kiss."

"You'll really teach me how to kiss?"

"I said I would. Didn't I?" The thought of kissing her shouldn't feel like torture, but he'd already endured a most pronounced suffering in his loins most of the day, and this task was bound to stretch him to the brink of his willpower.

"Will it be a kiss like those saloon gals know how to give?"

"*No.*" He suddenly regretted his offer. "Definitely not. You don't need to learn those sorts of kisses."

Her eyes opened in wide surprise. "Oh, yes I do. Those are exactly the kind of kisses I need to learn."

He swiped his fingers through his hair realizing he should stop this right now. It was too late though. The girl would be gravely disappointed. If she possessed a temper like her Pa Jargus, she'd probably toss him out of her tree.

He needed a serious element of danger, a scary outcome that would limit her eagerness to be kissed. "There are many types of kisses. And I'm warning you that if you don't learn how and when to use each kind of kiss, well . . ."

"Well what?" Her eyebrows drew together with concern.

"You could find yourself in very grave trouble."

Utopia bit on a nail. "I should know what I'm getting myself into. What kind of trouble is there in kissing?"

"Pollinated is exactly what girls get if they don't learn when and how to use the right kinds of kisses for the right kind of man." A true statement if ever he'd uttered one. It set off alarm bells in his chest just thinking about her pollinating.

Her eyes grew wide. For a moment, Utopia sat silent and bit on her fingernails. Then she slapped her kneecaps, having made a decision on the matter of whether to proceed. "Well, I can't shy away from the facts of life all my life. What kind of kisses are we starting with?"

He'd just failed at scaring her off. Now what? Maybe he could make the kiss such a tedious, confusing task she'd lose interest in trying. "You just said it."

"Said what?"

"Starter kisses. You're on starter kisses."

"I can do starter kisses." She shot to her feet. "Let's get to it."

Lance reluctantly stood and faced his opponent in all her eager glory. He swiped his sweaty hands on his pant legs and stared intently in her big, wide excited eyes. *Have mercy.* This was a mistake. One big mistake.

"Okay. Pay attention. The placement of hands is very important in starter kisses. Okay. Now." He paused for a big breath. "Okay. Here we go. There should be no contact of your body to the body of the fellow you plan to kiss. I mean other than your lips, of course." He pointed at her. *"This is very important.* You got that?"

"Got it." She licked her lips.

"Don't do that."

"Do what? All I did was . . ."

Did her naiveté have limits? He pointed at her mouth. "That's a wet kiss. A . . . a stage two kiss. And you're not learning those." Sweat beaded on his forehead, and he swiped his shirt sleeve across his brow. "Now the first thing you do is pucker. Like this."

To demonstrate he drew his lips into a small circle.

Her eyes focused intently on his mouth. She copied. "Wike this?"

"No. No. No. Not like you're tasting lemons. You need softer. A pucker is softer. Relax your mouth. Imagine you're blowing billowy seeds off a dandelion."

Lance squished and massaged the corner of her lips with his fingers. Her mouth felt so soft and pliable to his touch. He watched her mouth slowly form a seductive circle. His mind fell into a trance and imagined a kiss of those lips. She'd burn a man to cinders. This was a clear signal he needed more complicated kissing instructions.

She'd been practicing puckers during his mental dilemma. Her lips were opening and closing like a fish nibbling bugs on the surface of a pond. "Okay. Stop. That's enough puckering. You're ready for the next step."

"Oh, good. My lips were getting a mite tired of pucker practice."

"Now when our lips come together, you've got to remember that starter kisses can't last any longer than ten seconds. So you have to count to ten."

"But how can I count to ten if my mouth is puckered?"

"You'll have to count in your head, or you can mumble count out the corner of your mouth like this. Un . . . ooo . . . eee. Once you reach ten then your lips must stop the kiss. Remove your mouth from the man's immediately. You got that?"

"Right. Count to ten then pull my mouth off. I got it." She re-puckered and tried to count out the corner of her mouth. "Un . . . ooo—"

"Oh. There's one more thing."

She let out an exasperated sigh and rolled her eyes. "What now?"

"Your eyes will want to close when you do starter kisses. That's not allowed." His finger waggled in a no-no action. "You must keep your eyes on the end of your nose, or his nose, whichever is easier for you to see." His eyes crossed to look at the tip of his nose in another professional demonstration.

Her body jittered up and down in anxious anticipation. "I got it. Stare at a nose. I'm a pretty fast learner. Let's get to this."

"We have to get close to each other. But remember rule number one, or is it number three? There's to be no body touching."

She took two steps toward him.

Lance halted her. "That's too close. Take one step back."

Utopia took two steps back, frustration clear in her scowl at the delay. "Is this okay?"

"You're good right there. Now lean toward me."

They put their faces to within inches of each other. Close enough that she could feel his breathing on her cheek. His puppy dog brown eyes looked deeply into hers, and the palms of her hands began to sweat. She wiped her palms on her pants. His eyes intently locked on her lips and pulled her closer. The pull of him tugged her so strong, it took all of her will to wait for him to tell her to make mouth-to-mouth contact.

No more was said as his lips drew close to hers. Instinctively, her body knew when to move her mouth nearer to his. Her eyes froze on his luscious lips as they neared ever closer.

Then it happened. Her breath sucked in when the warmth of his mouth touched hers. Time froze. Her senses took in the smell of his sandalwood shave soap. It was hard fighting off the urge to close her eyes at the sweet sensations overtaking her body. She tried to focus her eyes on the tip of her nose, but her attention got sidetracked by the fact Lance had his eyes closed.

In a flash, his mouth quickly withdrew from hers.

She knew her mistake right off but pretended to brush over it. "How'd I do?"

He cleared his throat and looked away. "Fine. Fine. You did fine."

Something was definitely wrong with Lance. He paced back and forth. His fingers jittered nervously about. He shuffled across her tree floor in irritated movements.

THE COURTSHIP OF UTOPIA MINOR 57

"I think you forgot to count to ten. That . . . that's it. That's why I had to cut off the kiss. You . . . you definitely weren't counting like I told you to. It's not my job to count." Lance aimed an angry finger at her. "Girls are always supposed to be the counters. You got that? *Never forget to count*."

Why the heck was he hollering at her? Utopia put her fists on her hips. "Well, hell's bells. That was only my first starter kiss. I'll do better next time."

"See that you do."

Her kissing instructor seemed very angry with her. He was right, though. It must not have been the best starter kiss he'd ever had. What'd he expect for her first time? If he really wanted to know the problem, counting had been the last thing on her mind. Whether it had been a poor starter kiss lesson or not, she knew one thing. By gosh, by golly, she couldn't wait for stage two wet kissing. "I can do better. You want to do more practicing?"

"No. I mean . . . I think we've had more than enough practice for one day. Believe me when I say I can't take much more of this."

"Well, you don't have to be so snooty about it. Surely, forgetting to count can't make starter kisses all that horrible. I'm sorry. Really I am." How could she have been so stupid, messing up a simple thing like kissing? It made her wonder how bad she'd be at poking.

"It's nothing you did wrong. I should have been more prepared."

Was he telling her he'd left out some important details of starter kissing? She didn't have time for no half-ass kissing lessons. "Well, what in tarnation kind of starter kissing teacher are you, anyways?"

"A good one, if you are asking me." Lance paced back and forth. "Look, I think we should do something else. How about fishing? Don't you think that would be a good idea?"

"No fishing. The day's wasting and I have prospecting to do."

"What about me? Am I going to go along?"

"You can come along. I'll teach you some on prospecting."

"Uhh . . . I don't know if I care to spend my whole afternoon—"

"I owe you something for teaching me kisses. The least I can do is teach you something you don't know about."

She really wanted more kissing practice, but he was right. They had best get to mining. Utopia sat down on the edge of the platform to put her boots back on. Lance did the same. With the thrill of her first kiss still lingering in her senses, a worry crept into her otherwise perfect afternoon.

It dawned on her that once they both got out of the tree, it would be her turn to teach him gold mining. Panning wasn't anywhere near as complicated as kissing. What if he got offended at getting the little end of the horn on lessons and decided to cut off giving more saloon teaching? She'd better come up with a few difficult mining skills to keep him interested.

"Finding gold is hard work," she said. "It takes skills to know what to look for."

"I've seen how you work your wash pan. I might not get the same hip action going, but I'll give it my best. And I figure you'll show me the finding skills."

What hip action was he talking about? She stood up. "Well, let's get to it. You go down the ladder first. I'll be right behind you. That way I can roll up my steps once I'm down."

CHAPTER SEVEN

"Fine. See you below." Lance got half-way down the rungs when the rope staircase began to switch and sway from left to right. Such a motion drew his gaze upwards. Lance watched Utopia climbing down the rope. Her hips had the rope swinging like the pendulum in a grandfather clock.

He made it to the ground and continued to watch her provocative ladder act. "Hip action. It's all in the hips."

"What'd you say?"

"I'm thinking how sturdy your ladder is," he yelled. He'd consider this situation the most sexy and sticky predicament he'd ever pinned himself into. He was supposed to keep Utopia away from her gold hunting. If the fathers learned that he'd assisted her in gathering up her dowry, he'd be a dead man for sure.

Utopia skipped the last two rungs and jumped to the ground. She rolled the ladder up and tied off the rope. "Yew, boy. I never noticed how long it takes to get down from that tree."

"I didn't mind it." He smirked.

"Hmm. Right. Let's get to work."

They walked to the rocker several yards downstream. Lance knew he needed to be putting his brain to work on ideas to distract her from finding gold. He'd barely survived that brilliant kissing lesson idea of his. How disastrous would his attempts at distracting her from gold be?

Utopia placed her hands on her hips. "Now then, first we need our pans."

"I'll get them." Lance walked over to the tools on the ground and grabbed two pans from the pile. By the time he returned, she stood near the creek. He swallowed the knot in his throat. *Please, don't let her shirt get wet again.* "Here's your pan." Lance passed her one of the tins.

Utopia extended her arms, holding the pan out in front of her. "Now we got to ready our pans."

"Ready my pan?"

"Yep. Creek sediment swishes better if you ready your tool first. Watch me." Utopia held her item chest high. "Turn your pan so the bottom's facing you. Like so."

Lance turned his pan like she demonstrated.

"That's good. Now take it behind you to your backside, keeping a tight hold of the thing with both hands like so, then rub the pan on your bottom like this." Utopia moved the metal pan from side-to-side, back and forth across her butt.

It seemed a totally ridiculous thing to do, but he followed her instructions. "Can I ask you what the purpose of this procedure is?"

"It creates static. And static helps the gold separate from the sand and gravel."

"That makes sense," Lance agreed.

"You best rub faster. It'll take all day to build up good static at the rate you're swiping."

Lance moved his pan so fast he could actually feel the metal getting hot. Or maybe it was her eyes on his backside doing the warming. He felt plumb silly and relieved when she told him he'd reached a point of ample static.

"Now we got to shine."

"Shine? What the heck's that?"

"We seal in the static with a spit shine."

"A spit shine? You got to be kidding?" This couldn't be real.

"Nope. The static will stay on your pan longer once it is good and shined."

"I ain't doing it," Lance argued.

"Ooookay. You can work an un-spit pan if you want, but I wouldn't expect to find much gold if you don't shine." She spit in her pan and smeared it all around with her fingers.

"You're the expert," he grumbled. And like an idiot he spit and shined. "Now what?"

"We're ready to pan."

"Good. For a moment I thought you'd say we had to toss the pans to dry the spit."

Utopia's eyes lit up. She gave a happy smile. "Boy, I'm glad you mentioned that. I almost forgot that step." She turned her pan vertical and tossed it high in the air. She repeated the drying process several times. "Come on. Get to drying."

Lance shook his head. "For the love of Pete, this can't be a mining procedure."

"Are you calling me a honeyfuggler?" Utopia narrowed her eyes on him.

"The word never crossed my lips. To satisfy my own curiosity, how did you learn all this pan-prepping stuff?"

"Jargus taught me. He knows more about panning than anyone." Her hands and pan went to her hips in threat. "And no one calls him a honeyfuggler without him fixing their flint."

"Sorry. I certainly didn't mean to insinuate that you, or your fathers, are fugglers."

"I'll take that to mean you're apologizing. Now can we get back to our lesson?"

"Please. I'm all ears." Lance looked on while Utopia slowly walked out into the creek. "What are you doing? I thought we were going to pan from the bank."

"We aren't wearing these tall muck boots 'cause they're pretty. The water's not too deep here. What are you waiting for? Get in the creek."

Lance carefully inched himself into the water, testing for good footing while carefully making his way out to his instructor.

"Are you situated now?" she asked with a hint of annoyance.

"I think so." He hoped the water didn't get much deeper. He hated wearing wet socks.

"I'm powerful glad to hear that. Moving on to the next step, now we got to get some wash. You dip your pan into the creek, scoop up some silt and bring it out of the water like this." She straightened up holding a filled pan of water, sand and gravel. "Now you try it."

He followed her lead. "How's this?"

"Good. Now swish the water and dirt around in a circular swirl until the gold settles to the bottom of your pan." Utopia moved the pan in a well-practiced circular, titling motion.

Lance couldn't take his eyes off the movement of her hips. He wasn't built like her. It'd be impossible to duplicate the action of her panning. When she looked his way, he quickly diverted his attention to his own pan. "Like this?"

"No. No. No. You're way too stiff. Wait. I have an idea." Utopia emptied her pan and tossed it to the bank. She sloshed through the creek and came up behind him and clamped her hands on his hips. "I'll guide your bottom while you swish."

He felt her hands shove his bottom left and then force him to swing to the right. The directive of her hands, and their vicinity to his loins, had his blood boiling even though he stood knee deep in a frigid creek. "I'd like to try this on my own without your hands on me."

"I'm just showing you how to—"

"I know. I know. Hip action. I need hip action." Lance had to shed his reaction to her maneuverings and focus on panning and only panning. Soon he got into a rhythmic, synchronized washing movement. "I think I've got the hang of this."

"That's more like it." She gave his butt a hard pat. "Keep those hips working."

They both swished and swayed in the middle of the creek in silence. After about fifteen minutes, Utopia walked to the bank. "Okay. I think we've washed long enough. Bring your pan over here and let's see if we have anything."

Lance carefully held his pan ahead of him and walked toward the bank.

Utopia picked her fingers through the sediment on the hunt for shiny specks. "I've got nothing. Let me check yours."

He handed her his pan and watched her perform the deft hunt and peck skills to his creek muck. Her fingers suddenly stopped searching and her eyes grew wide. She pinched one teensy speck from the sand.

"Did we find something?" He leaned closer to see what she had.

"I don't believe it." Utopia held a shiny granule on her fingertip. "A flake. On your first dang try, you found a flake?"

"Is that good?" She didn't seem too happy about his find. Come to think on it, he shouldn't be happy about finding gold, either. "Is there something wrong with a flake?"

Utopia stared at her find. "I don't understand what it's doing here. This area's been washed out for years." She perused the hillside cliffs. "It wasn't here yesterday."

"I guess I used better static and spit than you." Lance watched her face scowl.

"Don't be silly. There's no . . ."

Lance now realized he'd been played the fool. "All that pan spitting, rubbing and tossing, those things weren't real panning preparations, were they?"

"That's not what I meant to say. I was being a . . ."

"A honeyfuggler?" he supplied.

She pointed her non-flake holding finger in his face. "Don't call me a honeyfuggler. We found gold, didn't we?"

"Yes, we did." Lance didn't know the reasons for all her shenanigans, but he'd not let her get the best of him. "And now we can split it fifty-fifty."

Utopia held her finger up and squinted at the speck. "Heck, there's no way to divvy up something this small."

"Well, you're the expert. Think of some way." Lance thoroughly enjoyed the rise of irritation showing on her face. "What in tarnation kind of prospecting teacher are you, anyway?"

"A darn good one, if you're asking me," she grumbled.

He reached in his back pocket for a knife and smirked. "Shall we take our flake to the bank? A flat rock might make the splitting easier."

"Look. This is plumb crazy. Why the dang thing's so small an ant might mistake it for a crumb and carry it off before we can put eyes to dividing it."

Lance put his hand over his heart. "What kind of partner would I be if I didn't give you a fair share?"

"Fair share?" Utopia squinted at the tiny dot on her fingertip. "What the hell are you talking about? This is impossible to have a share of."

"It was found in my pan. It would rightly be mine to keep. But I said we are partners and I'd split it. And I'm a man of my word."

"If you want to split hairs about the whole darn thing, your dang flake was discovered in my secret gold hunting place. The flake should be mine."

Lance crossed his arms over his chest. "I'll tell you what we'll do. We'll try to divide the fleck . .

. I mean flake. If the task is too hard, then I'll concede the teensy gold to you. Agreed?"

"I guess I'll never hear the end of it if I don't do this. Let's get to it."

Lance hunted around on the ground for a flat rock and made a selection. "This one will do. Bring *our* flake over here." Her expression looked so comical, he could hardly keep from busting out laughing. Utopia carefully swiped the flake off her fingertip onto the stone. He opened the switchblade and handed it to her. "Here's *my* knife. You may do the honors."

"Are we splitting hairs on which one of us has the tool for this splitting job?"

"No. Not at all," he replied with a smirk.

She took the blade from his hand, nearly slicing his finger. No doubt she had intended to pain him. Thank goodness for quick reflexes. He watched her ever so carefully place the knife's point on the tidbit.

She squinted at the knife placement and asked, "Is this where you want me to divide it?"

Lance bent down real close and made a lengthy inspection. He could smell her earthy scent. His chest touched her shoulder. She flinched. So did his heart. "No. That's sixty-forty. Move the blade to the left."

"I think you're being unappreciative of all my good teachings. If you were any kind of partner you'd—" A tiny puff of air escaped her nostrils, accompanied by a tiny *cheep*.

"You were saying?"

"Oh, no." Utopia looked all around the rock and then the ground with panic etched on her face.

He pretended not to know about her little nasal puff of air. "What's wrong?"

"It's gone. I sneezed and . . ."

"And what?"

"The dang flake—the darn thing blew away."

Lance choked on a laugh and added a cough to cover his blunder. "You lost my first flake. How could you?"

Utopia shot to her feet. "I didn't do it on purpose. If you hadn't insisted we split a flake, we wouldn't be without one now."

He met her rage face to face. "If you hadn't sneezed, it wouldn't have blown away."

"Ooooh, you. Here's your knife."

She flung the switchblade to the ground, implanting the blade clear to the hilt between his narrowly parted feet. If the blade landed any closer to either boot, she'd have severed a toe or two.

Utopia went over and collected up her tools.

Lance followed her lead. "I guess this means we aren't panning anymore?"

"You can stay here and pan all day if you want. I'm going back to camp."

At least for today, he'd successfully kept her from prospecting. He'd have to be equally bad at tomorrow's lessons. "I'll carry your tools for you."

She walked past him. "I'm as mad as a snared badger right now. If you know what's good for you, you'll not bother me. Or I might sockdologer you right in your smeller."

Before he could reply, she trudged down the hillside toward camp. He followed her fast-paced swishing behind all the way back to camp. *The gal definitely had some fine hip action.*

CHAPTER EIGHT

Tin Cup, Colorado

The Palace Oak Saloon was open for business, but at this time of day, it was hard to tell how good profits would be. Cyrus Langley rested his boot on the brass rail running along the bottom of the mahogany bar. He clasped his chubby hand on the lapel of his suit, and the paste diamond ring on his pinky finger sparkled. He withdrew a cigar from his mouth.

Cyrus viewed his newly acquired business in the mirror behind the bar. He gave himself a prideful smile and puffed a smoke ring in the air. His sudden ownership of the saloon came by way of a lucky poker hand. However, the months since winning the bar had not turned out to be that lucrative.

The responsibility of operating one of the town's more popular watering holes had certain implicit obligations. These included providing a good stock of whiskey for customers to get liquored up on, and secondly, sheltering pretty girls for men to enjoy. There was the rub of it.

Constant thoughts of financial ruin plagued Cyrus simply because his bar had no pretty saloon girls. His stable of prostitutes totaled three. The hauntingly boney Lil, with wrinkles so deep you could use her face as a washboard. There was boulder-bosomed Pearl, with her beagle bald head and an ever-changing supply of wig hairdos. And lastly, there was Sadie, a crab of a harlot past her prime at the age of thirty. The woman possessed a monthly cycle that hit like clockwork every two weeks, and during this spell, Sadie refused to work.

"Can I get you anything?" Risky Snoops, the bartender, asked.

"Hello, Risky. What gives today? Business seems slow."

"It'll pick up soon, boss, don't you worry. A cattle drive is due in town near sundown."

Cyrus took another puff of his cigar. He was in no mood for another one of Risky's perk-yourself-up speeches. "And how did you come by this information?"

"A trail boss, a fella named Gentry, came in earlier and booked all our upstairs rooms."

"Good." Cyrus gave a long draw on his cigar in deep thought. Even this bit of news couldn't stop his worrying on the problem that kept profits away. His recent gift of cosmetics should help. "Did you tell the girls to put on plenty of that face paint I got them?"

"Sure did. I told them to load it on good."

After Cyrus took over the Palace Oak, the first thing he did was take out a bank loan. He used the money to decorate the place with gilded mirrors, velvet drapery and a fine stage for bawdy entertainment. Simply put, the investment hadn't improved a thing. The saloon still had one big deterrent to profitability, his ugly dancehall girls.

He'd thought about replacing Lil, Pearl and Sadie. The only thing that made up for the unattractiveness of the harlots was the fact they worked for small wages. And until business improved, he couldn't afford pretty. It seemed he'd inherited a never-ending problem. The fact remained. He didn't have the heart to put the girls on the street. Not until he had replacements.

"Lil's already walking around with her new face." Risky pointed in the direction of three men near the door. "She's over there serving drinks."

The cosmetically enhanced Lil turned and headed for the bar. Cyrus slapped a hand to his cheek. "Great balls of fire. Look at her. Why she'll be the ruin of me for sure."

Luscious Lil slammed her drink tray on the counter. "Risky, I need me two whiskeys and four beers." Lil poked her long red nails in her frizzy, Georgia clay colored curls.

"Coming right up." Risky headed for the beer tap located at the other end of the bar.

Cyrus averted his eyes from Lil's bright rouged cheeks and poorly outlined red lips. He grabbed hold of the counter for support to fend-off a sudden case of lightheadedness.

Lil settled her hand on her boney hip. "Cyrus, is something the matter? You look pale."

"Oh, it's nothing." He cleared his throat. "How do you like the makeup I got you?"

"You want the truth? I think you've wasted good money."

He couldn't agree with her more.

The bartender returned and placed beer mugs, whiskey and glasses on Lil's tray and slid the completed order toward the flashy server. "Leave the boss alone. He's busy right now."

"Well, lah-di-dah. Huh. Cyrus, if you ask me, your business is down on account of him." She pointed a twiggy, red-nailed finger at the liquor server. "Take my advice and get yourself a friendlier bartender." Lil struggled to lift her order off the bar then turned on her wobbly heels, attached to her toothpick legs and sauntered off.

Cyrus shuddered at the thought of what Pearl and Sadie would look like. The sight of Lil set his mood and profit expectations low. He pointed his cigar in the direction of three gentlemen seated across the barroom. "Take a bottle of our best brandy and four glasses to that table in the far corner. After I talk with my friends, I plan to be in my office. When Travin comes around, you tell him I need to speak with him."

"Yes, sir," Risky said. "I'll send your boy back to your office as soon as he comes in."

Cyrus wormed his way through the saloon greeting patrons until he reached the table where the town's most prominent citizens now indulged in his limited stock of fine brandy. The Palace Oak was not the usual place he and his associates conducted their political business. He greeted Leo Dennison with a handshake. "Good evening, Mayor, it's been awhile. How's your wife?"

"Mary's fine. Her mother's moved in with us from back East though. Why my mother-in-law shows up at my house at election time is beyond me." Mayor Leo took a hefty gulp of his drink.

Next Cyrus offered a hand to the land assessor. "Hello, Harlan. How are things with you?"

"I've been better."

Finally, Cyrus offered a tentative hand to the bank president and second term territorial governor, Frank Sharps. The saloon owner felt the power of a political snub when his greeting was ignored.

"Sit down, Cyrus," Frank ordered. "This isn't a social call. We need to talk."

Cyrus took a seat. He nervously smiled. "What brings all of you to my establishment?"

"It's that menacing editor, Barris Baines," Mayor Leo said. "He's running a contest in that *Rocky Mountain Gazette* of his."

"What kind of contest?" Cyrus took a cue from the others at the table and poured himself a drink.

Mayor Leo pushed a newspaper across the table. "The election is ruined, I tell you. None of us stand a chance of being reelected."

Cyrus put on a pair of spectacles and perused the article. He slid the paper back to the disturbed Mayor. "So there's a contest. I don't see the harm."

"Look at the date, for crying out loud." Mayor Leo repetitiously jabbed his finger on the article. "It says the contest starts in June. The election's June 20th."

"Do we have to spell it out for you?" Frank interlocked his fingers and cracked his knuckles.

"Let's condense this problem down to terms you'll understand. Look around, Cyrus. Is this your usual Friday night crowd?"

Cyrus' shirt collar tightened like a hangman's knot around his Adam's apple. Frank was a most menacing man. Things like fingers, noses, and ribs had a way of getting broken if you crossed him. Not to mention he held the notes on practically all of Tin Cup's businesses, including his Palace Oak Saloon. "There's a big herd due in tonight. The place will fill up soon."

"If the contest doesn't end before Election Day, we can kiss our political careers goodbye." Leo doused down another swig of brandy.

Harlan tucked the article inside his jacket. "There won't be a soul in town to vote for us if this contest doesn't go away. Oh, why does this kind of stuff always happen at election time?"

"Hmm." Cyrus drummed his fingers on the tabletop and thought on what a possible shortage of voters would do for the election. "I don't believe we've ever had this kind of voter turn-out problem before."

Frank braced his elbows on the table. He clasped his hands in such a way that his pointer fingers formed a steeple. "We pay you quite a sum of money to guarantee our reelections each term. I'd hate to think our political futures are in jeopardy all because of some frivolous contest."

Cyrus reached for the brandy, and he poured himself a drink. The bottle rattled on the rim of his glass. "That article mentioned Jargus and Fergus Knudsen were the ones putting on this contest. I buy my whiskey from those Knudsen boys. Perhaps I could go and speak with them. Convince them to move their contest to another time."

"For crying out loud, is that the best idea you can come up with?" Leo exclaimed.

"Shut up." Frank tossed his drink in the Mayor's face and slammed his empty glass on the table. "Cyrus, you're going to end this contest."

The threatening tone hit home. "Gentlemen, don't fret." Cyrus felt sweat rolling down his back, his suit so damp with perspiration, it clung to him. "I'll simply go up to the Knudsen camp and ask them how long they think their contest will be. Not to worry. I'm sure everything will work out just fine."

Cyrus knew that cantankerous bastard Jargus wouldn't be easy to deal with. But it was either haggle with the Knudsen boys or get beat up, or receive much worse displeasures from Frank's henchmen. Cyrus pushed his chair back and stood. "Gentlemen, I'll handle everything."

Frank got to his feet and towered over the saloonkeeper. "Remember, Cyrus, my bank holds the mortgage on this place. I can call your note due with a snap . . ." He added the sound for effect. ". . . of my fingers."

"I'll take care of it." Cyrus swallowed a lump of fear and watched the banker leave. He tucked his spectacles back in his vest pocket and gave the remaining politicians at the table a slight bow. "Now, if you'll excuse me. I best get back to my work."

Cyrus ran for safety of his office with his chicken coattails tucked between his legs.

THE COURTSHIP OF UTOPIA MINOR   77

In his private quarters, he closed the door and somehow nervously staggered across the room. He lit the kerosene lamp sitting and an amber glow spread about the walnut paneled interior.

Cyrus circled around the mahogany desk and sat down in his tall leather-appointed chair. Within arm's reach behind his imperial throne, he kept a small bar filled with a variety of liquor. He poured himself a shot of whiskey and tossed down the liquid then banged his glass on the desk. What gal was so desperate she needed a contest to get herself a man? He knew the answer. An ugly gal.

He left his chair and paced back and forth with his hands clasped tightly behind his back. "Who can I trust to enter that contest and woo this girl to a fast wedding ceremony?" He thought out loud but no answers came to him.

The door opened and in walked Travin. The lad strutted into the office with a big grin on his lipstick-smeared face. "Hi, Pa. Risky said you wanted to see me?"

A seed of an idea sprouted in Cyrus' troubled brain. His one and only offspring happened to be very handsome and a lady's man. *The idea wasn't a crazy notion.* "Why, yes, son, I do. I do. Come in, come in. Have a seat. I'd like to talk to you about something very important. I really need your help."

CHAPTER NINE

The Bound to Be Lucky Mining Camp
June 1st

Lance couldn't pinpoint exactly when or how the fathers managed to wheedle him into another job. Nonetheless, he'd become the contest coordinator, in charge of making up the contest rules, registering contestants, and officiating the process by which the bride-to-be would pick a husband.

In a holding area down in the lower pass of the valley, two kegs and a rough planked board had been put together for a makeshift desk for him to work. Since early dawn, Lance sat before a long line of hopeful contestants issuing them courting numbers.

Almost noon now, the line of suitors had dwindled down to a handful. Wanting to be thorough, Lance spent this lull in the registration process double-checking the men's names against the corresponding contestant numbers on his other list.

THE COURTSHIP OF UTOPIA MINOR 79

"Excuse me, mister. Is this where I enter the bride contest?"

Hearing the squeaky voice, Lance looked up from his paperwork. *For the love of Pete, this one's nothing but a wet-nosed kid.* "Boy, are you even old enough to enter a wife contest?"

The lad yanked his newsboy cap off his head. "Mickey Crosby's my name, sir. I'm fourteen. I wouldn't be here if I weren't old enough, sir."

Exactly what age a fellow could enter needed to be clarified with the only father nearby. "Henry, this lad wants to be in the contest. Says he's fourteen. Your advertisement didn't stipulate an age limit. Do you want to let the boy enter or not?"

"Oh, please, mister. I've come all the way from Fort Riley to get myself a bride."

Henry shrugged his shoulders. "I suppose being a bit young's better than being an old buzzard that can't seal the marriage on the wedding night, if you get my drift."

Yeah. Lance got the drift. And the thought darkened his mood even further.

"The lad's traveled a far piece for a chance at a bride," Henry said. "He looks spunky enough to me. I say he can court."

That wasn't the answer Lance had hoped for. He handed the pimple-faced kid a slip of paper and made a notation of one-hundred-fifty next to Mickey's name on his list. This boy didn't stand a chance with the bride-to-be. That thought lightened Lance's sour mood some. "That's your contest number, kid. Don't lose it."

"This is a pretty high number, sir. Do you have any idea how long it will take to get to my turn? My ma says I have to be back by week's end."

"First, you have to win the luck of the draw. After that it's up to the girl to eliminate some of your competition." Lance stood and gave the boy a handshake. "Good luck."

"Thank you, sir." Mickey donned his hat and walked off with a bounce in his step.

Lance stacked his paperwork together and faced the father. "The day's getting warm, Henry. You ready to go over the rules with the contestants?"

"Ready as I'll ever be, I guess." Henry scanned the crowd and gave a short whistle. "I sure never expected this many folks to show up."

"I don't envy your girl. There are one-hundred-fifty registered suitors." Lance hated to think about Utopia's courting. He hated the sheer number of entrants even more. It was torturing him to no end thinking about her kissing even one man, much less each and every fellow in this multitude. "It's not too late to call this whole thing off."

"Nope," Henry said. "We're doing this. Oh, there's one small thing before we start."

Lance crossed his arms over his chest, waiting for the lead anvil to fall. It had to be a problem. The fathers always saved the troublesome details for last. "What is it?"

"I peeked in your parcibles. Now I know I shouldn't have. I saw your marshal's badge."

"You rooted through my things." Lance shot his hands to his hips. "Why'd you do that?"

"Jargus, Fergus and I wanted to be sure Utopia is safe around you. We wanted to be sure you didn't have a wanted poster out on you or some such. I feel much better about this contest now that I know we have some law around. We can't be none too careful. There might be some bad sorts amongst that crowd."

"It's not official yet. I'm resigning from the law at the end of the month. For now, I'm a reporter. You hear me? It's just me writing about this contest. I've agreed to chaperone during the courting but not as a lawman. Don't expect me to pull out my badge to break up every fight that erupts over your girl. That's your problem to handle . . . because . . . I need to keep myself unbiased. Are you hearing me on this?"

"When's this contest starting?" grumbled an anxious suitor, breaking into the tension-filled conversation Lance and Pa Henry were having.

Lance grabbed his hat off the desk and dropped it on his head. "I've said all I'm going to on the law matter."

"I didn't mean to snoop in your things."

"Forget it. We better get this contest started before these suitors string us both up."

They walked towards the hillside to the right of them and climbed up an outcropping of rock to be more visible to the crowd.

From the rock ledge, Lance had a good vantage point to look over the throng of eager suitors. It was time to get down to business. He raised his hands in the air for silence. "Gentlemen, when it is all said and done, in a few days, or weeks, one of you lucky men will be Miss Utopia Miner's husband."

The crowd cheered. Pistols randomly fired off, filling the airspace with a smoky haze. His inner lawman didn't like the fact there were so many weapons at an event that could become overly competitive. He'd have to put something in the rules about that.

"Quiet." Lance held up his hands. It took a moment for the crowd to silence. "I have some rules I need to go over before we can get this contest gets underway."

Henry stepped to the front edge of the ledge. "Lance, I'd like you to hold up on the rules a minute. I got to fix something that's wrong here." The father faced the crowd and scowled. "Clancy Stramps and Quincy Fraggert—you two don't belong in this contest. Both of you need to scat on back home to your wives." He aimed a warning finger toward the crowd. "If any of you fellas has got any improper intentions toward my daughter, or there's reason you can't lawfully be wedded, you best scat on out of here, too."

Lance patted the irate father on his shoulder. "Calm down, Henry. You're going to give yourself a heart attack. Let me handle this." He tweaked a thumb over the shoulder. "Boy, you sure can tell he's a father of the bride, can't you?"

The crowd laughed.

"Henry, Jargus and Fergus are Miss Miner's fathers. They'll take a shotgun to any man that gets out of line with their daughter. Is that understood?"

THE COURTSHIP OF UTOPIA MINOR   83

The suitors in the crowd silently nodded their heads.

"Now that we've got that important matter out of the way, let's move on. I'm going to draw seven numbers from my hat. The contestants with these numbers will be the first to go up to the camp and meet the lovely Miss Miner. The rest of you can head to camp in a bit and pitch your tents.

Lance paused, waiting for nods that the contestants understood.

"Each suitor will have one hour in which to court the bride-to-be. And since we don't want to wear the poor girl out, we're limiting the number of proposals to no more than seven a day. For those of you not courting, you'll need to find a peaceful something else to do. You can buy whiskey if you have a notion. However, since drinking and guns spell trouble, we'll be collecting all of your weapons."

"I don't turn over my gun to nobody," a belligerent man in the crowd hollered.

The lawman in Lance surfaced even though he'd said he wouldn't pull his badge in this contest. "Then leave." He waited to see how the man would react. When things remained calm, he continued. "Each of you will get your weapons back when you leave. Now if we're through with the rules then I'll draw the first seven suitor numbers. So listen up."

Reluctantly, Lance held his derby aloft and stirred the papers around with his free hand. The crowd fell so silent he could have heard a twig snap. His fingers toyed with the slips of numbers, not wanting to choose any but having to choose seven.

He pulled the first paper out of his hat. For the longest moment he stared at the number with a crushing pressure within his chest. A memory of Utopia and that day in her tree floor secret place instantly appeared in his mind. That first starter-kiss-lesson became so vivid he could almost feel her lips on his this very minute.

When he looked from the number in his hand to the crowd, he saw the sea of eager faces and struggled to accept what he must do. He couldn't blame any of them for being so excited to court. Yet, he did. He didn't want to start the contest. The knot in his throat grew tighter with each breath he took. Somehow he found his voice. "The first suitor number is seventy-five."

CHAPTER TEN

The first seven suitors trailed behind Lance, following him up the pass which was the only way in or out of the mining camp. The steep, rocky grade required a slow pace to navigate it safely. Lance let his sure-footed horse follow his nose. This riding time allowed him to catch a breather before his reporter and chaperoning duties kicked in.

Lance turned in his saddle and briefly scrutinized the contestants. Six were riding plow horses and one gent rode a mule. Most were dressed in their Sunday finest, all toting courting gifts. He couldn't help but think that a few of these suitors could be after the gold mine being offered in addition to the bride. Some of them probably didn't give a hoot who they married so long as they became rich. The notion of greedy suitors struck a bad cord in Lance's gut.

If he had anything to feel good about with regards to the courting contest, it was that he'd finally convinced the fathers to confess their scheme to their daughter. Jargus said he'd handle telling Utopia about the contest during the two days Henry and Lance handled the registrations.

At last, the group rode into camp. Lance glanced to Utopia's cabin and wondered how she'd taken the contest news. In the back of his mind, he sort of hoped she would refuse to have anything to do with the event, and she'd tell all these men to go to hell. He'd feel a lot better about owning his newspaper business if he could write only the one article on her decision not to be a marriage trophy.

"Is this the first batch?" Jargus asked.

Lance climbed down off his mount and walked toward Jargus standing not far from Utopia's cabin. "This is the first of the potential grooms. In my opinion, these suitors don't look too promising. One's not even out of knickers."

"You aren't the one that's going to decide, are you?" Jargus gave a spit to the dirt.

"That's a fact. Speaking of your daughter, where is she?"

"She's still in her cabin gussying herself up. I don't know what has her so chipper, but I'm real thankful for her good mood no matter the reason."

"Then you've told her about the contest and she's agreeable to it?"

Jargus abruptly turned toward the group of contestants. "You men can leave your horses tied up yonder by those trees. We'll be starting this here contest shortly."

The old man avoided his question, and that was not a good thing. Lance stepped in front of Jargus and blocked his escape. "Tell me Utopia's expecting these men."

"Dang-nabbit. I tried to tell her. She kept interrupting me." Jargus jerked his hat off and puffed up his chest. "Seein's how we're running out of time, I reckon you're gonna have to go in there and talk her into coming out."

"You're out of your mind." Lance's blood boiled. This time he'd put his foot down. There'd be no more contest duties dumped on him, especially this one. "No. Damn it. I've had it. Listen and listen good, old man. She's your daughter. You go tell her."

"I thought you'd say that." Jargus scrubbed on his cheek. "So I have another idea."

Lance threw his hands up. "I don't care. Forget your ideas. I'm not doing it."

"This is a good idea. You'll like this one. You see, you go sneaking up to the door real quiet like. But don't knock. Then you just barge right in there, round her up. If she ain't willing to come out peaceable, drag her out here the best way you can."

Lance tugged his bowler on his head tight, clear to his eyebrows. The snug fit did little to tamp down his temper. "Why do I have to fetch her? None of this was my idea."

"You don't have to lie to her like I do. She can always tell when I'm honeyfuggling."

"Then tell her the truth." This last word literally spit out of Lance's mouth.

Jargus wiped spittle out of his eye. "I suppose you're right."

"I'm glad you're finally coming around to the idea of telling the truth."

"Yeah. The truth is always best." The old man nodded. "I guess it's time you go in there and tell her everything. Word the truth anyway you like. But get her out here."

Jargus spun around and tried to scurry away. Lance quickly grabbed his arm. "Come back here, you ornery cuss. I'm not–" When he heard the double barrels of a shotgun locking into place and felt a poke in the ribs, he froze and glanced over his shoulder.

"H-hi there, Lance." Fergus aimed the weapon at Lance.

Jargus spit. "I say you're going in there to get her, or else."

"Or else what? I'm a whiskey sieve? I've heard that threat a hundred times in the last three days. You know what? I don't care anymore." Lance turned loose of Jargus' arm. "I don't think you have the guts to plug me. What do you think about that?"

"It's good to see you're finally growing yourself some backbone." Jargus took the weapon from Fergus and patted the stock of the shotgun. "But you're still no match for Betsy here. You say one more word and your guts will be spilled all over the place. Now go fetch her."

"Fine. I'll go. But there's something you should know."

"Yeah, sonny, what's that?"

"These shotgun threats are getting very annoying."

Lance strolled to the door of Utopia's cabin wondering how he'd tell her about this mess.

"Who's there?" Utopia really didn't have to ask. She'd recognize Lance's knock no matter what time of day he tapped on her door.

"It's me, Lance."

It only took four long steps for her to get to the door and pull it open.

He immediately took his hat off and gave a half-wave. "Hi."

She waved back and smiled. "Howdy. I looked all over for you. Where've you been?

"Your Pa Henry and I were down the pass doing something."

"It's good you were with Pa Henry and not Jargus, I think he's gone off his rocker some. Well … don't just stand there, come on in."

Lance entered the cabin and walked to the center of the room. Something about the look on his face, and the way his hands were squeezing that hat of his, told her he was in a standoffish mood again. Utopia closed the door and faced him. Today, the top two buttons of his tan shirt were unfastened, revealing a bit of dark chest hair which made him look–cuddly. His hat-mussed hair gave her a want-to-comb-fingers-through-it feeling. His brow had little beads of sweat upon it. It wasn't a stretch to say that looking at him caused a temperature rise in her, too.

She couldn't wait to share her surprise with him. "I'm sure glad to see you. Guess what I've been doing?"

"Uh . . . I don't know. Singing?"

"This." Wanting her surprise to really wow him, Utopia rushed across the space between them and placed her hands on each side of his lightly bearded face. She puckered up and planted her lips on his. Out the side of her mouth she counted, "Unn, ooo, eee, orr, ive, icks, evn, ate, ine, en." Then quickly released him and grinned. "I practiced. Did I do better? Did you like it?"

"Like it?"

Lance stood there looking stunned. She had this sinking feeling she'd not improved.

"Umm . . . you've mastered counting. And you did nose-tip looking good, too."

She'd not let on she expected more from him. "Thanks. I think that nose stuff is the hardest part of starter kisses. I always have this urge to close my eyes." Why hadn't he noticed her gussying up? "Did you notice anything else about me?" She fluffed a hand through her hair.

"Your hair. It's not in braids. I think I like braids, don't you?"

"I'll have you know it took me half the morning to get the tangles out. I think the vanilla I put in my wash water stuck some of it together. But it is smells real pretty. You want a sniff?"

Lance quickly stepped back, shying away from her like he feared she'd punch him.

"No. I'll take your word for it." His gaze drifted to her white peasant top.

Oh, yeah. His eyes were turning that deep brown color they always did whenever he looked at her chest. She stroked her hand along the neckline of her blouse, pretending to have a slight itch to scratch. "You like my shirt?"

"Where'd you get that top?" He fanned himself with his derby. "There's a bit much of you showing. Don't you think you should put something else on?"

She frowned. Why couldn't he say just one nice thing about how she looked? "I think it fits me fine. The outfit belonged to my mama." Boy, he sure was in a sour mood. Maybe Lance was hungry. "Why don't we eat? I've fixed us some lunch. Once I have your belly full, maybe we could get around to practicing some stage two wet kisses."

Lance jerked his hat back on his head and tugged the brim so low she could no longer see his eyebrows. "Since you've put your hat back, that must mean you don't want any vittles. That's fine by me. We can eat later. After we—"

"Utopia, I have something important I have to talk to you about."

"Can't you eat first?" She reached for the basket on the table.

His hand stopped her. "No. I need to tell you this right now."

Her heart skipped several beats. Only one thing could be this serious. She prepared herself for the worst. "Oh, my stars. It's bad news. One of my fathers has passed on."

"No. No. It's nothing tragic like that. Your fathers are fine. Please. Sit down would you? The sooner you know what's going on, the better you can prepare for it."

She sank into the nearest chair. Her eyes fixed on his serious face. "Know what?"

"Your fathers they have done something. Something . . ."

"What something?" Her Pa Jargus and Lance seemed to be having the same touched-in-the-head kind of illness today. "What in tarnation is the matter with you? You're more jittered than a mouse camped out in a barn full of cats."

"I'll show you what the matter is. Come with me."

Lance grabbed hold of her arm and pulled her up off the chair. He led her across the room and opened the door. Instant whoops and cheers greeted her.

"That's what I've been trying to say. There. Look them over. If you don't like any of these, there's one hundred-forty-three more that'll be camped on your doorstep by nightfall."

Utopia slammed the door and threw the bolt in place. "What in blazes is going on? What are all those darn fellas doing out there?"

Lance shrugged his shoulders. "Your fathers want you to pick out a husband."

Oh, no. This was the last straw. Her dander revved up tighter than a spinning top. She paced the floor, hardly able to keep from cussing Lance a blue streak. "I've told my fathers time and again. *I don't want a husband. A husband will ruin everything.* They can't make me take a husband. Not if I don't want one. Can they?"

"Well . . . uh."

Lance looked like he didn't know the answer to her question. "Well, can they?"

"You know it wouldn't hurt for you to consider the option, would it? I mean, since your fathers have gone through all this trouble of a contest and all the advertising."

"Advertising?"

"I know this is kind of sudden."

Lance made a reach for her shoulder. She brushed his hand away. Her eyes glanced upward to the empty shotgun rack above the door jam. "Where's my shotgun? Who took my shotgun? When I get my hands on my fathers, they better settle accounts with the man upstairs, for they'll be headed his way. "

The more she talked the madder she got. Then she eyed the picnic basket and dashed to the table, flipped the lid open and armed herself with two hard-boiled eggs. "I want you out of here. Now." She hurled one egg and it caught Lance in his ribs when he tried to dodge.

"Ouch. Stop it. Utopia. Be reasonable."

"I'll show you reasonable, you . . . *honeyfuggler*." She armed herself with more eggs from the basket and put every bit of anger into her next throws. Lance made a dash for the door and lifted the latch to make his escape. She managed to pummel his rump with three more eggs on his way out.

Utopia latched the door then dropped her spent body in a chair beside the table. The fathers really had outdone themselves this time. In the past, she'd only had one or two men to run off the mountain. Now there were gads to chase away. Lance said there were over a hundred. That number could fill two or three saloons.

An idea sparked in her calculating brain. She dashed to the window and pulled back the curtain and peeked at the fellas more closely. The men were fancy-dressed. Some had packages tied with bows in their hands. Presents? She needed to think on this. If there were as many men a coming to see her like Lance said, and if all brought her something, why that'd be a bunch of some things.

Hmm. Perhaps she shouldn't run these fellas off too fast. She let the curtain fall back into place. Utopia fetched her hairbrush and ran it through her hair, thinking things over.

This could be a perfect chance to practice dancehall things. All those beaus would be so busy wooing her, likely they'd not pay too much attention if she practiced skills on them.

She'd practice kissing. She'd practice singing and dancing. She'd practice every saloon skill needed. Utopia adjusted the neckline of her white top and fluffed her hair. "Fellas, we'll just see which of us has the most fun at this courting stuff."

CHAPTER ELEVEN

Lance shouldn't have been surprised by the reaction of the seven suitors when Utopia stepped out of her cabin, but all the same it stung a bit. The men's whistling kept on and on. Why shouldn't the suitors act like a bunch of love-struck hounds? Just look at how she was dressed.

Homer Dubois, contestant number five, couldn't contain his bug-eyed amazement. "That gal's prettier than daffodils in spring."

"That figure of hers is curvier than that pass we just come up," another suitor added.

Lance fisted his hands and willed himself not to take his frustration out on these suitors. After all, every bit of what they were saying happened to be the gospel truth. There was no denying the bride-to-be was a rare beauty.

Along with every other male, Lance's gaze traveled over her figure.

Utopia displayed a fair amount of curvy calves with her buckskin pant-legs rolled up to her knees. But it was her creamy expanse of shoulders in that low-cut peasant blouse that really had all mouths agape. Each suitor could easily catch twenty flies in their opened orifices. "You're acting like a bunch of the love-struck kids," Lance barked. "Stop your drooling and shut your traps."

Jargus leaned toward Lance. "I don't know what you said to her, sonny. My hat's off to ya. She seems agreeable to courting. Let's get started before she changes her mind."

Lance stepped up on the porch next to Utopia. "Are you sure you want to do this?"

She flicked her hair off her shoulder. "Sure. Why wouldn't I?"

"My rump's bruised where you hit my backside with eggs. You weren't too keen on the idea of these fellows being here a while ago. What changed your mind?"

"Presents."

"Presents? That's it? Presents?"

"Yep. I want lots of them."

Lance caught the curious gleam in her green eyes, a scheming, prey-in-sight kind of look. A man learned to stay clear of that kind of look from a woman if he knew what was good for him.

"I got mad for a minute, but I'm over it now. The truth is, my fathers are right."

Utopia moved her arm behind her back. He'd bet her fingers were crossing this very minute. Her strange country girl way of pretending she wasn't honeyfuggling.

"It wouldn't hurt me none to court for a bit. Who knows—I might like one of them fellas and change my mind about marrying." She smiled. "What am I supposed to do now?"

That comment stung him. It shouldn't but it did. Lance clenched his teeth and let his gaze drift along the low neckline of her white top. Chaperoning her while she was dressed in such a garment could lead to considerable thumping of someone, and he certainly didn't want it to be him.

Lance grabbed each puffed sleeve on her blouse and pulled the garment higher up on her shoulders. "For starters, why don't you go inside your cabin and put your digging clothes on."

"Heck, no." Utopia brushed his hands off her and pulled the blouse back down to where it had been. "I fancied myself up for some fun, and I mean to have me some. Besides, I'm supposed to be catching me a husband, ain't I?"

She had him on that one. He frowned. "No respectable young lady shows so much–"

"So much what?"

Lance shook his head. The girl needed another lesson. One on respectability. However, it would be too lengthy a conversation to take up with her right now. "Never mind."

He yanked the courting list out of his vest pocket.

"Those gifts the men have–they're for me, aren't they?"

"Yes. When a man is courting a lady, he'll give her a small token gift."

"Do I get to keep them?"

"Yes."

"Even, if I don't pick that particular fella to marry?"

"Any gifts you receive, you get to keep." Lance suspected gifts would be a big incentive for Utopia to put a little extra effort into her husband selecting. Then again, a girl with very few trinkets and pretties could possibly be tempted to earn herself bigger, better gifts. Earning gifts in all the wrong ways, like performing certain favors in exchange for pretty things.

He couldn't bear to think about what the lass might do to gain material wealth. The whole scenario sent his brain struggling to keep a lid on his sanity. If only he could think of a way to delay the contest a short while. A long enough delay to explain the dangers of taking these men's gifts.

Utopia stepped forward and addressed the men. "Which one of you do I court first?"

Lance about fell over at Utopia's unscripted and premature announcement.

"Me. Number seventy-five, that's me." A lanky man waved his hat in the air.

Lance pulled his blabber-gal back a step. "Why did you do that?"

Again, she swiped his hand off her. "It looks to me like you're stalling. So I thought I'd help get things started."

"You need to let me handle this. There's an order to courting, and you're messing it all up." His eyes again drifted across the low cut neckline, and once more, he grabbed a fist full of puffed sleeves and tugged the garment decent. "For crying out loud, keep this top pulled up."

"No." Utopia pulled it down off her shoulders again. "You go adjusting my shirt one more time . . . I'll . . . I'll . . . rip the whole thing off and go naked."

Lance knew she'd be brazen enough do what she said. "Wear it your way. See if I care."

"I will." She smugly smiled.

Lance tugged his derby down tight and waved the first contestant forward. "Utopia, this is Mr. Banniger Raspberry. You and he should take a walk and get acquainted. Banniger, you have one hour. I'll let you know when your time is up since I won't be far away. I'm the official contest timekeeper."

"Timekeeper?" Utopia scowled. "You mean you'll be watching what we say and do?"

"Your fathers insist I keep you safe."

"I can darn well take care of myself. I don't want to be spied on. You hear me?" Utopia jabbed her finger at his chest. "Keep away from my courting area or I'll quit right now."

How in the hell would he be able to do his reporter and guard duties if she wouldn't let him sit nearby? Then again, if the bride-to-be quits, it puts an end to everything. He had no intention of leaving this girl alone to experiment kissing lessons or anything else with strangers. But she didn't need to know that.

"Keep away. I darn well mean it," she warned.

"All right." Lance's arm went behind his back. His fingers crossed. "I'll stay away."

Utopia spit in her hand. "Shake on it."

Lance wondered if a spit-in-the-hand-shake negated his finger-crossed honeyfuggling. It must, for he suspected that was what she'd done a moment ago. He put his free hand in hers and for a minute he didn't want to turn loose of her. His newspaper career began now. He should be excited. Thrilled his plans were getting started.

Somehow his gut didn't agree with that logic. "It's time you get your courting started."

The fact he'd be doing his reporting from the shrubbery like some kind of peeping Tom had him plenty irritable. Maybe he'd gotten himself too personally involved with the subject he was to report on. That was a reporter no-no he'd be danged if he knew how to rectify now.

Lance took his watch out of his vest pocket and noted the time in his reporter's notepad. "Your time begins now, Banniger. You have exactly one hour."

Banniger offered Utopia his elbow.

Utopia walked arm-in-arm with this Banniger and they strolled along Coon Creek.

Lance did his best to be undetected and crept along the tree line, keeping out of sight. Every so often, he'd see Utopia point to a landmark and giggle or smile at her escort.

If a twig snapped, or his jacket snagged on a bush, Utopia would spin a quick look over her shoulder. Lance would freeze like a rabbit in fear of detection. Stalking through woods, ducking for cover, none of this was exactly how he'd expected to be covering this momentous contest.

The courting couple stopped in the clearing, at the spot where Utopia and he ate lunch the other day. Apple butter sandwiches flashed through his mind. When Banniger sat beside Utopia on the log, a sudden tinge of jealousy usurped that pleasant memory.

From his present vantage point, Lance couldn't hear a word of the couple's conversation. He needed a closer post to journal what they said.

THE COURTSHIP OF UTOPIA MINOR 101

Eyeing a spot directly behind the courting log, he decided to work his way to that location.

Lance crawled low through the wooded undergrowth, occasionally getting his pant leg snagged on sticker bushes. After about fifty yards of creeping, he reached a more suitable spying position.

This proximity to the log gave him much better hearing capabilities, but the visual angle was absolutely no good. Now he could only see the backs of his subjects. Banniger took Utopia's hand. Oops. No time to relocate. Suitor number seventy-five had started his courting. Lance readied his pencil on his notepad, prepared to take down every word of courting conversation.

"I have something for you."

Lance jotted those first words down. It was hot, and his clothing was drenched with sweat. He loosened his shirt collar and got back to reporting, focusing his main attention on Banniger for the moment.

"I can't seem to get the darn thing out of my pants." Banniger squirmed in an odd manner on the log. "It's small. But once I have it out. I think you'll like it once it's sized."

What small thing? And what sizing? The way the man leaned and jerked on the log suggested impropriety at hand. Based on what Lance just heard, it sounded like the cad was attempting to unveil his Johnson. Lance clenched his pencil and peered through the bushes.

During registration, he'd considered this contestant number seventy-five mild-mannered and not much of a threat to Utopia. Forget that. The lecherous swine was showing his true colors.

Lance couldn't see much sitting on his knees. From this angle it appeared Utopia now had her head in the man's lap.

"I can't wait to see it," he heard her say. Her comment shocked Lance and his pencil streaked a line across his notepad. Just what-in-blazes did she want to see?

"Here, let me help," Utopia offered. "My hands are smaller. I'll pull that thing out."

Banniger leaned back on the log. His legs straightened outward. The little man moaned.

Why, that no good swine. Lance still couldn't see the small thing. It must be real small. But no matter, the man's small whatever needed to have a stop put to it right now.

"That's it. You got it," Banniger yelled.

Lance hurriedly peered through the bushes trying to see the darn thing. He didn't want to jump to conclusions here. He needed tangible proof of misconduct first.

"Pull. Pull more," the moaning storekeeper begged.

Lance shot to his feet, and he got a shocking sight of Utopia stretched across the front of Banniger's elongated form, jerking and pulling on the unseen object. *What the . . .?* Lance leaned to his left then he leaned to his right. What the hell could she be doing?

Crap. This angle was no good for spying, and it was certainly too far for rescuing the girl if this courting of Banniger's went any farther.

"I can't wait to see it." Utopia continued to work at getting to the unseen item.

"One more pull should do it," Banniger moaned.

Lance stood on his tiptoes in a totally unhidden stance. The two log occupants were so busy they didn't see him. The couple's getting-a-grip trouble was giving him a headache. He never knew reporting could be so nerve racking.

"I got it." Utopia's head popped up. "Boy, I bet you feel better now that your what-cha-ma-call-it is out of there."

"Good things do come for those that wait," Banniger offered.

That tears it. He'd heard enough of this courtship, and so far he couldn't journal one damn word of it. Lance shrugged off his jacket and tossed it over a bush. In seconds, a nest of mosquitoes swarmed out of the disturbed foliage and began biting his arms, face and neck. He swatted and slapped at the pesky insects, managing to shoo some of them away. Unfortunately, the bugs returned with a hundred reinforcements.

The more he fought the winged assault, the more escalated the savage borage of biting became. *What the heck.* He couldn't concentrate under such an insect attack. Deciding to put distance between him and the home-base-bush, Lance ran a bit in the other direction, away from the bugs, away from the courting log.

Finally, shed of his obnoxious tormentors, Lance returned to his post, got back in position, hoping nothing much had happened during his lapse in coverage.

Utopia faced Banniger with her hands on her hips. "How can you ask me to do that when I just met you?"

"The next man you court is going to want you to do the same thing for him."

What? Lance couldn't believe his ears. Damn. He'd missed another important part of the couple's conversation.

"I must be honest with you, Banniger," Utopia said. "I don't know much about all this."

Lance had a plain view of Utopia's face. He detected a blush on her cheeks.

"You have a lovely hand for such a thing," the storekeeper replied.

Just what had this weasel gotten her hand to do while he'd been eaten by bugs?

"You deserve a girl who can do this better. I just learned starter kisses three days ago."

Starter kisses? Oh, no. He couldn't let her kiss Banniger's. He could stand no more of this.

Lance checked his pocket watch. The storekeeper had fifteen more minutes. But that could be changed—after all, he was the official timekeeper. He moved the minute hand on his watch up ten minutes then crept himself backwards from his observing post. Once safely away from the courting area, he jogged downstream a far enough distance to come out of hiding undetected. He then marched back up the path to confront the two lovebirds.

"Hi. What are you two up to?" Lance greeted, considerably out of breath.

Banniger looked confused and checked his pocket watch. "My time isn't up yet."

Lance glared at the man. "Oh, yes, it is."

"My watch says I still have ten minutes."

"And my watch says different. We go by my time. Official timekeeper, remember?"

The storekeeper faced Utopia. "It seems I must return you homeward posthaste, my dear. But, before we head back to camp, you need to open my gift."

Utopia tore the wrapping off and uncovered a small velvet box. She opened the lid and gasped. "This is the prettiest ring I've ever seen. Thank you, Mister Raspberry."

"Call me Banniger. Please."

Lance scowled. *A ring. The man gave her a ring.* Of course. Why wouldn't he? He was courting her. Utopia seemed real impressed with the gift. The notion that the storekeeper's flashy offering might win Utopia's hand in marriage disturbed him quite deeply.

Banniger removed the sparkly diamond from the box and placed the ring on her left hand. "It's almost a perfect fit. Like I told you before, we can have it sized. Miss Miner, I have a right profitable store and can provide for you. All I have will be yours if you'll be my wife."

Lance could do nothing but wait for mealy-mouthed Banniger to finish begging his proposal. Utopia continued to admire her ringed hand. Her ogling of the gem annoyed Lance to no end. He wanted to rip the darn jewelry off her finger and toss it in the creek. If only he could do just that, he'd feel much better.

"It's too soon for me to say which fella I'll be picking to marry."

"I understand. My only hope is that you'll keep me at the top of your list."

Utopia gave the storekeeper a pleased smile and crooked her right arm to her escort. Banniger put his hand on her arm. "Let's head back to camp," Utopia grinned. "I can't wait to show my fathers the ring you just gave me."

Lance fixed his eyes on the bride-to-be walking ahead of him. This time his focus wasn't on her hips. He watched her swooshing, swaying, waving hand proudly showing off her gift and cringed.

"This ring is really something," she gushed.

Lance rolled his eyes at her mushy response.

His newspaper job better be worth all this torture.

That was one courtship over, one hundred forty nine more to go.

CHAPTER TWELVE

Now back at her cabin, Utopia couldn't believe her surroundings. The camp looked like a hundred huge mushrooms had sprouted. There were tents pitched anywhere there happened to be flat open ground.

Of real interest to her were the few visitors she spotted still carrying around packages. Today, after only doing a bit of walking and talking with one man, she'd collected a real nice gift. And there would be over a hundred more coming her way in the next few days.

Utopia knew one thing. Taking gifts would sure make for one sticky problem of trying to get out of marrying up with one of these fellas. They all seemed to have their hearts set on her picking one of them. No matter. She had a goal, too. And saloon girls don't get married.

She agreed she'd court. She never said anything about marrying.

Her conscience did bother her though on whether she should keep Banniger's ring. He was a real nice fella, and his ring looked real valuable. That was the reason she wanted to keep it. But it would have to rain frogs before she'd pick him for her husband. Being a storekeeper's wife, living and working in a store, wasn't something she'd want to do for the rest of her days.

She turned the morality of keeping all the men's gifts every way she could twist the problem in her mind. In the end, her heart could find no sin in it. The sin would be in discouraging such a lucrative collection of goods. To her way of thinking, shirking gifts would be so, so wrong. If these men were crazy enough to bring her presents, she'd be the crazy one if she refused them.

Besides, some of the gifts might be things she'd need for her dancehall job. But sooner or later, she'd have to find a way out of picking a husband. Utopia bit on her nail. She just didn't feel like worrying about that right now.

For the rest of the day, Utopia made six more trips up the mountain with nary a one of the suitors giving her things that could be classified good saloon gifts.

The liveryman, Enos Christman, gave her a horseshoe. He told her dribble about how he'd be the luckiest man in Tin Cup if she'd marry him.

Fancy riverboat gambler, John Powell, did a few fancy card tricks then gave her the deck. Cards might be something she'd use once she was a saloon girl.

Reverend Pardee gave her nothing but an offer to perform the wedding service for a nominal fee. He'd do the ceremony for free if she picked him as the groom.

Something had to be done to sort the good gift givers from the waste-of-time gift givers.

Utopia spotted Lance sitting on a keg in the shade beside the whiskey barn eating an apple. When she approached him, she noticed his tan shirt looked grass stained and tattered. Not that she cared to count, but there were upwards of twenty or more mosquito bites dotting his handsome face. He started to get to his feet.

"No. Keep sitting. By the looks of your clothes, you could use the rest."

Lance sat back down. "I won't argue with you. I've been rather busy today."

"Looks like you were at it quite hard, whatever you were doing."

He tossed his apple core to the weeds. "Is there something I can do for you?"

"As a matter of fact, there is. I take it you decide whose turn it is to walk me up that hill."

"Unfortunately, yes. Is something wrong with how things have been going?"

"Well, yes. There is." Utopia held up a horseshoe. "My horse already has four of these. I don't need more." She tossed the horseshoe on the ground. "You can save us both a heap of aggravation if you weed out the fellas that don't have decent gifts."

Lance shot to his feet. "What?"

"You heard me." She crossed her arms. "I want you to find out what these men's gifts are. If it's not something pretty or saloon-useful, you tell that man he can't have a courting turn."

"How do you expect me to tell a man his courting present's no good?" Lance waved a sarcastic arm around. "Pardon me, sir. I need to find out if your gift meets up to the lady's standards."

"That sounds like a dandy way to weed out all of the no-good presents to me."

"And if they don't have a good gift, then what? I have to tell them to get a better one?"

"That's right. You might not want to be shouting when you say it, though"

She'd never seen a man's face get so red, so fast. Even her Pa Jargus' and that was saying something. Lance's hands fisted. His jaw clenched. He must be good and mad at her. No matter. She intended to have things her way. "Look, none of this courting were my idea. But, since I'm the one that's got to put up with all this matchmaking, I'm reaping me some rewards while I'm doing it."

"I don't even know what you consider good gifts." Lance folded his arms over his chest. "Can you give me some clues to what you have in mind?"

"I would like fancy dancehall girls things. Heeled shoes, stockings, and any other things you think a saloon gal needs."

Lance's mouth dropped open. "Of all the greedy females I've ever met, you take the cake." He shook his head. "I don't think any of these men have saloon presents."

Utopia flipped her hair off her shoulder. "I don't care how you sort. But you better sort. If these men want time with me they best have a decent saloon gift."

Lance didn't have an explanation for the change in Utopia. She seemed to have no care for what such saloon trappings would do to her reputation. He knew the girl had misconstrued notions about her career choice. But he thought their conversation had cleared some of that up. Utopia's lack of understanding of the difference between a lady and a harlot seemed to be the problem now.

A plan came to his mind. What better way to show the naïve girl the consequences of her unladylike job choice than to provide her the dancehall items her little heart desired? After Utopia donned such apparel, and received less than respectable attention from her suitors, she'd decide on her own to behave like a lady, get married and have a respectable happy-ever-after life.

He would make it his quest to see that every suitor was properly saloon girl gift supplied.

He pulled out the suitor list from his vest pocket and scanned the occupations listed for each contestant. His eyes stopped on the name Travin Langley. The information noted Travin's father owned a drinking establishment. He needed to talk to this man regarding soiled dove gifts.

Lance approached two gents, one old and one young, huddled off to the side of the middle shack. "Are you contestant number nine, Travin Langley?"

"Yes, indeed." The older man put a hand on the lad's shoulder. "I'm Cyrus Langley and this is my son. Have you come to tell us it's his turn?

I'm sure both his charm and his gift will impress the lovely girl."

"About the lovely Miss Miner," Lance started. "It is not your turn yet. I just stopped by to do a pre-courting check of your gift. That's a direct order straight from the bride-to-be's mouth."

"What gift?" Travin asked.

"Don't listen to my boy. Why he's brought her gift so perfect it will be the little lady's prized possession."

"Gentlemen, I must inform you that I need to screen all the gifts for Miss Miner. She'll not meet with any suitor unless I approve of his offering beforehand. Now if you can show—"

"That's insulting," Travin huffed. "Does she think she's the Queen of Sheba or something?"

"Would you excuse us for one moment?" Cyrus took his son's arm and pulled him off to the side for a private chat.

Lance nodded. "Take all the time you need."

The father and son's conversation carried on the breeze. Lance could hear every word.

"You did bring the lady a gift, didn't you?"

"I got a box of chocolates from Banniger's Mercantile before we came up the mountain."

"That's my boy."

"But Pa …"

"But what?"

"It all melted in this heat. It's one big brick of not very pretty chocolate now."

"You're a numbskull. Why did you buy chocolates in the middle of a heat wave?"

Lance could hardly contain his sniggers at the duo's gift dilemma. "Gentlemen, I don't mean to eavesdrop on your conversation, but I can offer a suggestion on a replacement gift?"

Cyrus' eyes widened with interest. "We would be indebted to you for such information."

"The lady your son plans to court considers the women in your Palace Oak to be some of the most beautiful saloon girls she's ever seen. In fact, Miss Miner happens to be a big fan of their many talents."

The saloonkeeper pulled his cigar from his mouth. Cyrus' head slowly dipped downward, and his eyes rolled upward. His face wore a skeptical expression. "You're pulling my leg?"

"No. No. It's the absolute truth."

"Please. Go on."

"If your son wishes to make a good first impression, he should present Miss Miner with a gift from one of your saloon girls. I have it right from Miss Miner's mouth that dancehall items are certain to gain a suitor the privilege of courting her."

"You don't say."Cyrus rubbed his chin in deep thought.

Lance could see the money wheels turning in Cyrus's head.

"I'll need a delay in my son's courting to make a trip to town to fetch the items."

Lance nodded. "I'll persuade the bride-to-be to postpone courtship a day or two. If I were you, Mr. Langley, I would bring back lots of saloon gifts. There's a tidy profit to be made."

"My thoughts exactly," Cyrus said. "Then there's no time to waste. Is there?"

CHAPTER THIRTEEN

Palace Oak Saloon

Cyrus pulled pantaloons and stockings out of Lil's bureau drawer. He tossed the garments into the opened suitcase on her bed. He waved the lacy garter in the air. "You have any more of these fancy thigh straps?"

"You got no business going through my things," Lil snapped. "I already told you I haven't been holding out on ya. I promise."

Cyrus dumped the dresser drawer contents on the floor. "I don't want money. I want more of these garters. You got any more or not? Help me out here. I'm in a hurry."

Wearing nothing but her stockings, pantaloons and corset, Lil paced the small confines of her room while Cyrus continued his frantic search. Her high-heeled foot stomped on the floor when he opened the second drawer.

"Now don't get all mad," Lil pleaded. "I stashed a little money aside but it ain't like it seems. I'm saving that money to pay it back to you in winter when things are slow."

THE COURTSHIP OF UTOPIA MINOR   115

Cyrus swore under his breath. Any other time if he found out Lil was holding out on him, he'd toss the hussy out on the street. Right now, he needed to be on his way with the goods. If any of Frank's friends spotted him in town, he'd rather forego the un-pleasantries.

Lil's stocking wrapped savings were pushed aside. "Keep your stash," he said. "All I want is trade goods. There's money to be made with your saloon trappings. Hand them over."

"Just how do you expect me, Pearl and Sadie to work if you take all of our things?"

Not finding any more items in the bureau, he tossed the last petticoat in the satchel and closed the case. A bit of lace hung out the sides of the luggage as Cyrus hauled it off the bed.

He pushed skinny Lil out of his way. The red feathered plume sticking out of the back of Lil's coiffure caught his attention. "I'll take this, too." He yanked the adornment from her hairdo, pulling a few strands of fuzzy red hair from her scalp in the process.

"Ouch. Damn your mangy hide, Cyrus. You come back here, you cur."

He left Lil's room, and the irate harlot followed right on his boot heels. She grabbed him by his coattails, putting quite a drag on his progress to the saloon downstairs.

"I knew you were a lowdown cheapskate, but you've gone too far this time."

Pearl and Sadie stood at the bottom of the staircase, their eyes red from spilled tears. Cyrus had already pillaged their rooms. He reached the bottom of the stairs and dropped Lil's belongings with the other plunder he'd gathered.

The three women's tearful wails echoed off the empty barroom walls.

"Look girls, I need these fancy duds. I'll return whatever I don't sell."

"Sell?" The gals flew into another fit of crying.

He covered his ears to drown out their anguished pleadings. "There's no use in me trying to explain. I said I'll replace everything soon as I can. Now clear out of my way."

Cyrus stuffed two cases under his armpits, grabbed the handles of two more satchels and made a step to leave. Sadie raced ahead of him and braced her back against the door to prevent his departure.

"You're a sneaky scallywag. You're hiring new saloon gals, aren't you?" Pearl bent down, grabbed hold of Cyrus around the ankles and lifted him off the floor, hanging him upside down.

Two of the cases dropped from his hands. He hung helpless in the big woman's grasp, with all the blood rushing to his head and barely able to breathe. "I'm not hiring new gals. I swear. Now put me down."

Pearl let go of Cyrus and he dropped to the floor with a hollow watermelon-sounding thud. He got back on his feet and straightened his rumpled suit. "I ought to fire you, and I will if you don't stay out of my way." He corralled his bundles back up then managed to finagle his bulky luggage to the door. "Get out of my way," he ordered Sadie. She stepped aside, and he hauled his load outside to the wagon parked in front of the saloon. He dropped his bundles in the pile of luggage he'd carried out earlier.

The girls followed him. Sadie clomped down the steps and perched her arm along the sideboard of the wagon. "Then tell us who the hell needs all our fancy duds."

"I don't have time to explain everything." Cyrus tossed one case then another into the back of the wagon.

The girls circled around him and left no avenue to escape. Each woman put a heeled foot on one of the remaining suitcases he'd dropped on the ground. The trio folded their arms. "We're not budging until we have answers," Sadie stated.

"Oh, all right. If you must know Travin needs some of this stuff."

Lil jabbed Cyrus' watermelon-sized stomach with her pointy fingernail. "What the hell does my Travin need with my pantaloons?"

"The things are betrothal gifts. I need the lad to court a gal up the mountain."

A shrill, wheezy gasp escaped the Lil's painted red lips. Her hand grabbed her heart in pained disbelief. "No. It can't be. Travin loves me."

Sadie and Pearl embraced their pitifully crying friend's shoulders. "How cruel can you be, breaking her heart like this? What kind of insensitive bastard are you?"

Cyrus couldn't stand the looks of contempt the gals were giving him. He inched close as he dared to Lil and put his hand under her chin. "My boy loves you. He told me so. This is a matter of life and death. My life. My death if I don't have these things."

"Why's he courting some new gal?" Lil whined into her hanky.

"He's doing it for me."

The women gave Cyrus a murderous look. They yelled in unison, "For you?"

He retreated back a step from the sharp verbal attack. "Now, Travin is helping me with a very important matter. When it's all settled, he'll get himself an annulment."

"Annulment?" Lil dug her fingernail into her boss's potbelly; this time, with enough force to draw blood. "You only need an annulment if you've married someone. Who is she?"

"He's being a loyal son. Loyal sons help out their father. I need the boy doing this."

"I've heard enough." Lil shoved Cyrus out of her way and headed for the saloon door. "You wait right there. I'm getting dressed and going with you to this camp."

"I don't have time to be dragging you along." Cyrus knew his words to be pointless. "If you show up in this camp, it will ruin everything."

Lil glared a no-objection warning. "You try leaving here without me and you'll be sorry. I'll fetch Risky's rifle and plug your bastard hide. No damn hussy's getting my man." The mad-as-hell harlot tramped across the saloon's threshold and slammed the door behind her.

"Where Lil goes, I go." Sadie said. "Come on, Pearl. Let's gather what few things he's left us. It looks like we're going on a little trip."

Before Cyrus could stop the two hussies, they were through the doorway and out of sight. Well—if the girls were going along, he'd make sure they all worked for their keep. This wasn't a pleasure trip. This was business.

He waited for the girls and packed more satchels and small trunks into the back of the wagon. The approach of a carriage drew his attention. Frank's buggy pulled to a stop in front of the saloon. Six rough-looking men on horseback pulled to a halt right behind the buggy. The riders bore menacing glares. This wasn't a social call.

Frank stepped from his carriage and dusted off his tailored blue pinstripe suit. He grabbed his gold-knobbed walking stick. The cane tapped along the side of the wagon as the banker strutted like a bantam cock on the peck for a fight.

The politician placed his polished Hessian boot on the bottom step of the saloon's porch. "Cyrus, I'm surprised to see you so soon. It looks like you're packing up to leave this town. It's not a permanent move, I hope?" Frank poked the tip of his cane into Cyrus's chest.

"No. It's nothing like that. I-I'm rounding up a few supplies."

"Supplies? Hmm. Now I find that interesting. Let's have a look at these supplies." Frank stepped over to the wagon. He pointed his walking stick toward the largest henchmen and motioned the man to check the wagon. The man immediately jumped down from his mount and lifted one piece of luggage onto the bench seat. He opened it for his boss' inspection.

Frank perused the contents of the case and used the tip of his cane to pick up a lacy negligee.

"These are unusual supplies. Explain your need for such frills."

Cyrus didn't know how far he'd get with any explanation. "These things are for the bride of the contest."

Frank gave a sarcastic chuckle. "I'll admit that picturing the young lass wearing such items stirs my interest, but please spare me the details. How are you progressing on ending the contest?"

Sweat rolled down Cyrus's back. His body was turning into one big yellow puddle. "I-I-I can say that the lady's doing well with her courting—although she's not settled on anyone yet. However, it's only been the first day of courting."

Frank took two steps and raised the gold knob of the walking stick to within inches of Cyrus's forehead. "How soon will the contest be over?"

Cyrus nervously focused on the glistening knob of the cane. "A very reliable source confided in me that . . . that the girl is fond of saloon girl apparel. That's why I need these items. My boy is sure to be picked the winner once he gives her such fine gifts, thus an end to the problem."

The cane bopped Cyrus's forehead. "You rattle on about a plan I care not. I don't intend to let things go too much longer before I take matters into my own hands. You know what I mean when I say that, don't you?"

Cyrus choked on a swallow. "I believe I do."

"In one week, there better be a wedding taking place. Do I make myself clear?"

There would be no hesitation on Frank's part to use brute force to end the contest. Cyrus had no way of telling how much of that force would be used on him. "That won't be necessary. Once my son's had his turn at courting, the lady will be as good as married. Contest over."

The henchman knocked the opened suitcase off the wagon, spilling all the white undergarments onto the ground. The thug of a man got back on his horse.

"Enjoy this fine day now, you hear." Frank climbed into his buggy. He flicked the carriage whip on the horse's rump and drove off.

The banker's goons rode off. Cyrus gave a tentative, unnoticed wave.

One week. His son had better get hitched. Otherwise, he'd be an orphan.

CHAPTER FOURTEEN

Late afternoon, Utopia walked into camp escorted by the last suitor for the day. Those men not courting were having a lively time. A campfire now blazed in the center of the field near the whiskey barn.

The non-courters were gathered around the fire eating, drinking or making merry. Utopia found that she couldn't walk from the whiskey barn to her cabin without a male offering a crooked elbow to escort her along.

She scanned the crowd looking for Lance but didn't see him. His presence had been conspicuously absent since her talk about gifts earlier today. Not to let his absence ruin her fun, she allowed a pair of suitors to perch her upon a stack of kegs near the camp's fire. Soon Utopia discovered that her every boon was eagerly serviced by one man or another. If she wanted water, a fella readily provided a cup. When she asked for a plate of food, like magic a meal materialized.

For the first time in her nineteen years, she actually felt what it must be like to be a saloon girl, to be admired and treated special. From her barreled throne, her throng of beaus entertained her with hilarious antics.

"I'm telling you true, the rabbits in Texas are this big." Charlie Fey demonstrated the critter's size with wide arms. "Our hunting dogs are even afraid to chase 'em."

The Scotsman, John Doble, chimed in. "'Tis that so? An' what do ye call such a rabbit?"

"Jackrabbits," Charlie answered.

"Now I can surely believe that. No doubt, a jackass like ye-self will know what a jackrabbit looks like when he comes upon one."

Laughter erupted from everyone.

Utopia wiped away gleeful tears. Her cheeks ached from laughing so hard. She giggled even more when the insulted Charlie Fey pummeled the big blacksmith with his hat.

This afternoon had been the grandest time of her entire life. She didn't want it to end.

Squeaking wheels drew the crowd's attention. The axels on the weighted wagon strained to support the load of trunks, tables, chairs and passengers. The potbellied driver pulled the tired team of horses to a halt. Utopia couldn't believe her eyes. There were three saloon girls onboard.

One of the women looked to be in her late thirties, with wild raven hair, wearing a gown of golden yellow trimmed with black lace. This dancehall belle stood up and braced her black stockinet leg on the wagon's bench seat. She waved. "Sadie's here, boys. Did ya miss me?"

Hoots and hollers went up from Utopia's suitors, and the men migrated to the new females like a swarm of bees in pursuit of tastier nectar. The dancehall girls cheerfully greeted the males and blew kisses while making wiggly moves with their legs and shoulders.

Utopia's heart felt like it would fly right out of her mouth. By gosh, by golly, real live, in the flesh, dancehall training just rolled into her life.

For a brief moment, she felt betrayed by the loss of her attentive suitors, which happened to be an ungrateful way to be looking at this unexpected blessing. She shouldn't blame the men. She could understand why they'd be attracted to such talented and beautiful ladies.

In comparison to these saloon gals, Utopia considered herself quite a plain specimen of a woman. No, extremely plain. These painted creatures had years of practice and an abundant confidence with using feminine charms.

"Hey, Miss Pearl, how about giving us a little shake?" one man yelled.

The lumberjack-sized woman named Pearl climbed down off the wagon. She turned toward the crowd and swished her rotund breasts from side-to-side in wiggled unison without once spilling the large mounds from her dress.

Admiration swelled within Utopia's chest to the size of a cannonball. She watched the tall siren continue to beguile the men with her swishing bosom.

One day, she would have the skills to do such a thing.

Then a thought came to mind. There was no better time than now to emulate what she'd just witnessed. All the men were still exceedingly distracted by the dancehall girls. Likely none of them would take notice if she practiced waggling since they were watching the real saloon gals.

Utopia rearranged her white blouse off her shoulders so her outfit resembled the low cut saloon women's bodices. Her breasts weren't the volume of this Miss Pearl's chest but maybe that small fact wasn't too important.

She pulled her shoulders back, stiffened her upper torso and shrugged her shoulders back and forth. Her slow motions produced nary a stir within her top, much less a juggled visual enough to grab a man's interest.

Giving this waggling a second try, she shook her shoulders harder and faster. This time her breasts wobbled a fair amount. The feeling wasn't all that physically thrilling. She'd even say it hurt a mite. It didn't matter whether chest shaking pleased or displeased her. If bosom wiggling was something saloon girls did, then it was something she'd learn to do, like it or not.

She opened her white top a tad and peeked inside to see how much movement went on when she shimmied. Putting a bit more force into her third shake of her shoulders, she watched her jiggling breasts.

"What are you doing?"

That all too familiar voice startled her. Utopia abruptly released her top and it snapped to her chest. Her head shot up and she spun around to find Lance grinning. "For crying out loud, you scared the crap out of me."

"Did you find anything interesting in there? If so, I'll have a look."

Not sure what he'd witnessed her doing, Utopia turned her nose up in indignation. "I ain't ashamed of practicing, if that's what you're referring to."

"Practicing? Just what kind of practice could looking down your top be?"

"I'm practicing girl stuff, and it ain't any of your business."

Lance stepped closer.

She backed away a bit. His dark eyes focused on her white blouse. She could swear her nipples tightened under his searing gaze. Her hand felt along the edges of her top to be sure she hadn't shimmied out of her blouse.

"Well—anytime you need some help with your . . . girl stuff," Lance flexed and squeezed his fingers like a person testing ripe plums. "Come see me. I've had lots of hands-on experience with those." She felt an immediate rush of heat within her bodice and sensed she should protect her breasts from his cupping hands.

Suddenly, in the distance she heard a woman's voice. Utopia turned her head toward the distraction. Giving no excuse for leaving Lance behind, she took off in the direction of the dancehall gal's calling.

"Wait. Where are you going?"

"None of your business," she said over her shoulder. "We'll talk later."

For the first time in days, there was something other than Lance to hold her interest. Right now, this saloon gal, calling for a fellow named Travin, beckoned her investigation.

THE COURTSHIP OF UTOPIA MINOR 127

A gent, with shoulder-length straw-colored hair, repeatedly yelled the name Lil from his position amongst the crowd. He stood out from the others huddled around him, waving a black hat wildly in the air. His voice could barely be heard over the din of jubilation going on around him. "Lil, I'm over here."

The skinniest of the three women on the wagon waved her arm. "Travin, I'm here."

This tiny Lil and tall Travin finally spotted each other and began to work themselves through the crowd toward each other. Utopia figured there would be some valuable lessons to be learned if she could get herself nearby when the eager couple got together. Wasting no time, she pushed and elbowed her way toward the spot she hoped would be the rendezvous location.

She arrived in time to catch the best parts of the pair's meeting up.

"Travin, you big lug," Lil cried out.

Travin corralled the small saloon gal about her waist. He lifted Lil, twirling her around and around in a circle. "How'd you get here? What are you—?"

Before the fellow could finish his word, the two of them got down to the most serious kiss Utopia had ever seen two people plant on each other. In studious fixation, she watched the talented saloon gal lock lips onto her man's mouth.

Unlike Lance's teachings, the couple's eyes were closed. Their mouths were wide open, so wide, she could see their tongues wrestling with each other. And forget counting. Heck, they'd already passed the number ten by a whole bunch.

The most interesting thing about the couple's joining was the fact that Lil wrapped one leg around Travin's hip, clear up to his backside. Once Travin had a good hold of Lil's raised leg, she brought the other leg up off the ground, wrapping it around the other side of him. That was one talented dancehall gal, kissing while perched in tall Travin's strong hands.

The moment became so intense, so heated Utopia momentarily felt the burn of their joining in her own lower extremities. Why, that Miss Lil and her Travin were like two grizzly bears grabbed with a powerful itch, both sorely in need of a tree to rub up against.

"Just what are you up to?"

Lance's voice startled her again. She spun on him. "Don't you have something better to do than follow me around?" How in blazes could she learn saloon skills with all of Lance's interruptions?

"You need some more help with something?"

"Do I look like I need your help right now?"

Lance folded his arms over his chest. "No. Not that I can see. But you have me wondering what you're up to. So—I've decided to stay close for a bit."

"Well, I don't want you around right now. Leave me be." She'd only turned away from the couple for an instant. "Now look what you've done."

"What?"

"They're gone. Oh, never mind. You wouldn't understand."

The leg wrap lesson was over. How disappointing. Then it dawned on her. If she really wanted to remember something it always stuck better in her brain if she put any such teachings promptly to use. And, beings how this was such a personal type of lesson, she wouldn't care to leg wrap on a strange man on her first attempt. She'd put Lance to some good use.

Instead of retreating from Lance's presence, she advanced. When close enough, she wrapped her arms about his neck. Her fingers twirled the wavy hair at the nape of his neck like she'd just seen Lil do to Travin's locks. "How would you like to go somewhere and do some practicing?"

Lance pulled her arms off his neck and moved her back a safe distance. "Utopia, stop it."

"Stop what?"

"The teasing."

"I'm not teasing. I'm practicing."

Her loudly uttered declaration drew the attention of other men nearby.

"I've had enough of this. We can't talk here." Lance needed to know what was going on in Utopia's busy little brain. Why she was acting like a common harlot. "You're coming with me."

He grabbed hold of her wrist and pulled her behind him, searching for a place for privacy.

"Where are you going, sweetheart?" One rather drunk suitor grabbed Utopia's arm.

"Sweetheart will be back in a minute," Lance snarled, removing the gent's hand from the lady's arm. He made one excuse after another to inquiring beaus on when Utopia would be returning to the celebration. The pair continued to wind through the crowd.

The whiskey barn was the busiest place in the camp right now, so privacy would have to be gained elsewhere. When they got near her cabin, he knocked on the door. No shotgun poked out of the doorway, and no sounds could be heard within. The fathers must be busy elsewhere. Lance pulled her inside and shut the door. He released her arm.

His fingers combed through his hair in frustration. One minute Utopia acted like this unbelievably backwoods virgin, in the next moment, she was like a seductive harlot on the prowl.

"Look I'm not saying you're dumb," he said. "But, some of the things you're doing aren't exactly smart. If you don't change your ways, bad things could happen to you. How a lady acts is a guide to how a man will treat her."

"You're right," she agreed.

Utopia gave a wicked smile and advanced toward him with shimmying shoulders. In self-defense he retreated and pointed to her wiggling bosom. "That's exactly the kind of actions I'm talking about. That will get you in trouble real quick."

"I figure you and me can work on my leg wrapping."

"What's leg wrapping?"

"This."

Lance had little time to react when Utopia wrapped her arms around his neck, made a little jump and both her legs coiled about his hips. She hung on him with her breasts pressed against his chest.

Simultaneously, his brain registered shock. His other organ registered excitement, and both reactions occurred in the same breathless moment. To keep from being bowled over with the weight of her clinging body, he braced her back against the door. This stability allowed her to pull him much closer. In accordance with his earlier kissing lesson terminology, she planted a definite wet stage-two kiss on him. *When had she learned that?*

He tightened his lips together and fought physically and mentally to prevent the intrusion of her flicking tongue into his mouth. In the end, his desire for a taste of her overrode his good sense. But not wanting to be a full participant in this kiss, he froze all other bodily movement, figuring that would eventually cause her to break her attack on him.

For one splendid minute, he was in heaven with the feel of her pressed on his enflamed loins. Her tongue and his explored. Lance couldn't get enough of her.

It wasn't long before her mouth left his. Her legs slowly unfurled from his hips. She stood looking at him with a puzzled look on her face.

"Are you done?" He kept his face stoic to show her he didn't like what she'd done, but in actuality, his head reeled from her kiss. He needed a moment to catch his breath.

"Are you just going to stand there or what?" she asked. "I can't do this all by myself. A little help from you would be nice."

This was the last straw. "Utopia, I meant what I said about men and their treatment of certain women. A girl like you, kissing like that, you're apt to lose your most valued symbol of love. Something that's supposed to be given to the one man you decide to make your husband. I don't know too many men that will take a used woman for his wife."

Her face reddened with ire. "You're wrong. I think saloon girls are treated pretty nice."

"Is that what this behavior of yours is all about? You're gathering saloon lessons by watching Cyrus' dancehall girls?"

"What's wrong with that? My mother was a saloon girl. She happened to be the most beautiful creature any man could want."

Lance pinned Utopia against the wall with his body. "You're not like Cyrus' girls. How can I get that through to you? Those men will take advantage of you if you give them a chance."

"You're wrong. I'll be the one saying what a man does with me."

"Oh, you think so? Let's see about that." Lance placed his hands on either side of her face. His mouth came down hard upon hers. His tongue begged entry into her mouth, which she readily opened for him. He knew this bad girl lesson was going wildly wrong, but he continued his assault anyway, possibly because he couldn't resist her.

If for nothing more than the want of a breath of fresh air, he stopped the kiss. Her head tilted back. He couldn't help himself. His mouth turned to her delectable neck, and he thoroughly enjoyed trailing kisses down the length of her throat. Lance detected her racing pulse throbbing beneath his lips. Without control of his lust, his hand worked itself into her top and cupped her breast. Her soft, warm mound fit his hand perfectly. His fingers tweaked her nipple.

This madness racing in his blood had a purpose, but what exactly that had been he couldn't recall. *Ill intentions, that's it. How a man can take her.* A sigh escaped her lips. *Have mercy.* Something had to be done, or he'd take her himself in another few moments, right on the wooden floorboards.

Lance yanked his hand out of her top, pulled away and inhaled a deep breath.

She pulled him close again, and like a relentless piranha, her lips nuzzled his neck.

In order to free himself from her seeking mouth, he pinned her against the door with a stiff-armed hold and inserted his free hand between his neck and her seeking lips. "Stop. You've got to listen to me. I want to apologize."

"What for?" Utopia jerked her head back and looked puzzled.

"There's no way you learned the consequences of wanton behavior based on my actions just now. I wanted to show you that once the wrong kisses are started then respectable conduct will lose to passion every time. I lost the battle, I'm afraid."

"The hell you say. You call that losing?" Utopia's breasts rose and fell with each of her winded breaths. "That was the most fantastic experience I've ever had in my entire life. Let's do that again."

"No. I can't. It won't happen again." Lance released his stiff-armed hold of her and reached for the door handle. He lifted the latch and glanced at her bewildered face. "At least, not with me, it won't. I'll give you one last bit of advice. Be careful with your kissing, sweetheart."

CHAPTER FIFTEEN

Utopia certainly wanted Lance's latest kissing lesson to continue. But by the time she pulled the door open to call him back for more practice, he'd run himself plumb out of earshot. One thing she knew for certain, she'd just gotten her first real saloon girl kiss. Lance had curled her toes, melted her insides and left her barely able to stand on her own two wobbly legs.

Her lips still felt puffy and tingly from the nibbling he'd done on her lower lip. For sure, he'd made her short of breath. With every touch of his soft lips, her body craved something more. When he nibbled on her neck, and his hand worked into her top caressing her like he did, her blood almost boiled her to cinders.

By gosh, by golly, he'd worked her into a sweat in places she never knew a body could sweat. No doubt about it, Lance had to be the best kissing teacher any girl could possibly ever have. No matter what risk came with his next teachings, she would give him her very best effort.

From the corner of her eye, Utopia caught a movement and turned her head to find the saloon girl, Lil, leaning against the corner of the cabin puffing on a cigarillo.

The dancehall gal tossed her smoke to the ground and slinked toward Utopia. "So, you're the one that's bringing the whole town to the hills."

The woman in the beautiful purple dress was an unexpected presence outside her cabin. "If that ain't the prettiest thing I ever laid eyes on. Are those long socks of yours made out of fishing net?"

"Don't play innocent with me, missy. Why do you have to be taking my man? Ain't having the whole town enough for you?" Lil pointed toward the campfire where the suitors were gathered. "Pick yerself out one of them and leave my Travin alone."

Utopia didn't rightly know what this tiny woman could be so riled about. "Maybe we should take the matter somewhere private. Why don't you come in my cabin and we can talk."

"Good thinking. We'll go inside." Lil stormed toward the doorway. "That way there won't be any witnesses when I scratch your slutty eyes out."

Utopia could hear the rustle of the woman's petticoats under the satin purple dress when the saloon gal sauntered past her and into the cabin. Lil perched her slim hips against the tabletop and braced one stocking clad leg on a chair.

This Lil was amazing; she sort of sauntered when she walked, and the room smelled like a big rose bush had taken root inside her cabin. Utopia couldn't cram all this amazing firsthand saloon training in her brain fast enough.

Lil pointed a bony finger right in Utopia's face. "You got a fight coming if you try to take my man from me."

Utopia backed up a step, fearing this ticked-off Lil might poke her eye out with that painted finger. "Travin's the fella you were kissing on earlier? He's your man?"

"I should say he is. And I intend to keep what's mine."

Utopia noticed that showy tall purple plume sticking out of Lil's hairdo. "I swear your hair is the prettiest I've ever seen on a head. And that feather, I really like that."

Lil's red-faced rant did a complete about-face. "Did you say you like my hair?"

"I sure do. Can I touch that big purple feather of yours?"

Lil fluffed her hair a couple times. "I guess you can have a feel. But don't mess it up."

Utopia feathered her fingers along the edge of the fine plume. Still in awe of the woman's hairdo, she gently tugged on one of Lil's frizzy banana curls. She let go of the lock and it recoiled to its original tubular shape. "Your hair's soft as cotton. It's real springy too. I'd love fancy hair like yours."

Lil slid her foot off the chair and impatiently tapped her foot on the floor. "Look here, missy. I didn't come to talk about hair. I come to get my man back. Travin and me, we–"

"Pardon me, Miss Lil, I don't rightly know this Travin you care so much about."

The harlot's face turned a volcanic red. "Listen to me. My boss took all my belongings.

He did the same thing to my two friends. Says he needs saloon girl gifts. My boss told me right to my face that Travin intends to court you with my things."

Utopia felt lower than a weasel that'd got caught robbing a hen house. Somehow this Lil was accusing her of stealing away her fella, and worse yet, stealing away all her belongings. "I'm sorry. Truly I am. I don't know that your Travin intends to court me. I want you to know I asked for saloon things, but I didn't mean for them to be your belongings."

Lil strutted back and forth with a condescending glare. "You won't be happy until you've nabbed the last man and my last dress. Why does an innocent like you need dancehall things?"

Why this Miss Lil figured she'd be able to use her dresses, Utopia couldn't figure that out. There were boards in her cabin floor wider than this skinny little woman. "Miss Lil, I don't think one of your dresses would fit me. I meant no harm by asking for saloon gifts. I just want to be like you and your two friends."

"You want to be what?" Lil's mouth dropped open and she staggered a couple steps.

"I should say so. Why, look at you. You wear pretty things. You know how to sing and dance. That takes a heap of talent and training. Your Travin's a lucky man. He's got himself a woman that knows how to make him happy in so many ways."

THE COURTSHIP OF UTOPIA MINOR 139

Lil lowered her chin a bit, and her brown eyes stared upward. "Is this some sort of act? Or are you always like this?"

"Best I can recollect, I'm always this way."

The swooning saloon gal braced her arms on the table for support. "I need a drink."

Utopia quickly caught the tiny woman and helped her to a chair. "Little Lil, you sit yourself down. I'll fetch some nerve tonic." She went to the shelf for her fathers' whiskey jug.

Utopia couldn't' believe it. After her and Miss Lil finished of the half bottle of whiskey, Miss Lil took her to a pretty roomy tent that was situated away from all the other tents the men had scattered around the hillsides. Miss Lil introduced her to those other two saloon girls, Miss Sadie and Miss Pearl.

They were real friendly and real talkers. They got to talking about makeup and fancy dresses and soap and one thing led to another. Now here she sat, being plumb naked, in a fancy bathing tub with frothy bubbles clear up to her chest. Utopia would laugh on this hoot of joy later. But right now, she soaked in the rose-scented water in a metal contraption that had come clear across the country from a place called Paris, Kentucky, and enjoyed every minute of this luxury.

"Life can plumb sneak up and surprise a body at times," Utopia said to Sadie.

"It surprises me every day."

"I sure do like this bar of rose soap. It's much better smelling than the lye soap I use. Can I keep it?"

"You can have it. Now, sweetie, you got to quit pulling away from me." Sadie struggled to lather up Utopia's long hair.

"But my eyes are burning." Utopia rubbed at the stinging suds, but her bubble-covered fists only made the problem worse. "I need some water to rinse off the soap."

"Well, Sassy Lassie, I reckon I can help you with that." Sadie put a firm hand on top of the sudsy head and pushed her fussing protégé down into the tub.

Utopia kicked and flailed. When her head came up out of the water, she gasped and sputtered for air, swiping soap suds off her face. "What'd you do that for?"

Sadie tossed her a towel. "It was the quickest way I knew of to rinse you off and shut you up at the same time. We've got a lot more work to do to have you ready for the dance. So, get out of the tub and be quick about it."

Utopia dried her hair in the towel then quickly wrapped it around her naked body. She felt embarrassed and totally unworthy to be in the company of the three dancehall women. Especially with the scrutinizing looks they were giving her unwomanly form.

Pearl gave a loud snicker. "Honey, let me fill you in on a little trade secret. There's no modesty to be had around here. If you can't stand being naked in front of men or women . . . then honey . . . you best think about finding yerself another line of work."

Utopia frowned. Why would Miss Pearl say something like that?

"Don't you fret on what Pearl says, you've got a fine body for being naked, which is more than she can say," Sadie said. "Come over here so I can see if my things fit you."

Sadie held a camisole up to Utopia's chest, then a pair of pantaloons at her waist. "I'm the only one of us that's anywhere close to your size. Some of my things might fit a bit snug. Here put these things on." The garments were handed to her.

Utopia put on the white cotton pantalets. The fabric felt so much better than her long wool underwear. The silky smooth camisole slid down over her head and covered her bosom in one slinky drape. She brushed her hands over the luxurious texture.

These undergarments were like heaven, and even if wearing such finery lasted only a short while, she'd enjoy their magic feel. "I surely thank you all for working so hard on me. The only thing that could make all that you're doing better is my ma's dancehall dress. I've been saving it for this kind of occasion. I could go get it."

Sadie brought over a lavender satin dress trimmed with black lace ruffles along the bodice. She tossed the exquisite gown on the cot. "Save your ma's dress for another time. My things will suit you fine. Let's get you cinched up in one of these."

Utopia stared at the stiff looking thing with long, dangling strings Sadie held in her hands. The stiffer than dried leather-looking garment didn't look like it'd be none too comfortable. "I don't think I want cinching. Why do I have to wear such a thing?"

Pearl gave a boisterous laugh. "Honey, it'll make your waist small and your tits big."

"If you want to be a saloon girl, you'll wear this and like it. So quit your griping," Sadie ordered. "Grab hold of something so I can tie you off."

If she wanted to wear that dress, she'd have to get strapped into this corset. Utopia looked around the crowded canvas tent for a good spot to hang onto.

There were four beds on the right side of this big roomy saloon girl tent. On the opposite side of the space, she spotted a small two drawer dresser with a swivel mirror centered across the furniture's back edge. That should be sturdy enough to hold on to. She placed her hands on the edges of the dresser. "I'm ready. You can go ahead and tie me into that thing."

Sadie wrapped the corset around Utopia's midsection and began tightening the laces. More than once Utopia lost her grip on the dresser. She grunted with each tug until Sadie declared her properly cinched.

When Utopia straightened, she couldn't breathe, every bit of air had been crushed from her lungs. Any attempt at taking in more air produced a wheezy, labored gasp. She could barely tell her saloon girl friends her problem. "I'm– cinched–too–tight."

Pearl laid on her chaise lounge, picking through a heart-shaped box of candies. She found one she liked and sucked the center of a chocolate-covered cherry into her mouth. "Stand up straight. You'll breathe in a minute. Honey, that corset gained you three pounds of tits. I'll have you know I once had me a figure like yours."

"Yeah, and you once needed only one bed for business," Lil crabbed. "Now you've eaten so much chocolate our tent's crammed with an extra mattress for that immense ass of yours."

Pearl chuckled and put the lid on the chocolate box and rolled herself off her chaise lounge to a stand. The big woman strutted over to the dresser and slapped a hand on her round hip. "You ain't lying there. This bottom is some prime real estate."

Sadie dropped two petticoats over Utopia's head and tied them snug at the waist. "Real estate that's no less than the size of Texas."

"I won't deny any man that diddles me will have plenty to plant himself in. Honey, come sit by the dresser. I'll fix your hair for you." The big woman removed a curly red wig from her head and draped it over the corner of the mirror.

Utopia gasped. "Why, Miss Pearl, you're bald as a beagle."

"I'm bald for a reason. Some men like redheads. Others, they like diddling a brunette and some prefer a blonde." Pearl pointed to a corner where a hat rack displayed several more fashionable hairstyles in assorted colors. "I can be whatever hair-colored gal they want to pleasure themselves with. That makes me quite popular."

Sadie picked up the lavender gown off the bed. She tossed it over Utopia's head and worked on the buttons on the back of the dress.

With sundown near, the interior of the tent now had a dim glow. Pearl struck a match to a kerosene lamp sitting on a keg in the corner. The red shaded lamp had teardrop crystals that flickered rainbow stars about the tent walls when Pearl carried the light over to the mirrored dresser.

Lil stood before the looking glass finishing up her primping before Pearl started on Utopia's hair. The shadows cast by the lamp's light added several more years to the thin harlot's face. Lil had changed into a royal blue and pink dress, of a similar style to Utopia's gown. Two short, fluffy blue plumes replaced the former purple feather worn in her hair earlier.

Not wanting to crush her fancy dress, Utopia made sure to lift the gown up before sitting her rump down the tufted stool.

Lil's eyes darted back and forth from her lip lining to Utopia's watchful stare. "Is something bothering you?"

"I never seen anyone paint their lips before."

"Well, don't get any ideas. I'm not sharing my face paint." Lil put the lid on her lipstick and tucked the tube in her bodice then walked away.

Pearl stroked a silver-handled brush through Utopia's wavy hair. "Honey, I'm going to make a few curls and pin them up like so. The rest we'll leave hanging."

Utopia glanced at Lil in the mirror then back to her hairstylist. "If it's not too much trouble, I'd like to have springy long curls like Miss Lil's."

"Hell, no. Honey, it'd be a sin if a man can't put his hands in such fine hair as yours. You leave the hair fixing to someone who knows what men want." She pinned a curl in place.

"Can I wear a big feather like Lil's?"

Lil strutted up behind Utopia and glared at her in the mirror. "No. Get feathers of your own from all your suitors out there." She turned her ire on big Pearl. "Ain't you spent enough time on her hair?"

Pearl patted Utopia's shoulder. "Never mind that skinny biddy. She's jealous. Afraid her man might like you better."

"Why, you slut, shut your fat trap." Lil charged at Pearl with red claws drawn for attack.

Sadie stepped between the two women and stretched an arm on each of their chests. "Enough. This night ain't about the two of you. And Lil, don't you go blaming your man troubles on this poor girl. I'll have no more of it, you hear me?"

Pearl nodded. "I second that. Now, honey, I think I'm finished. The men are gonna go plume crazy out of their minds when they get a gander of you."

"Something's missing," Sadie noted. She stared at their finished product. "Look at her feet. The girl needs herself some proper dancehall shoes, not those ratty moccasins."

Utopia frowned, feeling embarrassed her shoes weren't up to saloon girl standards.

"Aw, sweetie." Sadie patted Utopia's shoulder. "I didn't mean for that to sound like I'm speaking ill of your things. I only meant we need one more finishing touch."

Pearl put her fists on her hips. "I'm afraid my feet are too big and Lil's too small. And you're wearing the only pair of heels Cyrus left you. So what are we going to do?"

Sadie snapped her fingers. "What about your mama? Do you have shoes in your trunk?"

"No. But, that's okay. I probably couldn't walk in heels anyways. My moccasins will do me fine."

She really truly didn't care about what shoes she wore. The thing missing from her saloon girl attire was a pair of those fishnet stockings. Earlier, Lil had mentioned her suitors might give her a feather. Maybe one of her gifts would be fancy leg coverings. She'd have to wait and see.

Utopia splayed her skirt wide and twirled in a circle, catching her reflection in the mirror. She stopped her spinning, barely able to hold back the floodgate of happy emotions. "*Oh, my stars*, I can't believe what I'm seeing. I'm pretty. You've made me–"

"Beautiful." Sadie fluffed the ruffles on Utopia's bodice. "Now, now, let's have none of that. No crying or you'll muss yourself up." She pushed the newly fancied Utopia toward the tent opening. "It's time we take you out and show you off, Sassy Lassie."

CHAPTER SIXTEEN

Lance was under no illusions that Barris would accept an excuse of writer's block if he failed to turn in his articles each day for print. He reread what he'd drafted of the first day's courting. "Crap." He wadded the paper and pitched it to a pile of similarly discarded literary garbage.

His latest interlude with Utopia still lingered in his mind. It was all he could think on. He drew circles with his pencil on the blank page. He'd not written a single word worth ink.

So far, his big scoop of a story consisted of the girl's secret tree floor and that inappropriate starter kiss lesson with the bride-to-be. Writing about Utopia's soft lips, and how they inflamed a man's loins. This could be very problematic if the fathers learned what he done with their daughter. And he'd be guilty of total smut if he wrote about it.

Regarding his notes on Banniger Raspberry's courting, half the details he'd missed due to swarming mosquitoes. Barris wouldn't accept bug bites as a reason to neglect his article writing.

Then there was his totally unethical private meeting in the girl's cabin to consider. For Pete's sake, he'd put his journalistic tongue in the prize's mouth. And he didn't stop there.

Even now, his heart rate increased thinking of his hand on her soft, warm breast. He'd darn near sullied the girl. He couldn't understand his emotions which bordered on . . . on . . . a craving for her. Beautiful women weren't a foreign thing to him. What attraction drew him to Utopia? Why couldn't he keep focused on the most important thing in his life? *The Gazette*.

Utopia could ruin all his plans. He needed to stay focused.

Suddenly, the door of his shack burst open. In charged the three fathers with panic plastered on their faces. Lance's brain immediately registered that Jargus wasn't the only one carrying a shotgun. Now Henry and Fergus were armed. This must be serious.

"Don't tell me—there's another change to our article deal coming up." Lance put down his pencil and stood. He had a feeling he knew what their visit was about.

Utopia must have told them of their interlude in her cabin. He couldn't blame the fathers for their tempers. But, there were always two sides to a story. "Before you fellows jump to any conclusions, let me explain. Things did get a bit out of hand, or I should say . . . in hand, but that's beside the point. Nothing happened, I swear."

"What the hell are you doing in here?" Jargus fumed. "You're supposed to be keeping a tight tether on Utopia."

"Ha-have you seen what those hussies have done to our girl?" Fergus pointed toward the shack's opened door.

"Done what? Which hussies have done what? To whom?" Lance sprinted around his makeshift desk, past the fathers to the door to see exactly what all the commotion was about.

A lively tune filled the camp with merriment. He saw the glow of a campfire, and that Cyrus' wagon had been overturned to form a crude stage on which to present the night's entertainment. Flanked on each end of the makeshift stage were torch lights.

And horror of horrors, Utopia stood beneath the stars and flickering flames aglow in a black and lavender gown with the crowd cheering, catcalling and whistling.

Lance's eyes near popped out of his skull. He spun around to the fathers. "Where in the hell did she get that dress?"

Henry gripped his weapon in a white-knuckled hold. "It doesn't much matter now, does it? We want to know what you're gonna do about this."

"*Me? Why me?* She's your daughter."

Jargus leaned his whiskered face close to Lance. "We made us a deal. We'd let you write yer newspaper articles if you keep Utopia proper. It's time you start holding up yer part of the bargain. Now git yerself out there and see that dancing's all she does. You hear me?"

"Now, look here. Your daughter is more difficult to handle than you explained to me before I agreed to this deal."

"A deal's a deal. We shook on it," Jargus said. "There's no rehashing it now. So get out there and start guarding our girl."

"Our daughter wants to sow a few wild oats," Henry said. "You just need to see to it that the only oats she sows is dancing."

The fathers pushed Lance out the door of his cabin and kept pushing him toward the campfire. He tried to dig his boot heels into the ground to keep from being moved, but he only tore up grass with his futile efforts.

"You don't understand. Your daughter's sowing more than a few wild oats. She's —"

"H-here's your hat."Fergus shoved the derby into Lance's chest. "I-I think you're doing a good g-guarding job. "Y-you just need to do more of it."

Lance took his hat and stuffed it on his head. "I don't know how you expect me to protect her reputation when she's dressed like that. Those men are hungry as wolves for the sight of a pretty gal. If I interrupt the dance, there's no telling what that crowd might do to me."

"You're in charge," Jargus said. "They won't hurt you if they want a courting turn."

The fathers followed Lance until they reached the whiskey barn.

"Let our girl have a bit of fun," Henry said. "But don't let her out of your sight."

"I don't know why I have to do this." Lance headed into the throng with no clear plan on how to prevent Utopia's fun from going no further than dancing.

Sadie stood next to Utopia on the makeshift stage and waved her hands. The crowd went silent. "Men," she began. "Some of you've already had the pleasure of meeting Miss Utopia during courting. Others are still waiting for your turn. The girls and me, we noticed the bride-to-be didn't have a special dress for tonight's celebrating, so Pearl, Lil and me helped her out. What do you think of her?"

The sultry night air filled with men's cheers and shrill whistles.

Lance squeezed his way toward the stage with the maddening crowd so packed together it was like trying to mosey though a herd of thirsty cattle at a watering hole after a long dry run. No man would give him quarter.

"Now, men," Sadie raised her voice. "Utopia's a lady, and you'll treat her like such. She wants to learn how to dance. Are you all up to the task of teaching her some fancy dance steps?"

More cheers, whoops and hollers ensued.

"All right then," Sadie said. "Here's how we'll do this. When Rufus and Percy start their fiddles, each of you will have a turn to show Utopia yer best dancing moves. Every two minutes I'm going to ring this here bell."

Sadie held up a rusted cowbell and gave it a good loud shake. "When you hear me ringing, that's the signal the next man can cut in for a turn to dance with the lady of his choice, either Miss Utopia or one of us other females. You'll each be allowed two dancing cut-ins. Any one breaking the cut-in rule will be tied to a tree wearing nothing but his long underwear. That fella will stay tied up until morning. Is that clear?"

Lance had finally gotten to the stage but he'd missed what Sadie had been saying. The band began tuning up their instruments. He knew he needed to hurry, for once the music started, he'd never get near Utopia. A quicker way to the stage would be to run around the rear of the wagon to get to the other side.

"We will go by your suitor numbers," Sadie stated, "starting with the next gent to court."

"That'd be me. I'm next," Travin shouted.

"Then get me and the courting lady down from here and let's get this dance started."

Travin placed his hands on Utopia's waist and swung her down off the stage. The fiddlers raised their bows. The banjo player readied his pick.

Lance came around the corner of the other side of the stage right when the first notes were struck up on the tune *Old Susannah*. To his dismay and disgust, the Travin fellow spun the laughing Utopia off in a hopping two-step stride. Lance needed a new plan of distracting.

Figuring the fastest way to reach his objective would be to dance his way through the crowd, Lance looked around for a dance partner. The closest female happened to be Miss Lil, dancing with the lad, Mickey Crosby. Lance poked the youngster on his shoulder. "Sorry, kid. I have to cut in."

"Hey." Mickey scowled. "I didn't hear the cowbell."

More interested in keeping sight of where Utopia floated off to, Lance went up on his tiptoes, scanning for a glimpse of her auburn hair or that lavender dress. *Damnation. Where is she?* "Look, kid. Go find yourself a new dance partner."

"Did you hear the cowbell?" Mickey asked a nearby dancer. "That timekeeper fella says it rang. Did you hear the bell?"

There were several negative nods.

"Look here, mister. No one heard the bell. It's still my turn."

"Kid, I don't have time for your sniveling. I'm only borrowing Lil for a minute. Stay right here, and I'll bring her right back to you." Lance lifted Lil's petite frame off the ground and carried her off in a fluid spinning motion. He flowed along to the tune, dodging around all the men dancing with other men because they didn't have a female partner. Lance scanned over the bobbing male heads looking for Utopia.

Lil held on tight to her feathers. "In case you don't know–this is a dance, not a foot race. I can say one thing for your way of dancing. At least my sore feet get some rest."

"I'm not really dancing, Miss Lil. I'm trying to catch up to Utopia."

"So, she's charmed you, too?"

"Me? No. I'm her guardian."

"Hah. Some guardian. Why don't you guard her away from my Travin?"

Lance had no idea what Lil was harping about. At last, he managed to dance his way alongside of Travin and his lovely partner. "Utopia," he yelled over the music. "Utopia. I need to talk to you."

She put a hand behind her ear. "What did you say?"

"Put me down," Lil yelled in Lance's ear. "I want to dance with Travin."

Lance lowered his twiggy dance partner to the ground at the exact same moment Sadie's cowbell clanged. Miss Lil shoved Lance aside in haste to dance with her boyfriend. The next song started up and the big Scotsman, John Doble, filled the opened gap created by Lance's caught-off-guard displacement. John whisked Utopia off dancing to the song *Buffalo Gal*.

Lance's mouth dropped open. *Unbelievable.* She was gone again.

It took quite some doing but Lance managed to get around to Utopia during a third song. However, it resulted in the same outcome. The bell clanged and a new dance partner stepped in and snatched his lovely, swirling objective away.

Moving onto a newer, third tactic, Lance spotted Miss Pearl resting on a log with her blonde wig askew. The woman stood six foot-five inches in her bare feet. He'd ask this statuesque gal to scan over the crowd and point him in the right direction.

Lance approached the saloon gal, and waited until she had her hair twisted back in place. "Pardon me, Miss Pearl. Would you care to dance?"

"Sonny, I've been sitting here watching how you danced with Miss Lil. And, honey, I don't think you're strong enough to get my feet off the ground that high."

"*What*? No. You don't understand. I'm trying to catch Utopia. I carried Miss Lil so I–"

"Are you sweet on that little gal?"

"Who, me? Most certainly not. I'm her guardian."

Pearl chuckled. "Yeah. And I'm her mama. Never mind. If you need to catch up to Utopia, then look no further. I'm your gal. Come on, handsome, let's you and me do some dancing."

The big woman grabbed Lance by his arm and pulled him close, nearly smothering him in her abundant bosom. Next he knew, Pearl bundled him up tight, his feet left the ground and she carried him off in gigantic two-step strides.

Pearl towered a head taller than most on the dance floor and from Lance's new vantage point, he now had a grand view of every bopping head. "I see her. Move that way." He pointed left.

"Hang on, handsome. We're going for a whirl."

Lance's feet flew in the air nearly perpendicular to the ground. He clung to his dance partner, and when the tune increased in tempo, her dancing became more sporadic. Now he knew how Miss Lil must have felt with her similar along-for-the-ride experience. "Miss Pearl, I really should be leading."

"Stop your hollering. We're almost caught up to her."

A few more strides and Pearl pulled alongside big John Doble and Utopia.

"See, I told you I'd catch up to them." The big gal let her partner down.

The cowbell's clapper made one ding and immediately, Lance pushed the next man in line for Utopia out of the way, not wanting a repeat of his five previous attempts. "Thank you, Miss Pearl. I got her now."

A waltz now played. Lance wrapped his arms around Utopia's waist and waltzed her away. "Boy, I'm sure glad this is a slow song. I'm winded after chasing you all over the place."

He paid not much notice to the minor storm brewing along the sidelines of the dance floor. Lance swirled his lovely partner past the stage area with his attention focused on how light his lovely dance partner was on her feet. He waltzed Utopia past some upset fellows; Mickey Crosby, Quincy Adams, and three other men, all of them in heated discussions with Sadie.

Utopia's eyes sparkled, and Lance heart skipped several luckiest-man-in-the-world heartbeats.

"I'm glad it's a slow tune, too. I can hardly breathe in this dress."

"You look beautiful." Lance offered. He'd never seen anything to compare to her.

She giggled. "Why, thanks. I feel pretty. Miss Pearl says I gained three pounds of tits."

Lance's brain jerked in shock. "What did you say?"

"Three pounds of tits. I do have them, you know?"

"Yes. You do. And they're hanging out all over the place." A hand tapped Lance's shoulder. He shooed the distracting man to go away. "I'm dancing with the lady. Leave us be."

The lumberjack man grabbed hold of Lance's arm and pulled him to a halt. "I'm afraid not, mister. Sadie's sent me to enforce the cut-in rule."

"Cut-in rule? *What the heck's a cut-in rule?*"

"It's a rule you must have missed hearing about. You've cut in too many times."

Lance hadn't cut in on Utopia but once. He figured the cut-ins with Lil and Pearl didn't count. And besides he had an excuse. "Cut-ins don't pertain to me. I'm in charge of the contest and this dance."

The lumberjack stood silent with his bulging-with-muscles arms folded across his chest.

Hmm. This wasn't a good thing. Perhaps knowing the particulars of this rule he supposedly had broken would settle things. "Exactly how many times do you figure I cut-in?"

The big bouncer man held up five large fingers.

Lance eyes shifted a look left. Besides the black-bearded man in front of him, two equally threatening tradesmen now joined them.

"This cut-in rule doesn't apply to me. You see, I'm under orders by the girl's fathers."

These two extra men each took a side and grabbed Lance by his arms.

"Orders?" Utopia hollered, putting her two cents in the matter. "My fathers gave you orders to be watching me? I guess you lied when you said I was pretty. It's all part of doing your job, is that it?"

"No. I think you are pretty. Your fathers—they want me to see your oats are sown safely."

Just then, another tune began to play. And a new fellow grabbed Utopia away from the discussion to dance.

This couldn't be happening. Not again. "No, wait. Bring her back here." The *Virginia Reel* now being played drowned out his words. Lance tried to break the lumberjacks' hold. "You fellows have got to let me go. The girl could be in grave peril. I promise I won't cut in anymore."

"You're right about that, mister. Your dancing is over for the night." The first lumberjack pulled back a big right fist and punched Lance's jaw. Upon painful impact, his world went black.

CHAPTER SEVENTEEN

Utopia looked over her shoulder, trying to see what had happened to Lance. No longer able to spot him anywhere among the dance crowd, she turned her attention to her new partner.

The man yelled in her ear, "My name's Clevis Mudd."

"Hi, Clevis. I'm Utopia."

"Everyone knows who you are, sweetie pie."

"I'd like it if you called me by my name. In case you forgot, it's Utopia."

"I meant no offense, miss. My memory slows when I've had me a few drinks."

Hmm. She looked around, mainly to avoid the man's ogling eyes. Making small talk with drunken strangers wasn't too pleasurable, but she knew this was part of a saloon girl's job. "It a nice night, ain't it? The full moon's real pretty."

"Shoot, little lady. The stars and moon don't compare to you." Clevis sniffed her neck. "You sur-r-r-re smell pretty. Like a bed of roses. Speaking of beds, I'd like to have you in one."

Utopia leaned away from him a bit for she couldn't say he smelled anything nice. "Thanks.

And no thanks." She wished this song would hurry up and end. Her dance partner again sniffed her hair. Before she knew it, he went to sucking on her neck like a leech. Utopia braced her hands on his chest and managed to keep him at bay. "Hold on there, Clevis. I think you better keep your mind on your dancing. The way you're swaying we both could fall over and get trampled."

The music picked up tempo and the dancers around them separated into a handholding line, bouncing and jogging to the tune of *Camptown Races*.

"Come on, sweetie pie, this is one of my fav-o-rite songs. You hang onto me and I'll do the rest." Clevis was a good size man with a gut as round as a huge boulder, but that didn't prevent him from hooking onto the tail-end of the dancing line running past him.

"No. Wait." Utopia tried to pull away from the man, but they were off to the races with the rest of the crowd. The dancing line snaked around in a zig-zagging circle, moving so fast she could barely keep up. Utopia tapped her dance partner's shoulder and yelled, "Clevis, I can't catch my wind in this dress. I need a rest if you get my drift."

The man grinned and released the hand of the dancer in front of him. "Surrrre, sweetie pie, I get your drift. I could use a good rest myself." He winked

She wasn't sure if the man had something in his eye, or if he was just being friendly, Utopia winked back. "A rest somewhere quiet would be nice." She knew snookered when she saw it all those times her fathers tied one on. No doubt about it, Clevis needed to sleep off his stupor.

"Sweetie pie, I'm a fella that likes to rest in private." He winked at her again.

Utopia winked back again, only this time she figured the man didn't have anything in his eye. He must have a blinking trouble going on in addition to his drinking problem.

A walk would do the man some good so she obliged him by strolling in the moonlight some. She led the way and Clevis followed along, having a few stumbles here and there as he strolled. Utopia could feel the man's eyes on her backside. Only Clevis didn't give off any tingly and exciting sensation with his looking. It was totally different than when she had Lance strolling behind her. Clevis' gazing gave her the willies.

They'd now walked such a distance that only a few fiddle notes could be heard, and Utopia figured their stroll had probably gone far enough. Ahead of her, she could see a glow shining through the canvas of the saloon girls' tent. Maybe that would be a good direction to wander. If the girls were there, they could give her some on-the-job training on how to get rid of the drunken fella. Right about now, that was one lesson she wished her brain already knew. "You know what, Clevis? I think I better check on my sick friend. She's feeling a bit poorly, and I promised her I'd come by and see if she needs anything."

Clevis wrapped his arm about her waist. "Surrre thing. We'll go check on your friend."

Utopia managed to get her staggering companion into the girls' tent. On the dresser, the kerosene lamp with the red shade and dangly crystals glowed, but to her regret no one was home. Something about bringing Clevis here when the girls weren't around seemed not too good an idea all of a sudden. She'd get the tipsy fella to a bed then go find the girls and let them know they had an overnight guest.

She removed her arm from around the half of the man's waist she had a hold on. Without her support of him, the drunk immediately lost his footing and reached out for her to gain his balance.

"No. No. Clevis. You go right here." It took some doing, but Utopia turned him around and toward Lil's cot. "You stretch yerself out and get some rest. Sleep will do you a world of good." No matter how much she pushed on the swaying man, he wouldn't sit on the bed.

Clevis waved his arms about the air. "Nah, nah, nah. I won't lay down unless you're comin' wiff me."

The next thing she knew, the man had his hand on her right breast. Utopia didn't know if Clevis touched her by accident, or if he planned it that way. No matter, she intended to put a stop to it. She knew how hot-tempered her fathers got whenever they drank too much. She'd be careful on the asking nicely.

"Listen to me, Clevis, I'd really like it if you'd put your head down on that cot and take yourself a little snooze."

"A snooze? I don't want no damn snooze." Clevis belched. He straightened up a moment, but stumbled and wrapped his arms around her to keep from falling.

His weight caught Utopia off guard, and they both fell onto Lil's cot with Clevis on top. If that don't beat all, now she was trapped beneath more than a couple hundred pounds of drunk, and try as she might, she couldn't roll the big tub of lard off her.

Clevis started kissing along her neck, leaving a trail of slobber. This was a far cry from the great neck nuzzling she'd gotten from Lance. By gosh, by golly, what little common sense the good Lord ever gave her was gone, or she wouldn't be in a pickle like this.

Utopia wiggled her hands between her neck and the fool's drooling mouth. "Now, Clevis," she growled. "I don't know what you have in mind, but I'm telling you right now, you're doing whatever it is alone."

Clevis clutched the shoulder strap of her dress. Next thing she heard was a rip.

Oh, my stars. Utopia made a fist and pummeled Clevis' back. Her hitting got his attention for a second, and he sat up some. "Look what you've done, you snookered pig. You've torn my dress, and it ain't even mine. I borrowed it. Now git off me you big lu—"

Clevis stuck his tongue in her mouth. Eew. Gosh Almighty, just this once, she wished she'd kept her blabbermouth shut. Clevis tasted and smelled like a rotten potato. That beef stew dinner of hers wasn't far from coming up.

The thrills, chills and skills of Lance's kissing flashed in her mind. There were definitely two kinds of kisses. Good ones and bad ones, and this was a really, really bad one.

Her brain connected this drunk's actions with her fathers' talks about poking, with the girls' talks on shagging for money, with Lance's warnings on kissing, and it all made sense. She needed to act and very quickly, or she'd have her first poke with this man.

She needed to do something to end this horrid, wet kiss. Pinned as she was, she had but one weapon to use. Utopia chomped her teeth on that part Clevis had stuck in her mouth. The man immediately rolled off her, whimpering and holding his tongue.

She scurried off the bed.

"Damn you. Why, you little she-devil. So—you like it rough, do ya? Come back here."

He grabbed Utopia around the waist and pulled her against him, her back to his front.

The really riled drunk stuffed his grubby hand inside her bodice and clamped onto her bare breast. Utopia inhaled several jagged breaths, trying to keep her wits about her and not panic. She was in some pretty big trouble and needed a plan but her insides were shaking so bad her thinking had stopped working properly. She was so . . . so stupid and cursed herself for getting trapped like this. And then part of her was good and mad, too. Utopia wanted to rip the man's head right off.

"Clevis, I'm warning you for the last time," she growled. "Get your damn hand out of my dress, or you're gonna be sorry."

The drunk had a good hold of her, and the more she pulled on his hand, the more his hold tightened. An escape came to mind. Her fathers had mentioned whenever a fella got to manhandling a woman, there was one sure-fired thing a girl could do to stop him.

This was one time she sure hoped that her fathers weren't honeyfuggling.

Utopia reached down to the front of the man's britches. She got a hold on his hardened poke-stick and put a real bear-trap hurt on him. He screamed bloody murder, pulled his hand out of her bodice and shoved her away from him.

Clevis grabbed between his legs and dropped to the ground. He wailed and writhed, holding his pained member.

Utopia had her wits about her now, thank heavens, and made a greased lightning dash out of the tent and ran for the safety of her cabin.

Once inside her own abode, she secured the bolt on the door.

She scurried to the cook stove and took a bottle of whiskey off the shelf. Her hands were shaking so badly, the bottle rattled on the tin cup's rim as she poured herself a drink. She gulped down the contents then sat down in a chair and poured a second drink.

Bundled up emotions of fear, panic, revulsion, and confusion swelled to the surface. She swiped away the never-ending stream of tears trailing down her cheeks. Nothing like this had ever happened to her before.

This had been such a wonderful day. Why'd Clevis have to go and ruin it?

All day long, the suitors behaved themselves. Not one of them treated her badly during their courting time. But tonight, during the dance, they'd acted different, grabbing and nuzzling on her. She didn't care for this part of becoming a dancehall girl. Singing and dancing is all that interested her. And Utopia figured poking would be even less enjoyable than what she'd just been through. She needed to come up with some way to avoid such behavior in men before she'd be able to work in a saloon.

The more liquor she drank, the more her anxieties mellowed. A few things were sorting themselves out. When she wore her buckskins and muck boots, the men's manners were fine. Only when she wore the saloon girl dress did their behaviors change for the worst. That settled it then.

She'd not wear fancy dancehall gowns until the girls trained her on how to make drunken men behave themselves.

CHAPTER EIGHTEEN

Utopia knew she wouldn't get a wink of sleep until she had some answers to these puzzling questions crammed in her head. She set out to find Lance and have a long talk. He wasn't in his cabin. She'd already checked there twice. It was near midnight. Most of the camp's occupants were bunked down after a wild night of dancing and drinking.

The girls said they'd last seen Lance being chased into the woods. That was where she'd go look next. The full moon overhead bathed the path along Coon Creek in a fair amount of light. About fifty feet ahead of her, Utopia could see the courtship log and headed that direction until a gentle breeze blew something against her feet. She picked up the brown derby and knew immediately the hat belonged to Lance, and with her heart in her throat she scanned the area looking for him.

Going a bit farther along the path, she found a pair of boots and a torn blue chambray shirt on the ground. Utopia picked up the garment and a whiff of that familiar shave-soap scent drifted to her nostrils. Without a doubt, this was Lance's shirt.

Utopia looked toward the creek. In the pale moonlight, she glimpsed something floating half-in and half-out of the creek. She dropped the items she'd collected and ran toward what could be a grizzly scene. Panic crept back in her soul, only this time the emotion hit her like a sledgehammer, enough to stop her heart. Reaching the water's edge, she hesitated to look down, holding her breath until she gained the nerve to face her fears.

She let out a huge sigh of relief when the jeans floating in the water were lacking a body to fill them. But her worry weren't over. Where was Lance?

She heard a faint moan coming from somewhere to the left of her. A man's moan.

Utopia wrapped up the pants and boots in the torn shirt. She plopped the derby on her head and ran toward the sound. Not too far into the pines, low and behold, there was Lance tied to a tree, wearing nothing but his white long underwear. His head hung limp upon his chest.

She dropped all his belongings and ran to him. Lifting his head, she gasped. Poor Lance had dried blood from a cut on the corner of his mouth, and from what she could see in the dim light, his jaw looked swollen. She gently kissed his wounded mouth. "Lance. Can you hear me?"

Lance moaned, and slowly his eyes flickered open. "Utopia. Thank God you found me."

"Who on earth did this to you? I'll get Jargus to take his shotgun to the scoundrel."

"Never mind who or why. Untie me would you?"

"Are you sure you're okay? I could give you a look-over just to be sure you're not real bad hurt."

His head shot up in complete alertness. "No. I'm fine. Just get these ropes untied."

Judging by his reaction, there seemed to be nothing more than a busted lip wrong with him. But untying those ropes, well, now—she'd have to think on doing that. How often did a girl get a chance to investigate a handsome captive man? Never. She scanned his body with her eyes. His biceps and that broad expanse of muscled chest beneath his undergarment, he looked perfectly fine to her, but wait one minute. What was that on his chest?

Her eyebrows shot up, and her eyes widened with surprise. Why the man had hair peeking out of the v-neckline of his long underwear. "You know, on second thought, it's probably a good idea I inspect you for broken bones."

Lance squirmed and kicked. "I'm fine. Just untie me."

She hid her snicker. Heck, the silly man couldn't go anywhere or do nothing to stop her. He should save his energy. "Now, you be still. I'll be gentle with my inspecting."

"I don't need you inspecting me," he spat. "My bones are fine. Untie me right now."

"I'll agree with you on that 'fine' part. Just the same, I'm inspecting. I guess the best place to start is your chest. You won't mind if I have a peek just to be sure your ribs aren't busted?"

"As a matter of fact, I do mind. Now, damn it, Utopia. You need to listen to me."

Of course, she had every intention of ignoring him. This was her chance to explore a man she really cared to see all of. Her fingers slowly worked at painstakingly unbuttoning his long underwear one button at a time. Her innards were fluttering and flapping like a flag on a windy day with the excitement of revealing her captive's fine body.

The last button of his underwear came undone. Utopia slowly opened his garment then gasped. "Oh, my stars. You're sure a powerful sight for a gal to look upon." She wanted to touch him. Why not? She put her hands on his chest and swam her fingers back and forth. Why, he felt as warm and furry as a cat she used to have.

Lance sucked in a loud breath then squirmed like the dickens when she kept rubbing. "Utopia, stop. Please. Please undo the ropes. Or I'll tell your fathers about how you're acting."

"You're hairy, but you're oh, so soft. I like the feel of you."

His breath caught when her fingers swiped across his hardened nipples. What a coincidence. Her nipples had responded in the same way when he'd touched her like this.

"U-to-pia. This is no way for a respectable young lady to behave. Whatever you're looking for, I swear I don't have it. And I swear I'm not injured so cut me loose."

"I'm checking you to be sure, so save your wind." Utopia was enjoying her exploration a bunch. She roamed her fingers down his ribcage

THE COURTSHIP OF UTOPIA MINOR 171

and halted, shocked to discover he had a scar on his left side. She opened his garment wider. There was the evidence of a once grave wound between his second and third ribs. "Where'd you get this scar?"

"You want to check my teeth, too?" Lance crabbed. "If you must know, it's a souvenir from Dodge City. Now cut me off this tree, please."

"No. I'm not finished with my checking. So far, the top half of you seems perfectly fine. Now I'll check below. You could have yourself a busted leg. Maybe even two."

Lance really started wiggling at that announcement. Just to be sure he didn't work himself out of his bindings, Utopia tugged on the rope to be sure the knots were good and tight.

"Utopia, stop this. Now for the last time, untie me. I don't have a broke anything."

Boy, if only the man knew how true that was. Ignoring his tirade, she bent down and slid a hand up one leg of his long underwear. She squeezed his firm calves and marveled at how muscled even that part of him was.

She heard another sharp intake of breath from Lance. Her mind snapped to a vivid memory of how much she'd liked it when he'd touched her chest. Her breath had hitched in her throat at such touching cause it was so pleasurable. Did that mean Lance liked what she was doing?

"You're fuzzy as a little bear cub, everywhere. Does this fur go any higher?" She'd find out. Her hands drifted up to his knees.

"Utopia. Sweetheart," he whispered.

His soft pleadings drew her attention to his face. Lance's forehead was sweating like he'd been running on a hundred degree day wearing three pairs of underwear and a buffalo robe.

"You must stop. Please, sweetheart. Untie me."

She stood, knowing she'd probably taken this inspection far enough. She decided to untie him, but when she gazed into his brown eyes and saw how dark and steamy they looked, something came over her.

Utopia snuggled up close to Lance. "I have a powerful need to kiss you. A need I can't control my thoughts from having even if I wanted to. I hope you don't mind."

Lance's gaze drifted to her mouth. "Please," he whispered. "You musn't."

She placed her hands on his chest and slowly moved them upward.

He must have wanted the kiss as badly as she for he leaned his head forward enough to get her arms between him and the tree. With her arms about his neck, and her breasts pressed against his chest, her heart was beating so fast her lungs were having a hard time keeping up.

When she kissed him, zing, zang, wow. Her blood turned to liquid fire. She didn't have to ask him for a wet stage two kiss, his tongue did the stroking, and she eagerly allowed him inside her mouth.

Utopia's fingers possessed a mind of their own and drifted into the curls at the nape of his neck. All the while, she wanted the warmth of him and crushed her body as close as possible. Once again, her lower torso responded in that way it always did when she kissed Lance. She felt a pool of moistness between her legs.

One of them moaned. One of them groaned. She didn't know who made those sounds.

But even as good as his lips felt, she realized something seemed to be missing with this kiss. His touch. Her body craved the feel of his hands exploring her. Especially her breasts, she'd liked it when he did that.

Utopia walked behind him, and worked at undoing the ropes. He waited patiently, as patiently as a man that had just been molested could wait. The second he was freed, Lance turned and grabbed her hands before she attacked him for another sizzling kiss. His eyes caught notice of the strap on her gown. He'd been so distracted by his temptress, he hadn't noticed her state of dishevelment. "Your dress is torn. What happened?"

She hurriedly pulled out of his grasp and adjusted the gown so the rip wouldn't show as much. "Nothing happened. I just tore my dress on something."

"Utopia, I can tell by your tone and your face you're not telling the truth. Please tell me what it is." She strutted back and forth before him in a perturbed fashion, chewing on her nails. He'd never seen her so disturbed.

"It's nothing much, a fella got me down on Lil's cot is all. The man got himself a bit drunk it weren't his fault. But don't worry. I gave him something to busy himself with."

For Pete's sake. Lance should have been watching after her. "You weren't hurt?"

"Heck, no. I did get a mite scared for a minute though." She held up the dangling strap. "I'm real sad my dress got a little ripped."

Did this mean she did or didn't have sex? "You didn't do anything other than dance tonight did you?"

"No." Utopia crossed her arms over her chest. "I can't say I did nothing special at all."

Thank heavens. "I can't tell you how relieved I am to hear you say that."

"Well, that's relief for you, I guess. It's nothing but a big problem for me. I got to learn what poking is all about. How you do it. I need to know if I like doing it. By gosh, by golly, my new job depends on it."

"We talked about this. Good girls don't need to know all that much about poking until after they're married."

In the next instant, her eyes scanned down to the prominent protrusion evident beneath his long underwear. Mesmerized interest appeared on her face. "You know what? I'm going to get out of these fancy bloomers I'm wearing, and then you and I can have a poking lesson. I can see you're as interested in the subject as I am right now." Her hands started to lift up her skirt and petticoats.

"No." Lance hurriedly grabbed Utopia and pinned her arms to her sides to keep her from undressing. She was right about one thing. He couldn't talk about sex without thinking about her. "There's not going to be a poke lesson. You'll keep your bloomers on, young lady."

She turned and started to walk off in a fit of rage. Lance knew he couldn't let their conversation end like this. There's no telling what she'd do to retaliate. He grabbed her around the waist and pulled her against him, her back to his front.

"Oh, I get it," she raged, squirming and twisting mad. "I'm too ugly for you to poke. Is that it?"

"No. No. That's not it at all. You're pretty. Real damn pretty." Lance spun her around to face him. He put his hands on her shoulders and looked in her eyes. "You're very pretty. It's simply that you should wait. There's plenty of time for you to learn how to . . . you know . . . have a poke. But you need to find the right man and get married first. That's what respectable girls do."

"Folks can poke without being married," she argued. "I've seen it going on for days now. Men coming and going out of the girls' tent like free hotcakes are being handed out."

Lance was speechless. This conversation couldn't go on any more. Someone had to put the girl straight about things. "Utopia, your fathers must have left out a few important details about the birds and the bees. Let me get dressed and then we'll talk. I'll answer all your questions."

"All my questions? You promise?"

"I promise."

"No honeyfuggling?"

"No honeyfuggling. You go on over and have a sit on the courting log a minute."

For once tonight, she did as he asked. Lance slipped into his clothes, delaying the process so he could think on how to approach this topic without getting himself into sinful trouble? Not sure of what she all ready understood about sex, and what information she still misconstrued, he decided to let Utopia ask her questions. He'd fill in the blanks.

An hour of discussion later, Lance was satisfied he'd gotten the mystery of sex out of the way. He wasn't so confident about the one remaining issue. Did Utopia understand what being a saloon girl would do to her reputation?

"So there you have it. It's up to you to choose the right man, and preferably you get married before you decide to learn more on the poke subject."

"You're talking about that respectability stuff again, aren't you? Saving myself for that someone that wants me as his wife?"

"Every man on this mountain wants to marry you." Lance swallowed the sour taste that statement left in his mouth. "I guarantee they want to bed you. Do you think you can wait until you fall in love with someone?"

Her hands flew up in exasperation. "Dog-gone-it, Lance. You've gone and done confused me more. If I don't exactly know what love is, how in the heck am I supposed to know when I have the right fella I can give myself to?"

Lance had a knot in his throat at that question. It had been a long time since he'd allowed himself to care for someone like he cared for Utopia. He couldn't let his own desires hinder her from seeking out a proper mate. He brushed that wayward curl behind her ear. "That's something I can't help you with," he whispered. "You'll have to decide on your own."

There was silence. Utopia had all her answers now. Daylight would break on the horizon soon. Her courting would begin again, and he'd be back to chaperoning and newspaper duties, hiding and watching from the shrubbery while Utopia tested the boundaries of her new sexual awareness.

He'd be on the sidelines watching her choose a mate, totally regretting he wasn't her choice.

CHAPTER NINETEEN

What a nightmare of a night. The dance, that crazy business with the cut-in posse, his in-depth talk with Utopia. All-in-all, by the time he got back to his cabin, he managed to grab three hours of sleep before the fathers stirred him from his bed. It was no surprise his chaperone and reporting duties started early.

Utopia's courting had gone smooth as pie up to this point in the day.

The bride-to-be must have taken his talk on respectability to heart. She'd conducted herself like a proper lady all morning. He'd had no reason to come out of hiding and thump a man for getting out of line.

To his surprise, Lance discovered that innocent Utopia could handle misbehaving suitors all on her own. There were at least, at his last count, seven contestants bobbing like corks in the cold water of Coon Creek, easing the pain of a direct kick in the family jewels.

His coverage of the contest, although going smooth as silk for the bride-to-be, it was giving him an ulcer. Watching Utopia flirting, laughing and enjoying other men's company turned his temperament more sour than Jargus. He'd done about all the snooping around in bushes that he cared to tolerate.

As the official contest timekeeper, there was absolutely no call for him to be slinking around spying from the shrubs. No reason other than Utopia ordered him not to spy on her. He didn't care what she wanted. No more bug bites, thorns and bad vantage points for this reporter. From here on out he'd make his presence known. Her fathers' orders trumped her wishes. That was all she needed to know.

The only thing he'd have to be careful about was his note taking. If Utopia found out about his articles on her courting, she'd quit the contest, and he could kiss his newspaper career goodbye. He'd have to hide his journaling from her somehow. And he knew of a good cover, fishing. He'd enjoy a little relaxing fishing time on the bank right near her courting area.

Lance took his pocketknife out of his pants pocket, pulled a small pine branch from a nearby tree and carved himself a pole. He rummaged through some of the trash around camp and found himself a tin can then dug some worms. Completely equipped to fish, he'd go call the next suitor numbers then march himself to the creek and take up a front row seat on the bank, right out in the open to watch the courting show.

Grabbing the next courting number out of his pocket, Lance walked to Utopia's doorstep. The men quickly gathered around. "The next suitor to court the lady," He paused and glanced at the number and scowled. "The next number is . . . one hundred fifty."

"That's me. That's me," Mickey yelled, waving his slip of paper in the air.

"Wait here lad. I'll fetch the lady."

Lance turned and took two steps to Utopia's door and knocked. The latched lifted and she walked out. "Your next suitor is ready to court you, my lady." He gave a slight bow and waved a hand toward the waiting lad. "The boy's all yours for exactly one hour."

He turned to Mickey. "Mr. Crosby behave yourself."

"Oh, I will, sir."

The hopeful lad escorted his lovely, buckskin clad lady to the courting log. Lance gave the pair a head start then rounded up his fishing equipment and followed them.

Utopia and Mickey were already seated on the log by the time he caught up to them. Lance baited his hook and made his first cast. He took a seat on the creek bank thinking that this was first comfortable vantage point to chaperon and report that he'd had this entire contest.

Watching the fresh-out-of-knickers kid court should be pretty good entertainment.

"What's he doing over there?" Mickey Crosby asked.

Utopia wondered the same thing. Lance had no business there. "It looks like he's fishing. I'd say he's using the wrong bait. He ain't had a bite the whole time he's sat there."

"I thought my courting was supposed to be private. Can't you make him go away?"

If only she could make him leave. "Nope. I've already tried to run him off. He's the official contest timekeeper and won't budge." It was high time she showed the nosey snoop something of real interest to be gawking at. The lad's cheeks showed a fair amount of peach fuzz. "Mickey, just how old you are?"

"What's my age got to do with how much I care for you?" Mickey indignantly declared. "If you pick me for your husband, don't worry about me being man enough. My ma and me, we'll provide for you."

Utopia scanned the boy from his head to his boots. "Our ages may not bother you none, but from my side of things, I feel like I'm snatching a baby bird from the nest before he can fly."

"Aw, shucks." Mickey ripped his newsboy hat off his head. He rubbed his carrot-topped noggin in agitation. "I'm man enough to marry, dangnabbit."

She couldn't help but feel sorry for the lad. After all, they shared the same difficulty, a lack of hands-on experience. "I reckon you'd know if you're ready to marry."

Utopia narrowed her eyes on Lance. He sat there baiting his hook again.

"Don't mind me." Lance waved at her. "You two go on with whatever you're doing."

"Why can't he fish somewhere else?" Mickey scowled. "I don't like being spied on while I'm . . . aw, shucks. I can't abide an audience when I'm gonna get my first kiss." He glared at the distracting person by the creek. "Can't you make him go away?"

Lance cast his line into the water. "Get on with your courting, boy. I'm sure the bride-to-be's anxious to see what kind of gift you're giving her."

"I guess he's right." Mickey smiled for the first time. "You should open my gift." He handed her the brown paper wrapped package.

Utopia untied the blue ribbon and tore open the wrapping and tried to keep a frown off her face. "Well, I'll be . . . I've never seen a dress quite like this one."

"It's my ma's." Mickey beamed. "Ma said I could give you her Sunday dress for a wedding gift. Do you like it?"

There wasn't much she could she say about the pale green dress printed with tiny lilac flowers without honeyfuggling. "This lacy white collar's a real nice touch. This dress must be one of your ma's favorites. Are you sure she wants to part with it?"

Mickey's grin stretched from one pink ear to the other. "It's her Sunday-go-to-church-dress. We're Baptist. We go to church every day."

Utopia made a mental comparison of this simple garment to the fancy gowns her friends wore. There was no low-cut bodice. This garment would button practically up to a chin. The fabric wasn't silky, and the length brushed her shoe tops instead of being hemmed at the knees. What kind of woman wore such a plain dress? "You sure your ma wants to give me her Sunday dress?"

"It doesn't fit her anymore. Ma will be proud someone pretty as you can have use of it."

"Whoo-hoo, what a whopper," Lance yelled. His pole arched to the water with the weight of a large fish.

Mickey crunched his cap tight in his hands. "Does he have to fish there? Ain't I entitled to privacy?"

Utopia folded the dress and placed it back in the wrappings. She couldn't figure Lance's reason for being rude to Mickey. The poor lad's eyes were twitching he was so flustered. She pulled on Mickey's shirtsleeve to get his attention off Lance and back to her. "Don't mind him none. Pretend he's fallen in the creek and washed away."

"But, he hasn't. He's over there. And he keeps watching me. He'll know I don't know how to kiss a woman. Then soon the news will spread all over camp. I'll be a laughingstock."

"No, you won't. Kissing isn't hard. I can teach you starter kisses."

"Starter Kisses?"

Mickey looked puzzled. Starter kisses were too tame for this boy. The lad deserved better. Especially after the way Lance treated him. Even though she was only slightly sure she knew how to do stage two kisses, she planned to give the boy a pucker he'd never forget.

Utopia framed Mickey's face in her hands, put her mouth to his and stroked her tongue across his lips. It surprised her when the lad's eyes grew wide and crossed like he knew how to keep looking at the tip of her nose. That was good. Mickey must know this part of kissing. She continued to put her best effort into her tongue wiggling smooch and peeked around the side of Mickey's head, checking to see if Lance watched them.

To make it appear that she was really enjoying herself, Utopia moved one of Mickey's hands to her backside. Next she rubbed her fingers through the lad's pomaded hair in an exaggerated show of hair rubbing. It would really improve this demonstration if the lad would get more into enjoying himself. Utopia finally managed to get her tongue in Mickey's mouth. Perfect. She added a few very loud moaning sounds. She hoped her enjoyment noise carried clear over to Lance.

The minute she tried to wrestle her tongue with Mickey's, the rascal boy lost his balance and they both stumbled and fell over the courting log. Utopia landed sprawled on top of the lad.

Mickey rolled Utopia off of him and staggered to his feet. It was hard to keep from laughing at his hair all mussed and sticking out like porcupine quills. He stared at her with his eyes bugged out and his face beet red. Mickey swiped his shirtsleeve across his mouth, wiping off the kiss. "Why you're one of them loose women."

Utopia stood up, quite confused. "Didn't you like my kiss? I thought you'd like it."

"You thought nothing. My pa, he . . . he . . . ran off with a woman like you. He's probably in some saloon doing nasty stuff with a whore that kisses just like you."

More and more often, Utopia heard that word "whore" around camp. The men would mention it quite frequently around Pearl, Sadie and Lil. But she didn't get the gist of exactly what it meant. Apparently, Mickey knew the answer. "What's a whore?"

"It's a woman that'll give away her self-respect to any man that'll pay her two bits. *They're abominable creatures*," Mickey ranted. "If you're one of them, then you're abominable, too. My ma warned me to stay clear of girls like you. Only a nasty woman would kiss like that."

Utopia's hands shot to her hips. "I don't rightly like the way you're talking to me. Why would you say such mean things when all I was trying to do is be nice to you?"

"Yeah. I know what kind of nice you had in mind."

She never intended to be a nasty woman. Utopia glanced at Lance sitting over there still holding that fishing pole of his. Lance spotted her looking at him.

"What's the matter, boy? Are you two having a lover's spat?"

"I've had enough of him and you." Mickey slapped his cap on his head. "I'm sure my ma wouldn't approve of me bringing someone like you home to be my wife."

Utopia was fuming mad, packing enough anger inside her to stomp ten rats dead. This was all Lance's fault. If he hadn't been sitting there judging the lad's courting, then she wouldn't have overdone her kissing.

The lad's rejection deeply hurt her feelings. Utopia blinked back her tears.

"You keep my present," Mickey said. "The contest says all gifts are yours once we give them.

But I'd appreciate it if you wouldn't wear my ma's dress. You don't measure up to her standards."

Mickey turned and walked off.

That was it. Utopia stormed over to Lance. He deserved a piece of her mind. By the time she reached the creek, she'd built up quite a fuming mad. Utopia looked around for something to work off her rage. Seeing Lance holding that pole of his, she grabbed the darn stick and threw it into the creek and watched it float downstream.

Not totally in control of her temper, she grabbed his can of worms and tossed those in the water, too. For good measure, she kicked a cloud of dust at him. "Why'd you go insulting him like that? Because of you, I overdid my kissing."

Lance got to his feet and brushed the dirt off his clothes. "Hey, don't go blaming your conduct on me. I'm just keeping the courting time. " He cupped his hands at his mouth and looked toward the running-away lad. *"You still got ten minutes. Come on back, boy."*

A tear rolled down Utopia's cheek, and she angrily swiped it away. "Because of you that boy thinks I'm nasty. He's gonna tell his ma about me. Tell her how he fell into ruin kissing a whore."

"I warned you that bad things happen if you use the wrong kisses on the wrong fellows." Lance put his hands on her shoulders. "That lad is barely out of diapers. He wouldn't know a whore if she tore his clothes off. I wouldn't worry on what he tells his ma."

Tears welled up in her eyes at the thought of what this mother of Mickey's would say about her. "If ever I do get to a city, I won't be able to look folks in the face after he spread lies about me."

Lance brushed a curly tendril of hair behind her ear. "He probably will embellish his tale more than a few times. Just don't go to where he lives and your reputation will be just fine."

"Oh, wow, thanks for that information. That makes me feel much better about the whole thing. Get out of my way before I sockdologer you right in your smeller." Utopia shoved Lance aside. She stormed back to the log and retrieved Mickey's gift then stomped off for camp.

When she got back to her cabin, she went to her trunk and lifted the lid. She removed the upper tray and laid the neatly folded green print dress beside her mother's perfectly preserved red satin saloon dress. She ran her fingers over a few of the sparkly black beads on the bodice of her mother's gown. A tear rolled down her face. Today she'd learned a hard lesson.

There are two kinds of kisses.

There are two kinds of dresses.

There must be two kinds of women.

CHAPTER TWENTY

Lil stormed into her tent, barely managing to keep herself calm after what Travin had told her went on during his courting turn. "We got ourselves a big problem."

"What's bothering you?" Pearl adjusted her black wig on her head. "Did someone piss on your hair feathers again?"

"I've kept my eye on our girl most of the day. Nothing's changed. She's still got saloon girling on her mind. And I fear she's exploring on those kissing lessons of hers too much. Just look at this dress." Lil held up Utopia's torn lavender gown. "I believe the girl's done serviced her first customer."

Pearl took a seat on the chaise lounge, opened her half eaten box of chocolates and popped a candy in her mouth. "You mean to tell me after all the caterwauling those men did at the dance, how they pawed their grubby hands all over the personal parts of us–and her– you mean to say the girl's still got a notion of being like us?"

"She's even more determined than ever to be a dancehall gal." Lil angrily plopped down on her cot. "She's gone too far with these lessons of hers. The damn girl ear nibbled on my Travin this afternoon."

"Um, um, um," Pearl hummed, licking chocolate off her fingers. "We promised her mama, Della, that we'd make sure her daughter turned out a respectable lady."

Fully charged with mad, Lil paced the confines of the tent. "I knew those numbskulls Jargus, Fergus and Henry wouldn't raise the girl proper. We should have pooled our money, sent Della's girl to that boarding school back east when we had the chance. She was our friend and we've sure let her down. We let them no good men talk us into keeping her girl in this mining camp. Now look what we got to contend with."

"That's all bad water washed down the mountain now," Sadie said. "We'll just have to try some other way to set the girl straight. Perhaps we should tell her we knew her ma'am. Tell her about the promise we made to see she's a respectable lady?"

Lil shook her head. "You're forgetting the part where we promised Della we'd not tell her little girl what her mama did for a living."

"Well—whatever we do," Pearl said tossing her empty chocolate box aside. "I suggest we not dress her too fancy tonight. And another thing, I don't believe for a second the girl's had herself a man. But . . . why take chances she won't try. More than a dress could get ruined if we pretty up Utopia again."

"You're the brains of this outfit." Sadie tossed a pillow at Lil. "Get to thinking on this mess. What are we gonna do?"

"I don't have to think. I already know what we'll do." Lil pointed at Pearl. "Our big chocolate eater here gave me an idea."

※ ※ ※ ※ ※

"Honey, try these dancing shoes on." Pearl handed Utopia a pair of her size twelve heels.

Not wanting to be an ingrate, Utopia took the offered shoes, but there was no two ways about it, she was going to look plumb ridiculous wearing them. "Miss Pearl, I think I'll saunter better if I wear my boots."

"It's time you learn some sassy walking. And you can't learn that kind of a walk wearing boots," Pearl stated. "You can roll up all that extra bit of my stockings you're wearing into the toes of the shoes. Then they'll fit just fine."

Utopia sat on the end of Lil's cot and slid her feet into the big shoes. After plenty of stocking rolling, there was only so much hosiery she could cram in her footwear. When she stood up, the remainder of her extra, extra large stockings sagged in rippled gathers at her ankles.

The abundant layers of petticoat under her gown made it impossible to walk about the tent without knocking something over. "I feel like someone that's shrunk in their clothes. Are you sure I need all this?"

Lil folded her arms over her flat chest and got in Utopia's face. "Do you want to be a saloon girl or not?"

"Oh, I want to be like all of you." Utopia didn't want the girls taking offense.

"We want your first baggy clothing night to be special," Sadie offered. "Unforgettable."

"A baggy clothing night? What's that?" Utopia never heard of such a saloon girl thing. 'Course, there were any number of things she'd never heard of before the ladies came to camp. "How often do these nights where I have to wear this real big clothing come around?" It really didn't matter. She'd wear a furry bear suit in hot July if it would keep the men behaving long enough for her to learn tonight's lesson on playing cards.

"One evening, we wear our tight corsets and such, then the next night we put on our bigger stuff." Sadie informed. "That way our insides don't get crushed from being cinched all the time."

"Oh," Utopia replied. It all seemed to make some sense. "Why ain't all of you dressed for big-stuff clothes night?"

"This evening's your dancehall baggy clothes poker debut. We don't want to detract from the excitement when the men get sight of you. We intend to make you up extra special for the occasion," Lil stated. "Come sit down. I'll even share my lipstick with you."

Utopia eagerly took a seat at the mirrored dresser. Lil sharing her makeup and beauty tips with her had to be a dream come true. Lipstick would make her at least feel like part of her was pretty and it'd take her mind off how uncomfortable huge clothing feels.

Lil pulled the cap off her lipstick. "Open your mouth like this." She demonstrated in the mirror. "Now hold still." The harlot applied an ample amount of Persimmon Red lipstick to Utopia's mouth.

"I ho—" Utopia's heavily creamed lips made a popped sound on the "p." After that she was extremely careful not to close her lips until her lipstick dried some. "Will I 'e a-ule to talk with this lick-stick on?"

"Hush," Lil chided. "All saloon girls know you wear lipstick thick at first so it'll last through lots of kissing. You'll see."

Sadie added the final touches to Utopia's strange outfit by wrapping a shedding boa around Utopia's neck. "These red feathers will look great with your purple gown. Stand up, let us have a look at you."

Utopia wobbled to a stand, trying her best to keep her balance in Pearl's giant shoes.

"Honey, have a look at yourself in the mirror." Pearl helped turn Utopia.

When she got a gander of herself it wasn't pretty. Hideous was more like it. Several of the spindly banana curls Miss Pearl affixed on the top of her head now drooped in her vision. Utopia brushed the wayward curls out of her eyes so she could see the women's faces. "Somehow, I don't think I'm ready for my debut." She plucked a couple feathers off her gooey lips. "Maybe I should wait and have my poker debut on a tight-fit night."

"No, no, no. This should definitely be your debut night." Lil grinned from ear to ear. "After tonight, none of the men are going to forget you. No, sir-ree. You're a vision for the ages."

Utopia faced the mirror again and looked at her baggy clothes, overdone makeup and drooping curls. Lil was right about being hard to forget. It'd take a million years to forget looking like this. She shrugged. "If you say so."

Pearl shook her head and chuckled. "Umm, umm, umm. This is gonna be one great coming out poker party. No one's gonna be able to take their eyes off you. Enough with all the beautifying, it's time we showed you off."

Utopia exited the tent first, followed by Lil, Pearl and Sadie, who were all giggling so hard they had tears gushing down their faces. She wished they'd let her in on the joke. Right about now she could use something to take her mind off this oversized outfit they'd put her in.

The sun raged its daily departure by showing off in vivid hues of violet and red. Half-way to the improvised saloon, Utopia spotted Henry outside the whiskey barn lighting some torches. When he opened the door to go inside, a loud ruckus of crowd noise spilled outside.

"Sounds like the evening's already off to a good start in there," Pearl announced. "Whiskey and frisky men. Honey, you're gonna learn the ropes of our business tonight."

Utopia feared which sort of ropes Pearl talked about. Hopefully, they weren't ropes like the kind she'd had to untangle with Clevis.

The girls were halfway to the whiskey barn when a team of dapple gray horses hitched to a fancy buggy pulled into camp. A finely dressed man pulled the team to a stop in front of the women. Several gruff riders-wearing long dusters came to a halt alongside the carriage.

The well-dressed man tipped his hat at Lil. "Good evening, ladies. Aren't the three of you the gals from the Palace Oak? You're Cyrus' saloon girls, aren't you?"

Utopia noticed that Lil, Pearl and Sadie snubbed their noses at the man. Lil took her by the arm and walked her around the fancy rig.

"Pay him no mind. Keep walking, girl."

She leaned over to Lil. "Who is that man?"

"That's Frank Sharps." Lil pulled her along. Sadie and Pearl were close behind. "He's a man you need to stay clear of. You hearing me, girl?"

"I hear you." Even if Lil hadn't given such a warning, the man would be no one she cared to have a conversation with. She peeked over her shoulder. The man tipped his hat to her, flipped the reins of his team and drove on. A chill raced down Utopia's spine, the likes of which she'd never gotten from just meeting a person only once.

They entered the renovated whiskey barn. Utopia glanced to her left and noticed Pa Henry behind a makeshift bar serving drinks. The room was packed to the walls with tables, chairs and people. Utopia hadn't a clue where all the furniture had come from. Her fathers must have tapped into their surplus whiskey, for every table had a bottle or two sitting on it. And every table had a card game in progress.

"It looks like we picked a good night to teach you poker games," Lil said. "You go along with

Sadie. You watch what she does and follow her lead. Do whatever she tells you. I'll be back in a bit to check on you. I'm gonna go look for Travin."

"Let's go get ourselves in a poker game," Sadie said. She swayed her way over to a table.

Utopia followed the skillful woman's lead, but her overly large heels turned her attempt at a sultry gait into a wobbly swagger.

"I'll work this table and you can work that one." Sadie pointed to the next closest table. "I'll be sitting right behind you. Listen to what I say. Watch what I do. Then you practice."

"I'll try." Utopia could hardly hear over the noise. "Be sure you talk good and loud."

Sadie nodded. "I will."

Utopia made her way to her appointed table. Upon sight of the card players she'd been assigned, her spirits sank. This wouldn't do. Lance, Jargus, Fergus, and John Doble were the men at her poker game. By gosh, by golly, this wouldn't do at all. She needed a new table, but when she looked over her shoulder to confer with her mentor, it was too late.

The skillful saloon gal had already wedged herself between two men. Sadie tossed her boa over her shoulder and gave a cheerful smile. "Evening, boys, mind if I join you?"

Oh well, this table would have to do. It was time to start practicing and on who shouldn't matter much. Utopia flipped her red feather boa over her shoulder and oops, unlike her mentor's fancy flourish, her boa produced a flurry of feathers, infesting her poker table with a snowfall of plumes.

"What the hell?" The card players batted at the colorful fluff drifting into their game.

Undaunted by her shedding problem, Utopia forged onward. "Evening, boys, mind if I join you?" She tried not to be too obvious at plucking feathers from her sticky lips, but when her lip-plucking left the plumage stuck to her fingers, it was hard to stay unnoticed.

Utopia heard Lance's bark of laughter, and she turned a glare on him. He quickly covered his mouth and studied the cards in his other hand. She needed a place to wipe off the gunk and fast. A place came to mind, the underside of her skirt. Problem solved. She smiled and went back to work. "So, how about it, can I join you fellas?"

"Girl, what the hell are you doing?" Jargus growled.

Utopia giggled at the sight of Jargus with several feathers sticking out of his beard. "I'm working."

"Working at what? A chicken plucker? Where'd you get that getup? And why in blazes do you have to wear it around here?" Jargus took a sip of his whiskey only to get a mouthful of soggy feathers he had to pluck off his tongue. "I've had enough of yer fluff. Get those damn duds of yours away from me."

Undaunted by her pa's complaining, Utopia pressed on. She couldn't very well practice dancehall skills on her fathers. She'd have to pick either Lance or John Doble. She wedged her bulky skirt and petticoats between the two men and would sit on the first lap offered to her.

Lance batted at the swirling boa fluff invading his airspace. "Don't you have someplace else you can molt?"

"None of ye needs to be insulting me future bride." John patted his thigh. "Lass, ye ken sit your little tail feathers down on this sturdy knee."

Pearl's shoes were killing her feet. Utopia stuck her tongue out at Lance and gave John a pretty smile. "Why, thank you kindly. I don't mind if I do."

She wasn't settled on big John's knee but two seconds when the man's hefty arm wrapped around her waist and pulled her close. Utopia cringed. Her comfort level just rose to a huge worry. Utopia felt cornered, but she knew she had no choice but to push away her qualms if she wanted to learn saloon girl work. She told herself there was nothing to worry about. Lance and her fathers were here. They'd keep the man in line.

Utopia looked again at the other table to see what her mentor was doing. Sadie had her arm wrapped around her man's shoulder, and her expert fingers stroked in the fellow's hair.

Oh, thank goodness. She knew how to feel hair—she'd practiced with Lance. Utopia took one look at John and scowled. Her hair stroking just hit a big snag. The man wore a flat brimmed hat on his head. "If that don't beat all," Utopia muttered under her breath. That headwear would have to come off. She tapped him on the shoulder. "Do you mind if I take your hat off?"

"As a matter of fact I do. It's me lucky topper," John stated. "I won't be taking it off. T'would bring me bad luck."

Hmm. Utopia chewed on her fingernail. How would a saloon girl handle this problem? Utopia looked over to Sadie who still worked at hair stroking. The Scot's hat was a problem for sure. She could think of only one way to get John to part with his lucky hat.

Utopia leaned over and put her teeth gently on the Scot's ear and gave him a tiny nibble like Lance had done to her. She soon realized that keeping hold of a small earlobe with a ton of lipstick on your mouth was very difficult, if not nearly impossible to do.

"Praise be, lass, what in tarnation are ye slobbering on me for?" John leaned away from her and slapped his hand on the gooey side of his head. He glanced at his palm all covered in red. "Blimey. You've chewed me ear off."

By gosh, by golly, she didn't think she'd disfigured the man. Utopia turned John's head toward the light of the kerosene lamp hanging overhead. She swiped at his red hand and let out a relieved sigh. "I didn't bite your ear off. That's just a bit of my lip rouge."

"Bless me sainted mother, I ain't never been slobbered on so much in all me born days."

Utopia smiled. He'd have to take that hat off now. "I'll hold your lucky topper for you whilst you get yourself cleaned off."

John scowled, but nonetheless, he handed her his lucky fedora. He removed a handkerchief from his jacket pocket and dug in all the crevices of his ear to remove the lipstick.

Utopia used this wiping time to get more instructions from her teacher. Sadie's man was busily scooping in the winnings of a big hand, and her instructor rewarded her lucky man with a kiss on his cheek. Hmm. Another kiss wouldn't sit too well with her player. She decided to wait on the reward kissing part of the lesson if and when John won himself the money in the middle of the table.

"All bets are in," Lance called. "How many cards do you need, Jargus?"

"I ain't won a hand all night." Jargus tossed his cards on the table, and the table's settled feathers stirred back to life and flurried about the players a second time. The old man pushed his chair back and stood. "Enjoy your whiskey and feathers, fellas. I'm giving it up." He hobbled away from the game.

Lance waved the pesky plumes away from his area. He looked first to Fergus, then to John. "Jargus folded his hand that leaves the three of us. Big John, how many cards does that lucky hand of yours need to win?"

"I'll take one." John discarded his card to the pile, leaving a red fingerprint on the corner of the pasteboard.

"H-hey," Fergus called out. "H-he's marking the cards. That's cheating."

"Gentlemen, I believe this is a case of smudging, not marking." Lance pointed to Utopia.

For the first time, Utopia felt embarrassed, and more than a tad unsure of her ability to do this job she wanted so badly. So far she'd done everything wrong.

"I'm not cheating. It's the lass–she marked me with that red mouth of hers. Anyone calling me a cheat will not be saying it twice." Big John glared at Fergus.

"It's all a simple mistake. Settle down, Fergus. There's no call for name-calling. We can see John's not cheating." Lance took a handkerchief from his vest pocket and wiped off the card. "Let's continue our game, shall we?" He gave Utopia a stony look.

Utopia felt the sting of Lance's glare. Her darn kissing instructor always made her feel poorly about her skills. She stiffened her shoulders, more determined than ever to learn this game and prove to him once and for all that she was teachable and capable of doing this job.

Lance reshuffled the cards and dealt again.

John held his cards close to his vest, shielding them from Utopia's view. The man's lack of sharing his hand really irked her. Her dancehall job depended on this lesson. How would she be able to learn this game if no one helped her? "I have one teensy question."

"Can't it wait a wee bit, lass? I'm trying to concentrate on me hand."

No, dang-nabbit. She wanted to know what-beats-what in this game right now. "What's that lady card you just put with your other cards?"

John's eyes widened with shock. "Lass. For crying out loud. You're not supposed to be telling everyone what cards I've got in me hand. Sit there and keep that wee sweet trap of yours shut. Is that too much to be asking of you?"

Utopia scowled and pressed her lips tight together, highly offended at this man's attitude. He didn't have to be so rude about her one little question. She shoved the man's hat back on his head. "Here, have your lucky topper back. You must need it."

"I guess I do at that," John scowled. "I'm raising the both of you two bits."

When the Scot leaned forward to put his money on the table, Utopia got just enough of a peek of his hand. "How about that, every card you're holding is red. And they all have them little heart pictures on them."

"That does it." John shoved Utopia off his leg, dropping her to the ground in an abundant entrapment of petticoats and large clothing. "I've had enough of ye blabbing to last me the rest of me days. Gents, now ye know I have me-self a high flush. You'll have to show your cards and beat me fair 'n square, or fold." He reached in his pocket and tossed a slip of paper to the center of the table. "I'll even throw me courting number into the pot. I won't be needing it any longer."

"That b-beats me." Fergus tossed his cards to the discard pile.

Now that John's hand had been blabbed, Lance decided it wouldn't be sporting to pile more grief on the man. "I'm out, too. You won the pot." He folded the best hand he'd held all night, four of a kind, and placed his cards face-down with the others.

John chuckled and eagerly raked in his winnings. "Are we playing some more?

Utopia chewed on her nails and looked worried watching John haul in his winnings.

"Not for me." Lance pushed his chair back from the table. "Gentlemen, I believe I'll escort our feathery parrot to her cabin. I bid you both good luck and good evening."

He reached down and pulled Utopia up off the floor. "You're coming with me, Fluffy."

CHAPTER TWENTY-ONE

Lance held onto his stumbling captive's hand, forcing her to keep up. She lagged behind him because of her ridiculously big shoes. Impatient with her pace, he scooped Utopia up into his arms and carried her the remaining distance to her cabin.

Sizzling mad would be a mild word to describe his upset with her. He had no idea what he intended to do with this bundle of feathers and silk once he got the little hussy inside her cabin. One thing he did know. Tonight, her foolish saloon girl stuff would end once and for all.

There was light coming from the cabin. Apparently, someone had lit a lamp earlier. He reached her door and paused. "Do you mind? I have my hands full." His eyes directed her to lift the latch on the door and she complied. Once inside, he kicked the door shut, put her down then dropped the latch into place, barring interruption.

Utopia immediately bolted to escape him, but Lance grabbed her arm and spun her around. He put his fingers under her chin, lifting her head, forcing her to look at him for one intense moment.

All the while, he reminded himself to remain calm. "When are these lessons of yours going to stop?"

"I don't know. Maybe once I've learned salooning from real dancehall girls." She pushed his hand away. "Why are you always sticking your nose in my business, anyways?"

"We've already discussed this saloon dream of yours several times." He raked his fingers through his hair. "Damn it, Utopia. The work's not what you think it is."

She tossed her boa over her shoulder, sending several feathers fluttering. "So you keep saying. Only you never fill in the blanks of exactly what's wrong with saloon girls."

Lance let go of her and paced, hardly able to contain his frustration. "I don't want to shock you with all the details. You'll have to trust me. Give up this crazy idea before it's too late. If you continue, you'll ruin any chance you have at a decent life."

"No. I won't. My friends make a good living at what they do, and what folks think doesn't matter to them. I don't care about such things either. I plan to be just like Lil, Pearl and Sadie."

Without coming right out with the niceties of prostitution, he'd run out of ideas on how to get through to her. Utopia happened to be a free spirit with strong opinions. One of the opinions being she didn't care what others thought of her. Except—she did care what bad things Mickey's mother might say after she'd over-kissed the lad. Maybe now was the perfect time to fill her in on all the intimate details of whoring. It was the only ace he had left in his deck of ideas.

"Utopia, you're under the delusional assumption saloon girls have fun all the time."

"I'll admit sitting on laps, ear nibbling and hair rubbing on strange men to sell whiskey, none of that's too fun. I intend to skip doing those things. All I want to do is sing and dance."

"If you could keep it to singing and dancing that would be nice."

"Let's talk about something else. I'd like to play that poker game." Utopia scurried to the cook stove. "My fathers hide their cards from me. I guess they're afraid I'll learn bad habits."

Lance watched her root through each of the five books on the shelf above the stove. His mind flashed to the prior lessons he'd been forced to give the girl. What kind of trouble might befall him with card playing? "You shouldn't bother other people's things."

"Oh, they won't know about it. I'll put the cards back when we're done." She opened a book and from inside a rectangular cutout compartment, she grabbed the pasteboards. "Ha. Found them." Utopia returned the book to the shelf. "Let's get to our poker lesson."

Lance correlated this eagerness of Utopia's with the day in her treehouse. This would be complicated, and trouble, and he decided to leave while the getting was good. "I've changed my mind. I don't feel like playing poker right now. Why don't we forget all about this? I'm hungry. What say you and I go grab a bite to eat?"

Her bottom lip pushed out, her chin lowered, and her sorrowful eyes glanced at him.

His heart melted, along with any willpower to refuse her. "I can see I won't hear the end of it until I agree. I'll teach you the basics. That's all."

"Basics are all I need." She smiled and pulled out two chairs. "Sit down. Let's get started."

Lance swallowed a knot in his throat. He needed some sense pounded in his head. He joined her at the table and took the cards from her. "Okay. The most basic thing in poker is cutting the deck. We'll start with that." He reluctantly sat down.

"That sounds good to me." Utopia threw the boa over her shoulder, shedding a bit and eagerly took a seat across from him. "What do I do?"

"First, we make a wager." The blank look on her face said she was already confused. "We each have to bet on who's going to have the highest card." For crying out loud, the girl didn't even know the basics of basics. "Money? Do you have any money?"

"No." She worriedly bit her nail. Her hands crushed down the bulkiness of her petticoats and skirt. "All I got are a heck of a lot of Pearl's big clothing."

"It's not a good idea to play for clothes," he replied. "You could lose your shirt—I mean that dress, and sometimes lots more." The thought of her naked sent his brain reeling. "We should really go back outside." He started to leave his chair.

"You said we'd play. Can't we play a couple of times?"

His inner voice told him to walk, no run, away from this game as fast as he could, but his bottom plopped back down in his chair. He pointed his finger in her face. "We're only playing three times. Three articles of clothing is the limit. Understood?"

She nodded. A curl drooped over her eyes, and she brushed it aside. "Understood."

"And we're only going to practice cutting. Agreed?"

"Agreed." She smiled.

He undid his string tie and laid it on the table. "I wager this. What are you betting?"

"Hmm. Let me think." She nibbled on her nail while her other hand tinkered with her gown. "Boy, I don't know." Her nervous habit of nail biting changed to twirling a curl of her hair around and around her finger. "Umm, this is a darn hard thing to decide on."

For crying out loud, he was such an idiot. Her deciding on a bet could take all night. Lance gave cheating some thought. The problem being, it was pretty hard to cheat someone who didn't understand the basic concept of winning and losing.

"Oh, I know what I'll bet. Turn your head."

"What?"

"I said turn your head away. I want to get at one of these garters under my skirt."

It was hard swallowing the knot in his throat this time. He rotated on his chair to the extent the furniture's backing allowed. At first, he stared across the room at the stove until her movements, and rustling petticoats, forced him to take a peripheral glance at her.

She had her purple gown raised and showing a bunch of petticoats and an enticing, slender leg. Her fingers slipped under the lacy red garter and wiggled and worked the band down her thigh. She raised her knee toward her chest. Lance quickly forced his gaze back to the stove before he saw farther up her dress than he should.

"You can turn around now."

A moment passed, and Lance tried to decide whether to run for the door or face the table again. He turned back to the game. She tossed her bet on the table. "I wager this fancy garter."

He picked up the deck and shuffled, having a bit of difficulty, either because the pasteboards were so worn or his hands were too sweaty. He set the cards in the middle of the table, picked up the top third of the deck and showed her his card. "That's called a cut. I have a ten of clubs. Now you pick up a section of the stack that I left you and show me your card."

Utopia bent low and eyeballed the deck every which way a pile of cards could be stared at. "Wellll, I'm not sure." She leaned to the left. Her finger rested on her bottom lip while she studied the immobile stack. "This looks good." She reached for the cards then pulled back her hand. "But ..." She leaned to the right.

Lance drummed his fingers on the tabletop. "We haven't got all night."

"Be quiet, you'll jinx me." She ever so slowly made her cut and showed her card.

"That's a five of spades. Your card's lower than mine. You lose."

Her fist pounded the table. "Dang-nabbit. I knew I should have picked lower."

"You lost." Lance pulled his winnings to his side of the table.

"Now what?"

"We do it again." He wanted to keep her garter and threw his tie back to the center of the table. "I bet my tie again. Since you lost your garter, you'll have to find something else to bet." He grabbed the cards and shuffled while she decided on what piece of clothing to remove. He only hoped the item wasn't an essential piece of body coverage.

"I'll bet a shoe. A real big shoe. I think it should count like a double bet." She reached down, pulled off the heel and plopped Pearl's footwear on the table. "Say, can I try that shuffling stuff?"

"Sure, why not."

She licked at her fingertips and reached for the pile.

Lance spotted red all over her fingers and grabbed her hand to keep her from touching the deck. "Stop. First you need to wash that lipstick off, or you'll mark up the cards."

Utopia stood up, and without her garter, the large stocking slinked to the floor in a rippled bunch, covering her non-shoed foot. She quickly tossed the hosiery on the table. "There. That's my next bet after the shoe bet."

She looked down at her other foot. "I don't want this other shoe." She kicked her leg high, sending her other heel sailing across the room. It crashed against the door. Now shoeless, Utopia walked across the room with her surplus stocking flopping across the floor. She retrieved a damp rag from the washtub in the corner to wipe her mouth off.

Lance could see her efforts at washing off the lip rouge weren't going well. He walked over to assist. "You're not going about this the right way. Let me help you." He took the washcloth from her hands and gently rubbed his cloth-covered fingertips along her bottom lip.

As he wiped, her lips change from bright red to a luscious pink and the rhythmic beat of his heart quickened to unsteady knocks. "There," he whispered. "I think we've got you fairly unpainted." He hardly heard his own words over the drumming going on in his ears. Their eyes met. When her arms rose up and slowly wrapped about his neck, his last restraint of being a gentleman fell by the wayside.

Between the lamp's light in the room and the faint bit of moonlight coming through the window by the stove, Utopia's hair was cast in beautiful amber highlights. His gaze fell to her mouth. She was an angel. His angel.

Unable to resist her any longer, Lance wrapped his arms around her and pulled her to him. He kissed her. Not a pecking kiss. Not a starter kiss. He gave her a deep down, stage two wet kiss.

He finally ended their kiss only because he needed a breath of air. Lance looked into her eyes and wondered if he could stop himself from taking what he needed from her. His desire had gone far past the point of no return and he knew it. Now what to do about it.

Her eyes were lusty, a deep emerald color, and all too trusting of him. Lance took hold of the end of her billowy boa, and ever so leisurely, he slid the lengthy scarf from her shoulders, letting the feathery item spill to the floor.

"Ain't we going to play some more?" she whispered.

He brushed that wayward curl behind her ear. "Game's over, sweetheart. I forfeit the next hand." Lance pecked a light kiss on her forehead. "And the next." He pecked a kiss on her cheek. "And I forfeit any hands I play with you forever more." He pecked a kiss on her mouth.

"What's a forfeit?" she whispered.

Her question was an innocent one, and it certainly deserved an honest answer.

"It means I quit." Lance went down on one knee and put his hands on her stocking-clad ankle. "This baggy clothing of yours, you won't need to wear it anymore. Allow me to help you take it all off." He slowly moved his hands up her calf, taking great pleasure in feeling her leg from calf to knee. He moved his hand under her skirt and continued to explore up her leg higher.

Lance worked his fingers under the garter and heard a soft gasp from her. When he placed a gentle kiss on the inside of her thigh, he felt her shudder. Pleasuring Utopia could very well take the very life from him, but oh, he couldn't think of a better way to die.

He leisurely slid the garter down her leg, and right after, the stocking slinked to her ankle.

Lance raised her foot and slipped the first two articles of clothing off of her. He stood with the hosiery in his hand and let it float out of his fingers to the floor.

"So—that means I win?" she breathlessly asked.

"Yes, my sweet. Forfeit means you've won it all." He slid one arm around her shoulders, the other under her bottom and picked her up and carried her across the room, kissing her all the way to the curtained wall of her cabin. He had no free hands to part the drapery. "Do you mind? I seem to have my hands full."

She brushed the barrier aside. He didn't allow her mouth to leave his again until he laid her on the straw-filled mattress. Lance stood beside the bed, and one look into those luminous, trusting eyes of hers gave him a reason to put an end to what he craved to do with her. "If you want me to stop, you best say so now before I join you in that bed."

"I have to tell you something." She lightly patted her chest in calming little taps. "My heart's racing so fast I don't know if I can talk. Truth is, when those other suitors are kissing me I don't like it much. I only really like kissing you. And I think it's time I told you I don't think I'd like to be ruined by anyone but you. So—please don't stop."

"I wouldn't want you ruined by anyone other than me either." He kept his eyes coupled with hers and slowly pulled his shirttail out of the waistband of his jeans and undid the buttons of his shirt.

Lance took his sweet, sweet time undressing his sweet Utopia, and for once she was relatively silent. He posed her hands on her head and told her not to move an inch. Like the eager good student she wanted to be, she allowed him to caress her body. He proceeded to kiss her soft breasts, her stomach, and her thighs. Each time his tongue stroked across a sensitive part of her body she gave a few twitches, a few jitters, and more than a few sighs with an occasional hallelujah blurted out. He gave her credit for one thing. She kept her hands where he'd told her to.

What he loved about Utopia, his little vixen was a fast learner, and in no time, she had her pleasuring lesson down-pat. She eagerly practiced in no small dose her lessons on his body.

The night was young. Outside, a fiddle played a waltzing melody barely audible through the logs of the cabin, but soft enough to set the mood. He joined her in the bed. From that point on, he lost himself in her innocence. She explored him. He explored her. They loved each other passionately, and with abandon.

Lance couldn't say how much longer they had until their night of pleasure ended. Sunrise still could be a couple of hours away. He'd lost track of time after their joining. It had been slow, sensual and explosive. At least it had been for him.

They rested for now, their bodies too spent to do naught but lay in each other's arms. He was afraid to move, afraid to break the spell she'd cast over him. She was, for the moment, in a light slumber. He listened to her little snore. With her head resting on him, her breathing teased his chest hairs. Lance just wanted to hold her, enjoy the feel of her naked body against his.

Utopia had her leg bent and resting on his thigh with her womanly warmth pressed against him. He would need a bit longer to regain his strength if he wanted to make love to her again. And he sure wanted to make love to her again. He hoped he'd have forever to make love to her.

Relishing in the rose scent of her tousled hair that teased his face, his thoughts wandered. How had she wrapped herself so tightly around his heart? He made an analytical comparison of that tiny speck of gold they'd tried to split to this woman resting her head on his chest.

He now understood a man's crazy notion to hunt gold. Why a man would withstand unimaginable hardships, dangers and loneliness in pursuit of a mere gem. That once a small tidbit of the precious metal is touched, a man will do anything to protect his new-found treasure. Once that gem has a claim on his heart, he'll want more and more of it until the very want of his wealth consumes him body and soul.

Utopia was his nugget of gold. His treasure.

He knew what he wanted out of life now. And his wants had nothing to do with the law—or running a newspaper business. He intended to be truthful with her about how he had initially come to her camp to get a new start in life at her expense. If after he confessed all his snoopy dealings with her fathers, if she wasn't mad as a hornet and wanting to kill him for his article writing, then he'd ask her to marry him.

He intended to do right by her. How and where they'd live after they were married, he'd leave up to her. If she wanted to stay in these mountains, he'd help her find her rich vein of gold, even if it took them a lifetime. If she wanted to live in a big city, he'd run a newspaper in order to support them. He wanted to provided her a happy, respectable life and bless them both with lots and lots of babies. Hopefully, their children would be just like her.

Daylight was near for a minimal bit of light filtered through the tattered muslin curtain hanging over the window by her bed. Utopia's eyelashes teased his chest when she stirred awake.

She tilted her head to look up at him with a sleepy smile and gave a little stretch. "Is it morning?"

"Not yet, but soon." He rubbed his hand down her body, down to that wonderfully round bottom of hers. "You're so quiet. Are you all right?"

"Oh, I'm fine," she sighed. She rolled away from him onto her back and put her hands under her head.

Lance watched her profile. "You're never this quiet. What's wrong?"

"You promise you won't laugh?"

"I promise I won't laugh." He rolled onto his side facing her and brushed her long hair behind her ear. "My sweet, what do you need to ask me?"

"Is what we did with each other a one-time thing, or can we do it a lot more times?"

Lance smirked, trying to recover from her adorable question. He looked at her pretty blush and tried not to laugh. "I'll wager I can do it one more time." Already, his body prepared to have her again. He rolled on top of her and pecked a kiss on her forehead. "But it's going to cost you." He gave her bottom lip a little nip.

Utopia's arms slid around his neck. Her legs wrapped around his hips. "Judging by that grin on your face, I reckon I can get more than one time from you. What do you want to bet?"

CHAPTER TWENTY-TWO

Utopia opened her eyes and looked at Lance asleep next to her. She sighed with contentment. With the shadow of a beard on his face, Lance looked especially handsome this morning. Or it could just be the stars he'd put in her eyes last night that blurred all but heavenly thoughts for her lover. His chest breathed slow and deep as he slumbered.

Now that she'd made love with Lance, she felt different somehow. It was more than the fact their first joining felt different than the second time. Their first loving had been slow, filled with curiosity of learning about his body, him learning hers. The second time had been that bear-with-an-itch-to-scratch type joining, with both of them not able to stop loving until the rubbing, the desirous chafing and frictional heat inside each of them had been completely satisfied.

She let her gaze skim slowly down his muscular stomach to the blanket's edge covering his lower half. Her blood warmed, recalling the magic of his hidden extremity, and the pleasure it had given her.

With all the energy he'd pulled from her body during their lovemaking, it was a wonder she could even stir herself from bed. If the poor man felt as drained of life as she, it would probably be wise to let Lance have a bit more rest. Especially since she wanted to join with him again.

She slipped out of bed ever so carefully so she didn't disturb him. Utopia threw on her shirt, buckskins and boots, leaving her long underwear behind. That would be one less garment to have to get out of when they wanted to do more loving.

She'd get herself washed up at the creek. When she returned, she'd fix them a nice breakfast. Once fed, the man's energy should be revived enough for one or two more tumbles. Hopefully, they'd spend the day together. Any courting planned for today, she'd put off for tomorrow. In fact, she'd made up her woman's mind last night.

Woman?

Wow. When had she changed from a girl to a woman? It seemed impossible that she could feel so totally different than yesterday, all because of one night with one fabulous man. She'd taken Lance into her body, into her heart, and somewhere during their time together, he'd made her a woman. Now she knew she desired her man like Lil desired her Travin. Utopia wanted to wrap her legs, her arms and her heart tight around Lance and never let him go.

Utopia fetched a towel and bar of soap from her steamer trunk. Before she slipped outside, she took one more glance at Lance sleeping. She quietly shut the door and ran for the cover of the woods rather than taking her usual path to Coon Creek.

Slinking off to do her bathing wasn't her customary practice. But today she didn't think she'd be able to put on one of them poker faces like what she and Lance talked about last night. She feared even the mention of the word bed or undressing would be enough to set her face to blushing. A person's got no way of controlling a beet red face even if they were of a mind to.

Ruined was ruined and there's no use wishing otherwise. Besides, Utopia wasn't sorry for the loving she done with Lance. But it would be nice if he had the good sense to keep their lovemaking a secret until she could find a proper time to tell her fathers. If Jargus got wind of her ruining, he'd give her bottom a blistering she'd not soon forget. And she feared what he'd do to Lance.

Utopia had concerns now that she'd become a ruined woman. Why should she feel like keeping a secret about what she'd done last night? Lil, Pearl and Sadie bedded their fair share of men, and they seemed not to care who knew they did it. She now understood why men hovered around the girls' tent all night long. Now she completely understood why the men would want to pay the girls hard-earned money to get a poke.

But she didn't think joining with a fella could be any better just because a person gets married. If that be the case, everyone would be hitched. It didn't make much sense that folks should look down on certain women just because they made their living poking with a bunch of different men. Loving with a man shouldn't feel so darn good if you weren't supposed to do it, and do it often. She couldn't grasp the logic of this respectability stuff.

Utopia reached the creek and checked her surroundings before shedding her clothes and getting in the water. She lathered the soap and washed, with her mind rehashing her wonderful night.

The truth be told, Utopia knew there was no man on earth she would have ruined herself with other than Lance. And in the future, she'd certainly not turn him away if he wanted to do more lessons.

Finished with her bathing, she dressed. But that feeling of embarrassment or shame, she didn't know which, that feeling stuck with her and no soap or clean thoughts seemed to be able to wash the worry away.

How would she make herself look unsullied after knowing what she'd done with Lance?

Utopia took the graveled path back to her cabin. Along the way, Mickey's Sunday go-to-meeting gift crossed her mind. The lad had asked her not to wear his ma's dress. But it dawned on her that putting on the plain garb could make her look respectable and hide her ruination from suspecting eyes. It would soothe a lot of woes if she changed into the dress when she got to her cabin.

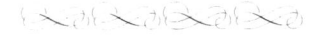

Frank approached the reporter's cabin. He checked his surroundings. Only a few early risers were sitting by the campfire area engrossed in coffee and a chat. He slipped inside the abode unnoticed and shut the door.

The makeshift desk caught his attention. Frank walked across the small room and rummaged through stacks of papers, coming across several articles regarding the courtship events of recent days. He glanced at the articles and scowled at not finding any mention of a closure date for the contest. How unfortunate.

This Lance had interviewed him several times in the past months, always asking questions that had a connotation of corruption attached. So far the reporter failed to link him to anything of an embezzlement nature. But it was only a matter of time until the man dug up smut to print in that rag newspaper. One dead reporter could solve that problem.

Things weren't to have gotten to a point requiring his personal intervention. However, at this late date, he wasn't willing to risk things going wrong all because he'd left the demise of one reporter, and the resolution of this contest, in the hands of his thugs. Any slip ups could ruin his political future, and he'd be damned if he'd let that happen.

Regardless of how the contest ended, that mealy-mouse Cyrus had failed him. Damn him. Nobody failed Frank Sharps without getting punished, and the barkeeper would be taken care of soon enough. With only two days left until the election, Frank knew he'd have to personally give the lass some strong incentive to hurry her husband selection along.

And the matter wasn't so disagreeable to him now that he'd seen the bride-to-be firsthand. His one glimpse of her when he rode into camp yesterday had stirred his loins like no other woman had done for him in ages. He'd always prided himself on having a discerning eye for the fairer sex. No one could say Frank Sharps didn't know a rare beauty when he saw one, even if she happened to be caked in tons of makeup. And no doubt about it, this lovely miss could be political gold for him.

Those three harlots of Cyrus' had failed miserably in their attempts to camouflage the girl's beauty under face paint and saggy clothing. Overnight, he'd thought long and hard on this contest, arriving at a brilliant solution. If everything went well with this new plan, he'd soon set up house in the governor's mansion with the lovely mountain beauty as his blushing bride.

First, he needed to know just how much the reporter had uncovered about his past. Frank spotted some belongings under the bed and turned his snooping there. He put Lance's saddlebags on the cot, opened the flap and searched inside the leather pouches, pulling out several sheets of notes and newspaper clippings. There were numerous notations in the margins regarding corrupt Denver developers and delayed construction of Tin Cup's business district. His name was boldly circled in a St. Louis article regarding embezzlement of bank funds. A scribbled notation on the top of the newspaper read "Sharps is linked to land swindles."

The articles confirmed his suspicions once and for all. The reporter knew too much. Frank needed to put an end to this long drawn-out contest, and at the same time, remove one meddling lawman turned newspaperman from his affairs.

A rap sounded on the door. Frank tiptoed from the bed to the door and put his back against the wall where he'd be hidden from view when the portal opened. He pulled a derringer from his vest pocket and waited.

"Boss. It's me, Carp," the hired gun whispered.

Frank opened the door and grabbed the man's vest. "Get in here before you're spotted." He pulled Carp Tagart inside the cabin and shut the door. "Well, don't just stand there looking stupid. Fill me in."

"I kept watch on that gal's cabin like you done told me to. That reporter fella and that gal were together all night. Just like you figured they'd be."

Frank leered at his lackey. "You're sure of that?"

The fidgety man ventured a look at his boss. "I wouldn't say so if I weren't."

Frank slapped Carp's hat off and it landed on the cot. "Don't get smart with me."

The gunman flinched. "I weren't being smart."

Carp and his two brothers weren't the brightest thugs that his money could buy in these parts. But Frank knew he had them sufficiently under his control. They'd do what he ordered without many questions and without much more pay than whiskey and a whore.

"I just saw the gal leaving the cabin carrying a towel. I think she's headed to the creek."

"What about the reporter?" Frank grabbed Carp's shirt. "Where's he?"

Carp shrugged his shoulders. "Best I know, he's still in her cabin sleeping off whatever he done with her last night."

Frank clenched his jaw. The reporter spent the night with his future bride, and there was little doubt what the man did with the lass. That bothered him some. He'd hoped to be the first man to enjoy her. So—she was no longer a virgin, he'd still have many pleasurable nights with her. He dusted off the sleeves of his black tailored jacket. "It's time I get to my courting."

"Courting? Why are you going courting, boss?"

He leered at his lackey. "I've changed my plans. Where are those numbskull brothers of yours?"

"Joe and Buck have gone to have a good talk with that gal Lil. By the time they're finished with the whore, she'll be telling everyone what you need her to say."

"Good. What about the others? Are they ready?"

"Yes, sir. JD, Percy an' me will take care of that reporter."

Frank put on his black Homburg hat. "Whatever you do to him, it's got to look like an accident. Remember that."

"Don't worry. Percy told me he'll make it look like the mine collapsed. He guarantees it."

When his thugs guaranteed something, a catch of some sort usually got put in the mix. Momentary foreboding flashed through Frank's mind. He shoved such inconsequential concern aside, for he'd personally oversee that things were done correctly. "This evening you and the boys need to be ready to stir up a mob against those three fathers when I give you the signal."

Carp nodded. "Will do, boss."

The two men cautiously stepped outside. Frank headed toward the courtship area to do a bit of persuasive proposing. Carp took off for the woods.

Lance awoke to an empty bed. The scent of roses from her pillow filled his senses. Where could his lovely redhead be? "Utopia." He anxiously watched the closed drapery, waiting for it to open, and for her to give him one of her radiant smiles. Knowing how readily Utopia explored him last night, and her curiosity for wanting to learn her lessons to the finest extent, it wouldn't be hard talking her into bringing that delectable body of hers back to bed.

"Utopia." Why didn't she answer him? He slipped on his long underwear and pulled back the curtain. Her shoes, stockings, petticoats and purple saloon dress lay in a pile where she'd removed them last night. Her buckskins, shirt and boots were gone. That didn't set well with him. She was off doing something, but what?

Lance got dressed and carefully cracked open the door and checked to be sure no one watched the cabin before he exited. Hoping to be unnoticed, he made his way across the open expanse of field between her cabin and his and quickly ducked into his shack.

Once inside, he gathered up his articles on the week's courtships. He stuffed the reports in his saddle bags and gathered what he needed to make his trek to town. Barris would probably be fuming because he'd missed yesterday's delivery of his precious contest news. It wouldn't hurt the old coot to miss one day of print.

Lance had much to do and very little time to accomplish all the tasks on his list. He figured he'd ask Fergus to be in charge of the courting until he got back from Tin Cup later this afternoon. He'd give the father clear instructions to stay real close to Utopia. Then he'd find his lovely lady, and no matter how much she begged, kissed or bribed him, he'd not tell her anything about his romantic dinner plans with her for later this evening.

Usually he headed for town just before the sunrise. He'd ride an hour down the pass to Tin Cup, drop off his articles, and then return to camp before Utopia started her morning courting. Today's late stir from bed had changed his routine some. Other things had also changed overnight.

Last night's affair altered his future plans, but in a good way. Today was the last contest article he planned to turn in. The odds were pretty much a one hundred percent certainty that Barris, and the throng of many suitors, weren't going to like much of what he wrote in his final contest article.

This afternoon, when Utopia's day of courting ended, Lance intended to take her away to some private and romantic place. Then he would get on his knee and ask her to marry him. If she said no—well, then— he'd have to get her to say yes. A visual of him persuading her to say yes flashed in his mind and made him smile. Evening couldn't come fast enough to suit him.

Most likely after he announced their engagement, the suitors would get in a huge uproar, maybe even organize another angry posse to run him out of camp. And he fully realized the suitors had every right to curse him for breeching his journalistic ethics. He wasn't even a registered contestant. To hell with all of them. Let the suitors scream and holler. None of that would sway him from claiming Utopia as his bride.

Lance wouldn't stand for anyone labeling Utopia a ruined woman. He intended to make things legal, give her a wedding with a beautiful dress, flowers, vows and his name. The whole works. And he'd be damned if he'd have a wedding ceremony performed with a grumpy old man's shotgun aimed at him with a gnarly finger on the trigger.

Now packed and ready to head to town, he'd looked everywhere for Utopia to no avail. Daylight was wasting. Lance didn't trust Fergus to could keep his secret. He decided to leave a message with Lil, mounted his horse and rode the direction of the girls' tent.

Lil happened to be sitting on a keg outside her canvas abode smoking a cigarillo.

He dismounted and removed his derby. "Morning, Miss Lil. I'd like a word with you."

The woman pulled her sheer robe together over her naked body, shielding herself in a semblance of modesty. "It's too early for business." She suspiciously eyed him. "Was that you I just saw sneaking out of Utopia's cabin a bit ago?"

Lance couldn't recall how long it'd been since he'd been caught leaving a gal's bed and blushed about it. "I was checking up on Miss Utopia, but she's not in her cabin."

"Ha, you were just checking, were ya? Guess you were checking her cabin for bed bugs, too." Lil laughed at her own teasing. "You said you wanted something. What is it?"

"If you see Utopia, could you tell her I had to go to Tin Cup this morning. I'll be back this afternoon. Tell her I have something very important I want to ask her tonight."

"You'll be back later. That's it? That's all you want me to say?" Lil took a long drag on her cigarette.

Did the gal even hear what he needed her to tell Utopia? "You won't forget about the important thing I want to ask her, will you?"

Lil stood and put her hand on her hip. "Look here, sonny, I ain't deaf. I'll be sure to tell her that you'll be proposing later."

"Who said anything about proposing?"

"Well, that's what you're intending' to do, ain't it?" Lil removed a flask from her garter, unscrewed the cap and took a swig.

Lance feared he'd made a big mistake confiding in this hussy. "All right, yes, I'm going to ask her to marry me. Right now, can't you just tell her I'll see her later? Can you do that?"

Lil put her flask back under her garter and rewrapped her negligee around her body. "Sure, I'll tell her. Now go on, git. I need to go grab me some beauty sleep."

THE COURTSHIP OF UTOPIA MINOR 229

Looking at the bags under Lil's eyes, Lance figured she'd been up all night servicing customers. That explained her grumpy mood. Then again. It didn't. Lil always seemed sassy. The thought crossed his mind to skip delivering the news articles. The hussy might sleep all day and forget to give Utopia his message.

On the other hand, if he didn't get these papers to Barris, that easterner, Horace Greely, still had his offer to buy the newspaper on the table. The editor would likely sell to him if Lance couldn't show him these articles. And if he didn't get paid for the articles, he couldn't buy a ring to give to Utopia.

Lance climbed in his saddle, put spurs to his mount, and headed his love-struck ass for Tin Cup.

CHAPTER TWENTY-THREE

Lil remained on her stoop after Lance departed. She'd give Pearl a little more early morning privacy since the big gal had given her and Travin some of the same a short while ago. After a half-hour of waiting, she walked to the tent flap and hollered, "I'm coming in, ready or not." She stepped inside.

Pearl tied off the belt on her pink silk robe and gave Lil a come-hither wave. "We're all done. You can come on in now."

The Scotsman was buttoning up his pants. "Miss Pearl, I'll be telling ye true when I say you've pleasured me well this fine morn. 'Tis been quite a spell since I've dipped into as bountiful and plush a female as ye."

"I must say I enjoyed that hefty dipping stick of yours." Pearl clamped her hand on his bottom and pulled the Scot up close. "I'll be calling you big bad John from now on."

John blushed. He put his hand on her shoulder and moved her back a bit. "Miss Pearl, I'd be honored if you'd dance with me tonight."

Pearl turned loose of the man's rump, walked to the dresser and picked up his straw hat. She sashayed back to her customer and plopped the hat on his red-haired head. Her arms crossed under her bosom. "I might have a dance with you if you're not too busy."

Lil tried not to eavesdrop on what could very well be the first romantic courtship she'd ever seen her friend have. Usually Pearl was all business, no getting involved with the customers.

"I intend to have my whole eve with ye, Miss Pearl."

The big gal's face drew a puzzled look. "Won't you be courting Utopia later?"

The Scotsman scowled. "I'm through courting the lass, I am. I withdrew me name from the contest. I'll not take me-self a wife that can't keep her mouth quiet during a poker game." John gave Pearl a quick kiss on her cheek. "I'll be having that dance with you later." He tipped his hat. "Good day, Miss Pearl. Miss Lil." He scurried out of the tent.

Lil strutted about in the close canvas quarters with one hand on her hip. "Well, well, well. I do believe you've landed yerself a fine strapping man."

Pearl took off her red wig and hung it on the hat rack. She grabbed her platinum locks off a peg. She looked at Lil by way of the mirror and arranged her new coiffure on her bald head. "Are you crazy? He paid his money for a flop like all the others."

"Hah, like hell he did." Lil thumbed the direction of the departed John. "That fella really likes ya. Why, it's written all over the man's face."

"I'll give the big Scot credit. He's plumb pleasing in the sack. He even thrilled my oversized and over-used money pit." Pearl swiped the tip of her little finger on her lower lip, spreading her lipstick. She paused and gave Lil a quizzical glance through the mirror. "You really think that Scotsman's sweet on me?"

"He asked you to dance with him later, didn't he?"

Pearl shook her head and gave Lil a skeptical wave. "Aw, like most men, he probably wants to try and talk me into giving him a free one."

Lil decided to throw in the rumor she'd heard about the man. "Word around camp is that big strapping Scot comes from some kind of clan royalty or some such. He's got pockets full of money and has some kind of a castle back in his home country. How do you like that? Sadie and I will have to get used to calling you Princess Pearl."

"Like hell. I'm not gonna run off and live in some run down, drafty ruin of a castle."

"Are you stupid, girl?" Lil's hands flew to her skinny hips. "Why wouldn't you hook yerself up with a fella like him? He's rich. He's not bad looking. And he's rich. Did I mention the part about he's rich? Think about it, you ninny. You'd have no more mattress work, except when you're pleasing him."

"Yeah, that sure would be nice," Pearl said. "My bodacious good looks won't last forever."

THE COURTSHIP OF UTOPIA MINOR 233

She turned on her seat, slapped her hands on her thighs. "You know what I might do?"

"No. What?" Lil rolled her eyes toward the tent's roof.

"If you're right about–well, everything you just said, I just might have to set my cap, or should I say my wig, for that big hunk of man."

"You. Do. That." Lil paused. It was the first that she noticed her other friend's cot didn't look slept in. "Where's our gal Sadie so early this morning?"

Pearl went behind the folding screen and grabbed her large pantaloons hanging over the top. "She never came back to the tent last night. Dang blame-it," Pearl grumbled. "I've been eating too much chocolate. I better lay off the sweets, or I won't fit my bloomers before long."

Lil shed her dressing gown and laid her naked body down on her cot. She turned on her side and supported her head with a bent arm. "Where do you think Sadie is?"

Pearl came out from behind the screen dressed in a cornflower blue dress trimmed with dusty rose-colored lace ruffles across the bodice and shoulders. She adjusted her bosom for a comfy fit. "Hell if I know. After the poker game ended, I saw her leave with a real scruffy looking pair. I overheard the hillbilly fella call the other gent by the name Joe. All I know is Sadie's been gone all night." Pearl went to her cot, sat down and put on her shoes.

Lil liked shagging in the woods every once in a while, but she knew Sadie was a comfort gal. Even if a man's pizzle happened to be made of solid gold, Sadie would no more service a fella in the brush and weeds than the man in the moon. The more she thought about their friend's long absence, the more worried she became. Lil got off her cot, grabbed her pantaloons and put them on. "I think I'm gonna get some clothes on and go see if I can find her. Just to be sure she's okay."

"I best tag along. If there's any trouble, your skinny ass couldn't run it off."

Lil and Pearl followed the worn path through the woods to the courtship log. They hadn't crossed paths with anyone. The girls weren't far from camp when they came to the small clearing. Lil remembered this as the place where she and Travin had made love the other night. Straight ahead, beside the fallen log, she spotted a frightening sight. Sadie's disheveled form lying on the ground. Her breath hitched, she pointed. "Look, she's hurt. That's Sadie over there. Come on." Lil took off running as fast as her skinny legs could dash across the space to her friend.

The girls reached their friend lying battered and lifeless with her clothing all torn. There wasn't any doubt as to what had taken place here. Pearl knelt and gently pulled Sadie's dress back down over her naked limbs. She swiped Sadie's sandy brown hair away from her beaten face, uncovering badly bruised cheeks and a bloody lip. "Oh, honey," Pearl cried out, softly patting Sadie's arm. "Sugar, speak to me."

No sound escaped Sadie's bleeding lips. Her usually luminous hazel eyes remained closed. Her eyelids were darkened, blackish blue and swollen.

Pearl rocked her friend against her soft bosom. "Lord, please help this poor working girl. She's done nothing to deserve this. Help her. Please, help her." When Pearl pulled her hand out from beneath the back of her friend's beaten head there was blood. "Oh my, God."

Lil glanced at a melon-sized boulder oozed with red. "Sadie must have hit her head on that rock. To me that wound looks real bad. I best run for help." She didn't want to overreact. Panicking would do no one any good. But if ever there were a time to be frantic it'd be now.

Pearl nodded. "Make it fast would you?"

"I'll make these skinny legs fly." Lil turned to make haste for camp when a hard-looking man jumped out of the shrubs and aimed a pistol at them.

"Nobody's going anywhere." The gunman sneered. "Git on over there."

In the next instant, he shoved Lil toward Pearl and Sadie. She glanced at her wounded friend and back at the gunman. "I suppose this is your handy work? You mangy cock-dogger."

"I have my orders," he replied. "Besides, that whore Lil got what she deserves."

"You no good—" Lil tamped down her rage for the man had just mistakenly called Sadie by *her* name. She'd keep her trap shut for once. Getting killed wouldn't do them any good.

The man spit to the ground. Lil glimpsed at Pearl and caught the rage stewing on the big gal's face.

Pearl laid Sadie's limp body gently back on the ground and slowly got to her feet. Her hands braced on her hips. "I saw you last night with our girl. Weren't there two of you cooties playing poker at her table? Where's that other fella? The real bright-looking one you were with."

"None of your business, whore. And don't be insulting my brother," the man warned.

"Oh, he's your brother," Pearl chided. "Then I see brains mustn't run in your family."

"Shut your trap, bitch."

"Pearl, keep quiet," Lil warned. "You're only going to make things worse."

"I recall your friend called you Joe. What orders you following, Joe? You're such a big man that beats up on helpless women. Why don't you put that gun down and try me on for size?"

"Didn't I tell you to shut your trap?"

"He's right, Pearl. Shut yer trap like he says. Mister, my friend Pearl's hard to call off once she's riled. I suggest you leave us alone and go on your way." Lil ventured another glance at Pearl and noticed those big feet of hers were inching forward. That confirmed her worst fears. Big Pearl was going on the rampage.

Pearl walked toward the man in slow, threatening strides. "Look here, sonny. You be a good boy and take your sorry ass away from here so we can get help for our friend. You mind what I say, and I'll have no cause to thump you."

Joe gave another spit to the ground. "And if'n I don't? What ya gonna do about it?"

"Well, now, sonny, I'm just about to show you what I'll do about it."

With each fearless step Pearl inched closer, the gunman took a retreating step back from her. Lil estimated the big woman stood two heads taller than Joe, and could likely get the drop on him if given the chance.

"Buck. Oh, Buck," Joe yelled. "Git yerself out here. Now." He aimed his gun toward Pearl. "I'm only telling you once more, bitch. Stand back or I'll put a bullet in you."

"If you think you can, go ahead, sonny."

Lil's heart jumped into her throat, pounding like there'd be no tomorrow. She clenched her fists tight and prayed the whole time Pearl kept advancing. Joe's wild eyes had that scared shitless and ready to shoot look about them. With no time to think about a smarter thing to do, Lil darted around Pearl and ran right at the gunman. She charged, raised her skinny leg high like a male dog peeing, reared back and kicked hard, nailing the scoundrel right in his scrawny balls.

The gun in Joe's hand aimlessly fired, whizzing a bullet straight through Pearl's platinum wig, barely missing her scalp by a half an inch. The slug lodged in a pine tree behind her.

"Ahhhhh. Shit. Shit. Shit." Joe fell to his knees, so doubled over in pain he dropped his pistol in order to hold his pained member with both hands.

Lil quickly snatched up the weapon and turned it on Joe, but their troubles weren't over. In her peripheral vision, she caught sight of some movement and quickly looked to her left and saw a second man running out of the bushes, headed straight for Pearl. "Watch out." Her warning came too late.

This second man jumped on Pearl's back. To Lil's amazement, somehow the big gal stayed on her feet. Pearl leaned her body forward, lifting the attacker's feet off the ground.

"Pearl, what the hell are you doing?" Lil managed to keep her shaky hand holding the gun trained on Joe, and she helplessly watched her superhuman friend stagger around with the big lout on her back.

Holding onto the man's arms to keep him attached to her back, Pearl began spinning in a circle. Slowly, she swayed and turned, her momentum picking up speed. With each rotation, Lil watched the man's legs fly higher and higher and nearly perpendicular to the ground.

"Big fella, you're along for the ride now."

"Wait. Stop." The man pleaded to deaf ears.

"I ain't stopping."

Pearl's spinning reached the pinnacle of human speed, and Lil could see the hillbilly's face showed signs of rotation illness. "Pearl, he's turning green. You better let go of him."

"Mister, my friend's right. I think it's time you and I part company." Pearl released Joe's arms, and when he flew off her back, Pearl crashed hard to the ground.

The man's boots hit the ground running full speed ahead. He staggered about, unable to gain his feet beneath him. Lil heard a loud thump and a grunt when his noggin crashed into an unforgiving pine tree. Hillbilly number two fell to the ground, unconscious, with a bloody crease on his forehead.

THE COURTSHIP OF UTOPIA MINOR   239

Pearl got up off the ground and swiped grass off her skirt. "Well, I don't think Joe, or his brother, will be giving us any more trouble." She ambled over to the crumpled and moaning Joe and grabbed a hunk of his mangy hair in her fist. She pulled him to a sitting position. "Joe, you and me, we're gonna have ourselves a little chat. What orders were you talking about?"

"I ain't telling you nothin'." Joe defiantly spit in his interrogator's face.

Lil had only seen her friend get this red, this upset, one other time. The end result of that incident didn't bode well for that fella either. "Mister, you shouldn't have done that."

Pearl gave the fistful of her captive's hair a hard yank. Joe squealed. To keep his scalp, Joe raised both his hands to his hairline in an attempt to free his locks from the woman's one-handed hold. Pearl reached her other hand down and grabbed the man's pecker in a vice hold. "Now, Joe, I'll give you one minute to tell me what I want to know. If you don't talk, then you're soon gonna be a bald man with a very high-pitched voice."

"Ahhhh." Joe squirmed and groan and cringed. "I'll talk. I'll talk."

Pearl released the weeping man's scalp and groin. "Lil, you best go fetch help for Sadie. I think Joe's gonna behave himself from here on out." She glared at him. "Aren't you?"

Joe nodded.

Lil smiled, partly relishing seeing Joe in so much pain, and happy that Pearl bare-handedly dealt out some justice for Sadie. "I'd do what my friend tells ya, mister. She missed her breakfast this morning, and that sort of thing gets her cranky." Lil gave Sadie one last look. "I'll be back in a flash with help."

Travin and Fergus carefully laid Sadie on her cot. The tent flap opened and Doc Cruthers entered carrying his medical bag. "You gents can leave now. Anything I might need, these two ladies can get for me."

Pearl gave Fergus and Travin each an appreciative hug. "Thanks for getting to us so quick. By the way, where did Henry and Big John take those two fellas that beat up Sadie?"

"Don't worry about them," Travin stated. "Those two thugs are being held in the old mine shaft for safe-keeping. Jargus is guarding them until Henry and John can fetch the law."

"Is . . . is Miss Sadie gonna be alright?" Fergus asked.

Pearl shook her head. "I don't know."

Lil put her hands on Travin's and Fergus's arms and escorted them out of the tent. "Both of you go on now. Fergus, you run the day's courting like Lance asked you to. Don't say a thing about none of this to anyone, you hear?"

"W . . . w . . . what if Frank sees his men ain't coming back?"

"Let's hope Frank doesn't miss his men none too soon," Lil replied.

The distraught father tugged on his felt hat. "I-I'll see that the courting gets started."

Travin gave Lil's cheek a peck. "I think I'll give Jargus a hand with keeping those two bandits under wraps. He probably could use a break about now. I'll see you later, Buttercup."

Travin and Fergus left the girls to their duties. Lil went back inside the tent.

While the doctor attended to Sadie's injuries, Lil pulled Pearl aside and pressed her for details. "So what did that pint-sized Joe tell ya after I left?"

"He said Frank Sharps is behind all of this. Joe rambled on and on about an election in between all his moaning."

"Did he say anything else?"

"Only that Frank has more of his henchmen going after Utopia's reporter fella. Joe made it very clear these other thugs don't intend to just rough Lance up. They plan to permanently put him out of the way. That's all I got out of Joe before he passed out."

Lil gave Pearl a reprimanding glare. "Some fine interrogator you are."

At Lil's harsh tone, Pearl's tender hold on emotions slipped into tears. Tons of tears.

"I'm sorry," Lil apologized. "That was a real mean thing I just said." She hadn't paid attention to how close her big friend's emotions were teetering on the brink of a breakdown. "Ya did a real good job corralling up those scoundrels and looking after our Sadie."

"I don't know about you . . ." Pearl paused to blow her nose in her hankie. "I have a hunch we should give Utopia's fancy reporter fella a heads up."

"That won't be necessary. Lance left for Tin Cup this morning. He'll be safely out of harm's way for a while."

Pearl let out a deep breath. "I guess we don't have to worry about Utopia getting mixed up in any of this trouble."

Lil bit on her long red fingernail. She wasn't so sure Pearl's wisdom held true.

"There's no worry, right?" Pearl asked.

"I'm not going to lie to you. It won't be easy keeping Frank in the dark about his missing men. Until we know more about what he's up to, we can't do anything that would make him suspicious."

"I'd sure feel better if we knew what that no-good ruffian was up to," Pearl added.

"Lance said he'd be back by late afternoon. Him being a reporter and all, he may have an idea on how to snuff out the scoundrel's plans." Lil glared at Pearl's lopsided hair piece. "Straighten that damn wig of yours. You want Sadie to wake up and see ya all mussed up?"

"All right," Pearl peeped. She blindly tried to straighten her fake locks.

Lil had never seen her big friend so upset. She tenderly adjusted Pearl's platinum hair. "I'm sorry I yelled at ya. You got to get a hold of yerself. I need you." Her own eyes started to shed a few tears. "Sadie needs you."

Doc Cruthers got to his feet. He walked to the washstand, poured a bit of water over his medical instrument and dried it with a clean towel draped over his shoulder.

"Well, Doc, is our Sadie going to be okay?" Pearl dabbed a hankie at her moist eyes.

The doctor packed up his bag. His eyes had that wait-and-see look. "Head wounds are the worst. She's in a coma. That's a good thing. It's the brain's way of trying to heal whatever trauma's been done. For the time being, all we can do is to wait and see. I have to ask this. Does she have any next of kin?"

"No. We're it." Pearl covered her eyes with her hanky. Her shoulders shook with a huge wave of emotional distress, venting all her pain in inconsolable tears.

Lil stood on tiptoes, wrapped her arms about her tall friend's neck, and pulled Pearl's head down to rest on her own small, supportive shoulder.

Together Pearl and Lil held each other.

They wept.

They prayed.

CHAPTER TWENTY-FOUR

Lance rode through the lower mountain pass headed south to Tin Cup. Along the way he rehearsed the proposal he'd make to Utopia when from high off a cliff to his right, a man jumped onto Lance's back and knocked him from his horse.

Two other men rode up on horseback just as Lance received a kick in the gut from his assailant. A rifle cocked. "Give it up, mister, or I'll feed you to the worms right now."

Outnumbered three-to-one, Lance resigned himself to captivity. His fingers swiped blood off the corner of his lip where his prior cut had been reopened. "What can I do for you gents?"

The man on horseback pointed his rifle Lance's direction then toward a mine shaft opening. "That way. Get walking, mister."

Obscured somewhat by overgrown shrubbery, Lance could make out a plaque above the entrance to the Bound to Be Lucky mine.

The rider dismounted and tied his animal's reins to a nearby shrub.

His captors forced Lance into the dark confines of the mine as far as daylight illuminated then his captors lit a lantern. Upon hearing voices echoing from a deeper area of the mine, the leader put a finger to his lips for silence. "There's someone ahead of us. Keep your voices down and tread lightly."

"Right, JD," one gang member loudly whispered.

"Shhh. Damn it. Carp, keep your trap shut."

Lance made a mental note of their names. The leader's name was JD and the other went by Carp. Again, a rifle poked in his back, and he was forced to go farther into the dark shaft.

Dripping water echoed its timeless etching of the cave's interior. A flickering light could be seen in the tunnel ahead of them. JD led the gang onward, toward the glow. Soon the voices grew louder, less echoed. Lance and his captors hid in the dark recesses of the mine's passageway. From where he sat, Lance could see Jargus sitting on a whiskey keg, with his back to the entrance. Travin wasn't too far to his right sitting on a box.

"Did the doc say how bad she was?" Jargus asked.

Alarm bells went off in Lance's brain. Had Utopia gotten hurt?

JD shot to his feet and sprang from the shadows. "Put your hands up, both of you."

Travin's hands flew up in shaky fright. Jargus' startled reflexes caused him to drop his whiskey jug. The crock broke with an echoed crash on the cave's floor. Jargus made an arthritic reach for the shotgun at his feet.

"Stop right there, old timer, or never sip whiskey again," JD warned. He shoved Lance toward the others. "You all sit tight and behave yourselves. We'll be out of your way real soon."

"Boss, look over there." Carp pointed to the left of the cave.

"What the hell?" JD scowled.

Lance noted the ringleader's response at finding what must be reinforcements trussed up like Thanksgiving turkeys. Some of the gang's plans must have gone off track. Lance thought he recognized the two hog-tied fellows. They were the two piss-poor poker players who'd lost a bundle at Sadie's last night. He'd wondered how these two not so bright sorts had so much money to squander. They'd been paid to do someone's dirty work.

JD walked over and untied the bandana gag from the smaller man's mouth. "You two knuckleheaded jerks better not tell me you've screwed up the boss' plan." JD removed a knife from his vest pocket, and dropped the blade on the cave floor. "Cut your brother loose."

"We wondered when you'd show up. Buck and me ran into a bit of trouble," Joe said.

"I don't have time for your lame excuses." JD turned to the quiet big fellow. "Buck, did you take care of that Lil gal like the boss told you to?"

At the mention of harm to his sweetheart, Travin gave a mournful wail that echoed through the cave and gush of tears ensued. What on earth were these fellows up to? Not only were Travin, Jargus and he at the mercy of these men, they'd harmed Miss Lil. But why?

"It weren't our fault." Buck gingerly dabbed at the dried blood on his cut forehead. "After Joe finished his poke on the gal, there was this giant lady. I come out of the bushes and climbed on her back but the woman got the best of me. Of us."

"A giant lady?" JD barked. "If you two aren't the stupidest bastards I've ever run across. Save your excuses for Frank. We got work to do. Joe, get the old man's shotgun and keep a watch on our prisoners." JD pointed toward a pile of tools. "Buck, get one of those sledgehammers and use it on that support timber. Carp, you guard the entrance."

The gang set to work following their leader's orders with no questions asked.

JD paced back and forth in front of his captives. "I just hate to be killing folks I don't know." He stopped in front of Travin. "Don't I know you from somewhere?"

"I don't think so," Travin answered in a sorrowful voice.

The man in charge snapped his fingers. "I know. You're that saloonkeeper's boy. I've had me a few whores in your pa's bar. Does your pa know he's got some damn ugly whores?"

Lance watched Travin's jaw clench at the bandit's insult of his girlfriend.

"And just who the hell are you, old timer?" JD asked.

"Name's Jargus. I own this mine. I'm the bride-to-be's father. Maybe you've heard we're having ourselves a marriage contest up in these parts?"

JD pushed the brim of his hat upward with the tip of his pistol. "That's why I'm here, dear daddy. I've been hired to put an end to the contest."

Lance followed the leader's gaze to the kegs of gunpowder and boxes of dynamite around the cave's interior. He looked back to Jargus and didn't like what he saw. He'd personally seen the old man's fuse lit a time or two and knew Jargus was set to explode any minute. "Jargus, don't you go doing anything foolish," he whispered. "Let me handle this."

Jargus glared at the ringleader and gave a spit. "You mangy cur of a she-whore, you intend to bury us in here, don't you?"

"The only one we came here to bury is that reporter." JD snickered. "Can I help it if you two happened to be in the wrong place at the wrong time?" The gunman used his foot to slide a jug across the floor to Jargus. "Here, old man, have a final drink on me."

The riled Jargus left his keg seat and charged toward the ringleader like a bull seeing a red flag. Before he got two feet, JD fired a warning shot at the old man's boots. Jargus stopped in his tracks, but the bullet ricocheted off the floor and wall finding a direct hit in Buck's left buttock.

Son-of-a-bitch!" Buck dropped the sledge hammer on the cavern floor and grabbed his hurt bottom. "I've been shot in my ass." Blood trickled between his fingers.

JD went over and gave the hurting Buck a shove. "You always seem to have your big ass in the way. Get on your horse and get out of here. Joe and I will finish this."

"I'm not gonna be able to sit a horse," Buck whimpered.

The leader gave Buck another shove toward the entrance. "Then walk, you big moron."

Lance eyed the stacked kegs of gunpowder and boxes of dynamite. Being blown to bits isn't how he wanted this all to end. "Mister, unless you plan to get blown to smithereens with us, I wouldn't fire off any more bullets."

The leader eyed the dangerous boxes and holstered his pistol. He picked up the sledgehammer and handed it to Joe. "This needs to look like an accident. Joe, it's time you get to work. Pick up where that numbskull brother of yours left off."

Joe picked up the sledgehammer, hauled the weight of it back and then struck the timber one hefty blow. The whack loosened small rocks. Whack after whack and soon the confines of the mine filled with dust, making it difficult to breathe or see. One last hit and the first support crashed to the floor. Joe tied his bandana around his mouth and nostrils and went to work on the second beam.

Panicked and looking for a way out, Lance puts his shirt over his mouth to stave off inhaling the suffocating chalky air. Travin and Jargus were doing the same.

JD held his bandana over his nose and issued orders to Joe. "When I give the signal, I want you to give the last timber one or two good hits. When it starts to give, you clear out."

"Right." Joe raised the sledge and pounded the nearest timber. Debris rained down on his boss and fellow thugs.

The irate ringleader took off his hat and pummeled Joe about the head. "Wait until I give the signal, you damn idiot." JD ran for the direction of the exit then yelled to Joe, "Hit it."

Joe gave one more huge swing and ran toward the exit as the last support gave way.

The noise was deafening. Rocks and debris crashed down, sealing off the exit, trapping Jargus, Travin and Lance in the total darkness of the mine.

Lance covered his head with his arms. A good-sized chunk of rock hit him on the back of his head, nearly knocking him unconscious. Blood streamed down the left side of his face.

The trio coughed on the dust for several minutes, hardly able to breathe.

When finally the cloud of dust settled, Lance took stock of the situation and how bad it was. Yes, they were trapped, but at least they were alive. "Travin, Jargus, are either of you hurt?"

"I'm just dandy."Jargus pummeled his shirt sleeves to shed dust and wheezed and coughed.

It figures that the old man would be too ornery to meet his maker without one last drink. "I should've known you'd survive a cave-in with only minor bruises."

"I'll minor bruise your sorry ass, you sniveling-nosed reporter."

Travin threw a rock at the wall. "Hush up. In case anyone's interested in me. I'm fine."

Thank heavens they'd all made it through the mine collapse without grave injury, but what were they to do now? Lance walked about the accessible areas of the cavern looking for anything that might be of use. Farther back in the mine, he found a lantern and blew dust off the globe to see if it was operable. Being careful to stay well away from any boxes labeled gunpowder or explosives, he struck a match to the wick and turned up the lantern's flame some to shed light on their surroundings.

Now, Lance would be the first to admit he hated communicating with Jargus even on a pleasant day, even under pleasant circumstances, but he had to face facts. The old man knew this mine and this situation called for some conversation. "Old man, do you happen to know if there's another way out of here?"

Jargus thumbed toward the debris blocking the exit. "You're looking at it."

Lance glanced at the entrance, and his hope of escape sunk to a new low. As Jargus so astutely pointed out, the entrance was completely shut off. The odds of leaving this mine any time soon were slim to none.

The old man made his way to his keg seat. "If I got to be trapped in a mine with somebody, why did it have to be you two?"

"I love you, too," Lance quipped.

Travin paced back and forth looking around his surroundings. "When I left camp, Henry and John were headed to Tin Cup to fetch Sheriff Mays. With any luck, they'll pass this mine on their way back to camp."

"So what?" Jargus growled. "They won't even notice the mine's collapsed. A cave-in can't be seen on the outside."

For once, Lance agreed with the old man. There wasn't much hope someone on the outside would see the caved-in mine shaft because the entrance was hidden by shrubs. Things weren't going in their favor. "That isn't the worst of it, gentlemen. I suspect that Sheriff Mays is in Frank Sharp's back pocket. He'll do whatever he's paid to do. Even cover up our murders and harm women."

Jargus glared at Lance. "And do you mind telling me how you know all this?"

"I've been working on a story involving corrupt officials and bad business deals going on in Denver, Golden City and even in Tin Cup. My investigation can connect Frank to a company, Consolidated Elite. Frank overbills the government for construction costs on his business projects then pockets the difference. The graft is hidden in his false bookkeeping."

Travin took a seat on a dynamite crate. "I never saw my pa talking with Sheriff Mays, only those others. All I know is my pa kept saying the contest would interfere with voting."

Lance crossed his arms over his chest. "Frank plans to end this contest so the election can go on as scheduled. He can't risk losing political control of the business district project."

"Well, hell. Why didn't Frank move the election day or hold the voting in our camp?"

"Too late for that. His opponent, Christian Fuller, is showing much stronger support this election. With Frank's main constituents living around this area, he needs every vote to win. Your contest has many of his voters far more interested in your lovely daughter than his re-election. Frank's a desperate man."

Mention of the suitors highlighted the second most important item on Lance's mind at the moment. No better time than now to do his asking. "About your lovely daughter, sir, I–"

"I'm through jawing." Jargus pointed to the powder keg under Travin. "My good lad, open that box you're sitting on and get each of us out a jug."

Travin lifted the lid on his seat. "Holy, cow. There's enough whiskey in here to keep us skunked until Christmas." He passed out three jugs and put the lid back on the powder keg. Travin sat down and pulled the cork on his own personal supply of whiskey to drown his sorrows. He held his jug high. "I want to make a toast. I'm sorry I'm going out of this world without making love with my Buttercup one more time." Travin swiped tears from his eyes and took a swig.

The fellow looked crushed. Lance knew exactly how the lad felt. His thoughts wandered to Utopia and doubts on whether he'd ever see her again. But, *damn it*. As long as there was a breath in him, he'd try to find a way out of this mine.

Lance took a seat on one of the kegs of gunpowder. Perhaps he'd have just a small nip before he broached the topic of marriage. He uncorked the clay vessel and raised it high to make a toast of his own. "Here's to the loves of our lives, my friends." He took a swig and choked on the burn streaming in his throat.

The men sat tipping their whiskey for a bit.

Jargus sent another scathing look Lance's direction. "You yellow-tailed paperhanger. What's bothering you? Speak up. What's on your mind?"

Did the crusty jerk just call him a chicken shit? That was it.

Lance slowly put his jug down. "I've had enough of your insults and shotgun bullying." He pointed his thumb to his chest. "No one calls me a chicken shit unless I say they can. You're one cantankerous old fart. You know that?"

He looked down and spotted the wooden stock of Jargus' weapon trapped under a large boulder. "Ha ha, look there." He pointed. "You don't have your shotgun anymore. Now you're nothing but a crabby old coot with no bullets. Ha."

Lance took another drink. "And another thing, I have something veeerrrry important to say to you." His eyes started to blur and his stomach churned. His speech was becoming slurred. Although the whiskey wasn't helping his pronunciation, it had abated his anxiety about asking for Utopia's hand in marriage. "It's like this, sir."

"Like what?" Jargus put down his jug and got to a hunched stand. His eyes narrowed. "You got something to be telling me? If it's about Utopia, I'll have the whole of it. I know what you're gonna say. Why, it's as plain as the nosey nose on your face. Utopia's ruined, ain't she?"

Lance staggered to get to his feet. Once steadily standing, he looked up from his feet to find himself confronting, not one, but two irate Jargus'. "Well, um . . ." He took a stab at trying to find his pockets to shove his hands into. Not locating any pant openings, he crossed his arms over his chest. He paused and swayed a moment. "Sir, I won't lie to you. It was me. I ruined your daughter."

"Here, here," Travin cheered. He raised his jug in a swig of a toast.

Jargus flung his empty jug and it sailed through the air on direct course for Lance. He managed to duck enough that the vessel flew over his head and crashed on the mine's wall, breaking into pieces and fumigating the mine with the odor of one-hundred-fifty proof whiskey.

"You mangy cur. I'll kill you with my own two hands." Jargus ran for a pickaxe lying along the wall. Taking firm hold on the handle, he hefted the tool in the air and charged.

Lance dashed and stumbled around the debris-cluttered space, avoiding the man's attack. "Jargus, put that axe down. Let me explain. Travin, can't you help me?"

The uncontrollable father wielded the axe in another wild swing. Lance ducked then scrambled the other direction. Lance dodged the blade a third time. "Travin, do something, would you? He's trying to kill me."

Sulking Travin hiccupped. "I'm not involved. It's 'tween you an' yer future father-law."

"Father-in-law? Like hell I'm gonna be kin to him." Jargus growled. "They can hang me for murder first." He raised the axe high over his head and charged again.

Lance ducked the whooshing swing that narrowly missed implant in the top of his skull. It was amazing how fast a man sobered up when being chased with an axe. "Damn it, Jargus, put down that axe. You don't want my murder on your hands. What would you tell Utopia?"

"I'll make something up. I'll not have a no good sonny-in-law like you."

Jargus was a bit winded from his labors by now, based on his heavy breathing. If Lance could avoid him a few more times, he'd be safe.

The old man hefted the axe for another go at hair splitting and his grip slipped. Lance ducked and the axe sailed across the cave, its sharp point wedged in a crack in the mine's wall. Jargus scurried across the cave to retrieve his weapon.

Lance hurried after Jargus and grabbed him about the waist to keep him from prying the axe from the wall. It took an astonishing amount of strength to keep the old man held in check. The two tussled and struggled with all hands clenched on the wooden handle when the axe broke free of its hold in the rock and clanked to floor.

Both men fell in a heap on the cold hard surface.

Jargus reached for the pickaxe, but when his hand touched on the pointed tip of the tool he froze then angled his fingers toward the lantern's light. "Well, I'll be a monkey's daddy."

The old miner went into gleeful chuckling. He struggled to stand without using the hand his eyes were fixed on. Once on his feet, he roared with laughter. *"Eureka."*

Lance had no idea what had come over Jargus all of a sudden but was glad the coot had settled down. He stood and dusted himself off. "You snarly old fart, did you have an epiphany?"

"No. Lookee here." Jargus swiped his fingers on the axe's tip. "It's gold. We've done struck gold." The old man picked up the rock at his feet. He did a little jig, holding the gold dust for the others to see. "Wait 'til Utopia and the boys get a gander of this."

"Gold? Where?" Travin hiccupped. He staggered to his feet.

It was like déjà vu. Lance recalled finding gold with Utopia. How he'd insisted they divide that teensy tiny flake. The look on her face when she'd sneezed and the miniscule fleck blew away. "Might I suggest a fifty-fifty split?" Lance smirked.

Jargus spit to the floor. "In yer dreams, sonny-in-law."

CHAPTER TWENTY-FIVE

Utopia entered her cabin and found her bed empty. Where had Lance gone? Disappointed, she spent the next twenty minutes brushing her hair, figuring he'd stepped outside to relieve himself. She anxiously anticipated he'd walk in anytime now. But he didn't. A half-hour later, her mood had turned plumb aggravated.

She hurled her brush at the wall. By gosh, by golly, she'd go find the man and hog-tie him to her bed. Her plans were to repeat what they'd done last night. The hugging, kissing and she planned to practice lovemaking until she had it well learned. It'd be a grand way to spend the day.

Dressed in Mickey's mother's Sunday go-to-meeting dress, and satisfied with her appearance, she left her cabin to go in search of Lance. Barely a step out the door, Fergus grabbed her by the arm. "Where ha-have you been? The suitors are waiting for you."

"But Pa–" Before she could tell her father about calling off courting for the day, he pulled her down the steps of the porch and walked her toward the campfire.

"L-Lance put me in charge of courting today."

"He did? Where is he? Why isn't Lance running the contest? I need to talk to him."

"L-Lance said he'd be back later. Until then, h-he said I'm in charge of courting."

Quicker than flies on fresh fruit, Fergus matched her up with the first suitor. From that point, her day dragged on miserably with beau after beau. There'd been a Bryce, a Clancy, a Spenser and Larry. Probably all fine men. But every single one of the lot turned her stomach, especially when they kissed her. None of these men stirred her insides like Lance did.

The last man she courted for the day was Hennessey Englewood, Tin Cup's proud as a peacock postmaster. The man happened to have possum-poor sight, and Utopia had to help the man dodge ruts and holes until they finally reached the courting area. Right off, with barely a howdy-do, he handed her his wedding gift.

On the way to the log, Utopia had been as rude as she knew how to be to Hennessy. So rude she now felt bad about her bad manners. "I can't take a gift from you, Mister Englewood. It would bother my conscience something terrible after how I've been toward you."

"I know you said I'm not someone you're attracted to. You made that quiet clear in a rather harsh way. But nonetheless, I admire you for coming right out and speaking your mind. The truth is I've got no one else I can give this present to. You should take it. Please."

"I guess so. Hand it here." Utopia tore off the ribbon tied around the large square box. She opened the lid and gasped. Her heart fluttered. "Why, it's a crown."

"The jeweler in town said the stones are only paste."

She removed the crown from the box and examined the rainbow sparkle of the jewels. "Paste or not, this sure is pretty."

"Like you." Hennessey stuffed his hands in his pockets. "When I saw this fancy crown in a customer's order that'd not been paid for, something told me this would be a perfect gift for you."

"That was real nice of you. This is the best courting gift I've gotten. Can I try it on?"

"Allow me." Hennessey placed the glittery crown on top of her head then took hold of her hands. His eyes squinted in order to try and see her more clearly. "I imagine you look like a princess. Could I have a kiss for such a gift?"

Utopia stepped back from the man a bit. "I think I best be getting back to my cabin."

The man started whimpering like a pup, and she didn't have the heart to be rude again and refuse him. Placing her hand softly on Hennessey's cheek, she put her mouth to his, letting this little peck of a kiss stretch the whole of a slow half-minute.

When she ended the smooch, she noticed the little man's eyes remained closed. He whispered, "Emily" then his eyes popped open when he realized he'd spoken the name aloud. He adjusted his bow tie and cleared his throat. "Thank you for that. My wife, Emily, she's the last woman I've kissed in quite a spell. She passed on five years ago."

"You must miss her very much."

"Oh, I do. She's the only woman I ever loved or ever will. I mean you no offense, miss."

"None taken." Utopia smiled. "What was your wife like?"

He wiped a tear off his cheek. "We had many common interests. She made me laugh."

Utopia remembered when Lance mentioned the kind of wife he'd want. Those very words "common interests" were on his list of necessities.

"Emily helped me in the post office without her I couldn't have done the work. What with my poor eyesight and all. I crossed my fingers and hope you'll pick me for a husband. Not that I expect you to love me. I know it's a long shot, but would you like to work beside me at the post office? Like Emily did. And be my wife of course. I can provide for you."

Utopia bit on her nail, not wanting to hurt his feelings. "I don't see how I'd be of much help to you. I done told you I can't read."

"Yes, you did say that." Hennessey's brow furrowed. Then he perked up. "I could teach you how to read."

"I got along without reading this far, I'd best leave it be. We should get back to camp."

"Before we go, let me just say I think you're a smart lass. I know you'll pick a husband well-suited for you. And I want you to know I harbor no ill feelings if I'm not the one you pick to fill those shoes for you."

"I appreciate you saying that." But he didn't understand the real reason he'd been turned down. She'd never be a wife to any man. Saloon girls don't get married. She even heard Lil, Pearl and Sadie mentioning that very thing the other night. Utopia took Hennessey's elbow and led him back down the graveled path.

They chatted about things other than courting until at last they reached her cabin. "Well, thanks again for the crown." She removed her hand from his crooked elbow.

"I hope to see you again." Hennessey's face turned solemn. "I'm sorry."

She was puzzled. "What for? You didn't do anything wrong."

"I didn't mean to put you on the spot about choosing me. It's just that I'm so lonely. All I want is a companion. The days are all the same when you don't have someone to love."

This time Utopia had to swipe a tear off her cheek. "I'm sorry, Hennessey. But I don't think I would make you a very good companion or post office helper. You and I–we don't have those common interests you mentioned earlier."

"I suppose not. Well, I best be off." He cleared his throat and departed.

Hennessey stumbled and tumbled his way back to the campfire.

That's the blindest man I believe I've ever seen. As she reached for the latch of her cabin door, Utopia spotted Fergus and another man coming toward her. She paused.

"Utopia, wait up," Fergus called out.

THE COURTSHIP OF UTOPIA MINOR 263

"What is it, Pa? I'd like to take me a bit of a rest." The stranger now stood next to her father, and she instantly recalled where she'd seen this person. He was the fella with the fancy carriage and the devilish manners. The man Lil had warned her to stay clear of.

"If I might be so bold, I'd like to make my own introduction. I'm Frank Sharps, at your service, madam." He removed his hat and made a slight bow.

This man Frank took her hand and pressed a kiss upon her fingers, and she took an instant dislike to the slobbering gent. She yanked her hand away.

Frank straightened, giving his thin handlebar mustache a tweak. "I do hope you won't take offense, Miss Utopia. I've implored your father for a late afternoon courtship."

"I'm afraid I'm through courting for the day." Once again, she reached for the door latch.

"Please reconsider. I don't need but a half-hour of your time."

If Pa Fergus wasn't standing near, she'd tell the no-good to go fetch horse dung. Utopia resented the man's smugness. "Well, Frank, I just told you, I'm tired. You're too late for any courting today. Besides, I've pretty much settled my mind on somebody already. So you'd be wasting daylight."

Frank took her by her elbow and escorted her a few steps away from Fergus. "I don't believe time spent with such a lovely creature could be construed a bad use of time." Frank put his hat back on and pressed his hand over his heart.

"Please allow me a small half-hour of your precious company." He crooked his elbow and waited for her to accept. "I do insist."

Utopia glanced to her father. Fergus looked worried. "What's wrong, Pa?"

Fergus fidgeted with the felt hat in his hands. "Y-you best give the man his courting time. D-don't you worry. I'll be nearby."

"That won't be necessary. I promise I'll return your girl safe and sound." Frank stared Fergus down with a stern glare.

Her heart skipped a beat. What did her pa mean don't worry? "Where's Lance? I should probably talk to him about this."

Fergus shook his head. "*No.* Y-you go courting with Frank like I tell ya."

This stranger seemed to be pushing his weight around. If hell didn't already have a devil, this Frank character could surely fit the bill. The man's aloof overpowering attitude bothered her to no end. She'd go to the courting log and give him exactly two minutes of her time. That was all he was entitled to. "Very well, mister. If you want courting time, let's get to it."

When he reached for her, Utopia jerked away and tromped off for the path to the courtship area. Frank had to hurry to keep up with her strides. Along the way he made small talk, but she refused to respond to any of his dribble. When they reached the clearing, she spun on him and braced her hands on her hips. "This is it, the courting area." Utopia splayed her arms pointing out the expanse of clearing surrounding them. "Frank,

THE COURTSHIP OF UTOPIA MINOR 265

you best be quick with your proposing. Your time's ticking on a fast watch."

"Very well, my dear, as you wish. I too, like to get to the heart of matters expeditiously." Frank extended his hand in a wave along the log. "Please, have a seat while I 'get to it' as you so eloquently stated."

Utopia sat and crossed her arms under her bosom. Frank's eyes drifted to her chest. He seemed to be mentally putting his filthy paws on her breasts. Every muscle in her body tensed, but she swore to not show him her fear.

Frank redirected his gaze to her face. "You mentioned that you have made your choice of a husband. It wouldn't be that Lance fellow now, would it?"

Her breath caught at the mention of her lover, piercing her heart with jagged concern. "Who are you? What are you? Are you some kind of mind reader?"

"No, no, no, my dear." He chuckled. "I'm not a mind reader. It so happens, an employee of mine came to my quarters early this morning. My man seemed quite distressed over something. When I begged him to tell me what bothered him, he informed me that you and this Lancelot Jones fellow spent the entire night together."

Utopia's brow furrowed with worry. She channeled her distrust of the man into outrage. "What business is it of yours?"

"Allow me to continue. As I was saying—my man feared you might come to harm, and he put his ears, and eyes, at your cabin's window to investigate. The lantern beside your bed provided him ample light to take in all the details of your evening. I dare say the poor chum blushed recounting what he'd seen."

Her stomach roiled with nausea. She and Lance had given a peeping Tom a naked show.

"Knowing my intentions to court you today, my employee felt it his duty to alert me to the fact that you may no longer be a lady untouched by a man." Frank took a reverent, condescending stance.

A scalding blush surged to Utopia's face. Her tongue tied itself in a million knots and she failed miserably to utter any saving grace response to his gossip.

Frank's eyebrows shot upward in feigned surprise. "Say it isn't so. Deny that you were alone in your cabin with a man the entire night. Deny it if you can."

Her eyes looked down in avoidance. She said nothing.

"Everyone knows what goes on between a man and a woman when left alone in a bedroom. Why, if I were secluded with you and a bed were available . . ." He left the rest unsaid. His beady eyes trailed a lusty gleam to her bosom.

Utopia fidgeted with the lace collar on her Sunday dress and fought to erase Frank's filthy visual of a scene of her joining with him from her mind.

Frank stepped close. He raised his hand to brush a curl behind her ear, and she shrugged away from his repulsive touch.

"Dare I ask you again, my dear? Did that man help himself to your virginity?"

His question brought a rush of rage to her insides like none she'd ever faced before. She poured hate into her glare she gave him. "You, sir, have a filthy mind. Who I share my time and anything with is *none* of your business."

"That is true. Nonetheless, where is this Lancelot of the west now?" Frank stretched his arms wide and looked to his left and then right. "Where is this man who's been so fortunate to dip himself into that goddess sweet body of yours before marriage?"

Utopia looked to her tormentor with pleading eyes. She wanted him to stop. The pain and embarrassment were too unbearable. "Enough with your insults. What do you want?"

"I'll get to the point. I wish to be your husband, my dear. I intend to marry you regardless of your virginal imperfection. I'm not too late in asking, am I? Has this Lance proposed?"

Impossible to hide the "no" from her face, she stiffened her shoulders and held her head high. "I'm not certain Lance intends to propose, but I know I will agree to only marry him and no other."

Frank removed a gold watch from his vest pocket and flipped the lid open. "My, my, you were right. Our time's gone by way too fast. I best finish what I have to say. This man, who stole your heart and virginity, he'll not be returning to you any time soon. Lance will never surface again if you don't agree to be my bride." He clicked the watch shut and put it back in his pocket.

"What have you done to Lance?" She shot to her feet and raised her hand to slap Frank.

He quickly grabbed her wrist and held her firmly in his grasp. "Why, my dear, you've wounded me, or tried to." His free hand went to his chest imitating his heart pained him. "What kind of man do you take me for? I would do nothing to hurt you. Nothing, I say. For you stole my heart the moment my eyes fell upon you yesterday."

Frank took her hand firmly in his and pressed a kiss on her fingers. She tried to pull free but he countered her move by yanking her close against him. "I only wish to offer you salvation from social ruin. That is more than your Lancelot seems willing to offer you. He's left you for parts unknown. I will make you a governor's wife, a pillar of the community."

Utopia struggled to get out of his hold. "You're lying. Lance wouldn't just leave. He's around camp somewhere. I know he is. You're a liar." She held back tears, determined not to let this bastard see her cry.

"My dear." Frank chuckled. He released her, and she stepped away from him. "I have no cause to lie to you. The man's headed to Tin Cup this very minute to print the scandalous details of your affair in his newspaper. If you don't believe me go speak with your friend, Lil. Perhaps you'll believe the truth from her."

"I'll do that. Lil would know where Lance is." Utopia held out a glimmer of hope that the braggart was lying. She headed for camp in a dead run, leaving Frank to choke on her dust.

CHAPTER TWENTY-SIX

Utopia hoped Lil would be able to prove Frank lied, but upon entering the girls' tent she clutched her stomach and gasped. The late afternoon sun filtered the canvas interior in a peachy soft glow. Sadie lay on the farthest cot with her head wrapped in a blood-soaked bandage, her body still and almost lifeless. "What on earth happened to her?"

Lil left her friend's bedside vigil and promptly escorted Utopia outside. "Two men attacked her. They beat her to within an inch of her life and helped themselves to a free one."

"A free one?"

"Girl, we don't spread our legs with lots of men because we enjoy this work. Bedding down with men, that's how Sadie, Pearl and me make our living shagging. Sometimes men can get rough. The fellas that did this to Sadie took what they wanted while she laid near to dying. When Pearl and I caught the bastards, they had said they were just following orders."

"What did you say about orders?" Utopia knew one person who could shovel out orders like stable men shoveled dung.

"Orders is what the man squealed when Pearl questioned him. The fellas done their dirty work all wrong but they don't know it. I should be the one lying in there. Not Sadie." Lil's eyes watered. "They tried to kill the wrong woman."

Utopia bit on her nail and wondered if Frank could be the one behind all the evil-doings.

Lil dried her eyes with her sleeve. "What is it? I can tell by the way you're chewing your fingernail to a nub there's something bothering you. Spit it out, girl."

"It's about that man you warned me to stay clear of. I went to the courtship log with him this afternoon and he told me—"

"Didn't I tell you to stay clear of that fella?"

"I couldn't. Fergus said I had to court him."

"Git on with it. What did he tell you?" Lil's hands formed tight fists.

Utopia took one look at the stress on Lil's face, and her own worry surged to a new level of panic. "Is it true that Lance left for Tin Cup this morning?"

"Yeah. Lance came by our tent early this morning. He and I talked a bit."

Please. Let Frank be a liar. "Did Lance tell you what his plans were? Was he going to that newspaper to post articles? Did he say when he's coming back?"

Lil scratched her nails in her mess of hair. "I think so. What with finding Sadie all hurt and rounding up those two thugs, I'm sorry. I can't remember what Lance told me to tell you."

Before Utopia could ask Lil another question, Pearl and Fergus came charging toward the tent area like their shoes were on fire. Pearl was so winded she had to brace her hands on her knees to catch her breath. "Have either of you seen Travin?"

"Travin?" Lil grabbed Pearl's shoulders. "Has something happened to him?"

"There's nothing to be getting all stirred up about. At least, I don't think there is," Pearl stated. "But Fergus has been real shaken up ever since his run-in with Frank earlier."

Fergus looked at Utopia with watery eyes. "F-Frank made me send you courting."

Pearl patted the father on the back to calm him some. "Fergus says this Frank near broke his arm to get himself entered in the contest. He's rambled on and on pert near all afternoon. It wasn't until it started to get late in the day that I noticed Travin hadn't come back from relieving Jargus at prisoner watching."

"What prisoners? What checking up?" Lance hurt, Fergus threatened, Henry's getting a sheriff. Utopia couldn't fit the jumbled pieces together. "What in the blazes is going on around here?"

"There's too much to tell right now," Lil stated. "I'll give you the short version. We caught them fellas that done hurt Sadie. Travin and Jargus are holding them at your fathers' abandoned mine. I sent John and Henry to Tin Cup to bring back the sheriff."

Utopia shot her hands to her hips. "And you're just now telling me about all this?"

"All that matters is that you know it all now. What we need to do now, we need to make sure Frank's not going to try and rescue his buddies. At least, not until John and Henry get back with the sheriff."

Fergus put on his hat floppy felt hat. "I . . . I'm going to ride down to the m . . . mine and check on Travin and my brother."

"Pa, I'll go with you." Utopia didn't want to be around in camp with that Frank, especially since Lance wasn't around to protect her. "I'll fix some food to take along. I'm sure Jargus and Travin are hungry." She looked at her friend's and her pa's face. "Come on. You all stop worrying. Jargus probably talked Travin into pulling a cork with him. That's all this is." She hoped drunk was only the worst of Travin's tardiness.

Utopia waved at her father. "We need to head out before it gets dark."

"You two be careful," Lil warned. "And take a shotgun with you." Lil turned to Pearl, ripped her blonde wig off and plopped on curly brunette hair instead. "I'm tire of seeing you in that pale looking scalp. Pearl, I want you to mingle by the campfire. Entertain those suitors with that monstrous chest waggling of yours. Whatever you do, keep a watch on Frank and his thugs. I'll stay here and look after our Sadie. Now everyone's got their part of the plan to do. Hop to it."

"Bye, Miss Lil. Bye, Miss Pearl. Come on, Pa."

THE COURTSHIP OF UTOPIA MINOR   273

Utopia and Fergus left the girls' tent and ran to her cabin.

Once inside her abode, Utopia removed Hennessey's tiara from her hair and placed it on the table. She gathered some food from the cupboard and packed it in her picnic basket.

Fergus rounded up the bed rolls and had just set them on the floor next to the table when there was a knock. "I-I'll get it." He walked to the door and lifted the latch. Instantly, he was thrown backward by the force of the door being kicked open. Frank and his thug forced their way into the cabin, and the brute beside Frank shoved Fergus to the floorboards.

The gruff henchman secured the door. Frank stood nearby and removed his hat, hanging it on a peg next to the door, making himself quite at home. "Good evening, my dear."

Utopia ran to her father and helped him up off the floor. She glared at her intruder. "Usually folks wait until they are invited before they just up and walk into someone's home."

Fergus rubbed the shoulder he'd fallen on. "Y-you gents have to leave. We got—"

Fearing her father would alert Frank to their plans, she cut off his words with a squeeze to his hand. "This isn't a good time to talk. We were just on our way out."

"I can see that." Frank strolled over to the table and lifted the napkin covering the picnic basket. "Is this fine smelling chicken for Jargus, Travin or Lance? I can save you the trouble of delivering it."

A shot of fear short circuited her heart. Utopia walked toward the table. It was impossible to control her shaking hands but she managed to recover her basket from his clutches. "It's such a nice evening. Fergus and I've been looking for the others. We're going to enjoy our afternoon meal outside. Have you seen them?"

Utopia shifted her gaze a tad to the side of Frank's head and watched Fergus slowly inching his hand toward the latch of the door. Her heart jumped in her throat and lodged there. Their intruders seemed to not be watching his movements. She hoped and prayed he'd escape.

Frank pulled a chair out from the table and took a seat at a right angle to the door.

Utopia intended to keep his attention focused on her and not the door. She fidgeted with her lacy dress collar. "So, Frank, what can I do for you?"

He folded his arms over his chest. "My men are making certain that nothing will interfere with my evening plans that include you. I've come to ask if you'll be my guest for the campfire festivities."

"And if I say no, then what?"

"That would be a big mistake. Travin, Jargus and Lance are my prisoners, at my disposal, or not. If you cooperate and my evening goes well, I'll disclose their whereabouts."

"What rock did you crawl out from? It must a huge one for you're a whopper snake."

Frank shot to his feet. "My dear, your sharp tongue is beginning to chaff my good natured attempt to make this an enjoyable evening to announce our engagement."

"I'd call you a lot worse names than snake if my father weren't listening." She glimpsed toward Fergus, with his hand nearly on the latch. Her eyes darted back to her abrasive guest.

Frank's eyes missed nothing. "Percy, stop him."

Fergus received a punch in the gut. He grunted and fell to the floorboards.

"Please–don't hurt him." Utopia bolted toward her father but didn't get two steps before Frank grabbed her wrist and pulled her back to him.

He forced Utopia into a chair, and pinned her down with his hands on her shoulders. "Percy, bash him where there will be no signs of assault. And you, my dear, if you wish to see this father of yours unharmed, you'll remain seated and quiet. Do I make myself clear?"

Burning tears pooled in her eyes as Fergus lay hunched on the floor. She nodded.

Frank sat down in a chair beside her and crossed one knee over the other. He snapped his fingers. Percy gave the helpless father a kick in the groin. Fergus gave another gravely groan and curled into a fetal position.

Utopia shot up from her chair. This time Frank yanked her abruptly onto his lap, holding her in place with an arm around her waist. He took the tiara off the table and placed it on her head. "How lovely. Like a princess. Soon you'll be my princess," he whispered in her ear.

She again bolted, and the tiara jarred loose and crashed to the floor. Again, Frank thwarted her escape with his superior strength.

"I admire your spirit, my dear, but it is futile to resist me and what I desire. Percy will stop his abuse of your father when I order him to and not before." The hold of her waist tightened. He nodded. The man obediently kicked and Fergus grunted.

Utopia shook with rage, her lungs so pained she barely had air to speak. "No. Stop. I'll do it. I'll marry you."

"That's much better. But now I'll have a kiss from you, my dear, to show me you're sincere about your pledge. A kiss or I'll order Percy to persuade you a bit more."

Utopia quickly pecked a kiss on Frank's cheek. "There. I kissed you. Tell him to stop."

Frank raised his arm in a bent elbow position, ready to drop his forearm like a lever to signal his man. "I'm afraid I'll need a more passionate kiss than that." His hand swiftly lowered.

Again, she heard a moan from Fergus and watched him roll in agony on the floor.

Her captor posed his arm yet again. His slate gray eyes gleamed with menace and pure enjoyment. "This is your last chance to save your father from some very grave pain. Your next kiss better be very persuasive."

The man had no conscience, no common decency. When she made no effort to comply with his demands, Frank smiled and moved the threatening signal ever-so slightly, giving her one last second to respond the way he wished.

"No. Stop." She needed no more encouragement. Utopia swallowed the bile in her throat and kissed her captor on his disgusting lips.

Frank entwined his fingers in her hair, forcing her head to tilt upward. And just when Utopia thought her misery couldn't get any worse, his tongue pressured her lips to part. She thought about biting him, but when his hand started to leave her hair, Utopia knew what came next, thus she had no choice but to yield her mouth to his tongue.

Her head swam with disgust. Her stomach churned with nausea. Would his kiss ever end?

His vile violation of her mouth stopped. "That's more like it." He released her hair, but to torment her further, he lightly brushed his fingers across her bosom before wrapping both his arms around her waist. "I crave you even more now that I've had a taste of your sweet mouth. I should do something about that."

Utopia followed his gaze which drifted across the room. Her heart gave a shudder. If he dragged her to her bed, she knew what he intended do to. And from what little she knew of the man, his loving wouldn't be gentle. She squirmed like never before to get free, but his strength overmatched hers tenfold.

"My heart will be dashed if we are not joined together in one way or another. Tonight."

"Tonight?" The shocking words plunged a deep gash in her gut. "No–please. You don't have to do this."

"Oh, but I do. I'm so smitten with you, I don't know if I can wait to make you my wife." Frank stood with her in his arms, holding her tight.

She felt her feet lift off the floor, leaving her no traction to aid her escape.

Frank carried her toward the curtained off area of the room. "I think you won't go willingly to the altar. So, why wait? I'll test the bounds of your love right now."

Utopia kicked her legs every which way she could trying to nail him in his shin or some other painful part. She dug her fingernails into Frank's hands and clawed like a bobcat, but he still kept his hold. He got her to the bed and tossed her on the mattress like a sack of flour. His body quickly fell on top of her. She froze with only one way to fight. Utopia spit in his face.

Frank swiped spittle out of his eye. "My dear, I'll make you sorry you did that." He pinned her arms above her head with one hand and explored her bosom with his free hand.

His pawing repulsed her, but a passel of stubbornness wouldn't allow her to be totally passive. She'd not agree to Frank's demands to marry unless she knew that Jargus, Lance and Travin were safe. "How do I know your men haven't harmed or killed your hostages already?"

"I can give you nothing but my word, my dear." He started to unbutton the top closure of her Sunday dress.

"All right. Stop. Promise to let all of them go, and I'll willingly marry you." Her breathing was rapid, her pulse racing. Utopia knew the man couldn't be trusted. But for the moment she had no other leverage.

Frank released her arms, slinked off of her body and the bed.

Once freed, she scampered to her father. Utopia assisted Fergus over to a chair then dashed to the washstand and fetched a rag. She dabbed the damp cloth on his forehead.

Frank walked up behind her, wrapped an arm around her waist and brushed her hair aside. He kissed her neck. "I suggest you make yourself presentable. We haven't much time."

Utopia fought to hold down the nausea threatening to erupt.

"And just in case you're thinking to pull a fast one over on me," Frank added. "When we get out in front of the suitors, or should I say my voters, my loyal employees will be watching. They'll be ready to declare that you are sullied goods, and that your fathers' contest is a fraud. I dare say there could be a lynching of a father, or two, or three. I'll do my best to dispel any such threat—but only if I you cooperate."

Her blood boiled so hot she could hardly stand the burn in her chest. "You're a disgusting bastard. I hope you *rot in hell*."

"Take her father outside," Frank instructed. "I'll be along momentarily." He leaned in and placed another kiss on her, this time on the cheek. "I'll be waiting for you outside. I'll give you ten minutes to get your appearance in non-disheveled order. Make me wait too long, and I'll be back in to take up where we left off in your bedroom."

CHAPTER TWENTY-SEVEN

Sheriff Mays made no hurry of his ride through the steep passage heading up to the Bound to Be Lucky Mining camp. John and Henry shared eye signals, silent urgings for one or the other to say something to the lawman.

Henry guessed it'd be him. "Do you think you could ride a bit faster, sheriff?"

"Hold up there, fellas. I think my horse has turned up lame." Mays pulled his mount to a halt and jumped down from his saddle and lifted his mare's front leg. "Yep, she's picked up a stone, all right." The lawman removed a switchblade from his pocket and worked at prying the rock from the soft cartilage in the animal's hoof.

Henry pulled his mule to a halt and dismounted. "We're almost to the first clearing. We could leave your horse here and double up riding my Betsy the rest of the way."

"And leave my mare for the wolves during the night? Hell, no."

John walked over to the injured horse and patted the animal's neck a couple times. "I could loan you me beast. I'll walk your animal to camp at a nice easy pace. That way the two of you can get to camp much quicker."

"I'll not put you out." Mays got to his feet. "I can take care of my own horse."

Henry couldn't stomach any more wasting time. "There's a woman at camp that's on her death bed. The men responsible could get away if we don't pick up the pace."

The sheriff wiped his brow with a bandana. "I'm not in much of a hurry to investigate a whore's beating."

Henry's usually calm, collected personality ignited in a fit of rage. "No matter if she's a saint, your mama or how she feeds herself, she's a *woman.* And one that's been beaten badly."

Big John got in the lawman's face. "No one deserves such a pummeling. As long as she's taking breaths, I'll be having ye show a little respect."

The sheriff brushed the Scotsman aside and grabbed his hobbled mare's reins. "If you two want to give your respects to the likes of her, then you go right ahead. I certainly won't stop you. So far, you haven't provided me any proof that Frank Sharps had anything to do with this bitch's injuries."

Henry swore if the lawman said one more ill-toned word about Sadie, law or no law, he'd get a dressing down for it. "Sheriff, we got two of the men that done the actual deed under armed guard at our old mine. One of the culprits named Frank as the person who gave the orders. What more evidence do you need?"

"The man ratted? Hmm. Sounds like you have one man's story against another's. I'll have to hear Frank's side of things."

"Just whose side are you on, sheriff?" Henry suspected he knew the answer.

Mays spit tobacco juice to the ground. "Well, now, I don't like your tone."

"I reckon we'll soon see which side of the law your Johnson swings once we get to camp." Henry grabbed his mule's reins and gave a tug to get her moving. "Come on, Betsy."

John grabbed the reins of his horse. The two men put the lawman between them as they continued on to camp.

Henry had nothing more to discuss with Sheriff Mays. Likely any justice for Sadie would have to wait until the circuit judge came back to the area in late September.

They arrived in camp after nightfall. Their animals were tied to the hitch post in front of the whiskey barn. Most of the activity in camp was outside tonight. The usual campfire blazed near the stage wagon and fiddle music played.

Along the edges of the rowdy crowd, Henry spotted Cyrus sitting off to one side of the fire. He tapped Mays on the shoulder and pointed. "There's who you need to talk to, sheriff."

The lawman headed the direction noted.

Henry followed right in the sheriff's footsteps, with John taking up the rear.

"Evening, Cyrus," Henry greeted. "Have you any word on how Sadie's doing?"

The saloonkeeper looked up. His gazed locked on Sheriff Mays. Both Henry and John noticed the

THE COURTSHIP OF UTOPIA MINOR 283

lawman and bartender seemed to be having a silent communication going on.

"Answer the man, Cyrus," Mays instructed.

The saloonkeeper's eyes shifted to Henry. "Doc Cruthers says she's got a fifty-fifty chance of pulling through."

"Is Frank around?" Mays spit to the ground. "I need to have a word with him."

To Henry, it appeared the saloon owner seemed to be quaking in his fancy boots. "Is there something bothering you, Cyrus?"

Mays stepped forward. "First you'll answer my question. Where's Frank?"

Henry scanned the crowd and spotted the upstanding, no good citizen in front of the makeshift wagon stage. "Frank's over there."

The sheriff tipped his hat. "I'll go have a talk with him." He walked away.

"I don't intend to let that lawman out of my sight." Henry took off after Mays.

John chased along. "Ye won't be leaving me out if there's going to be trouble."

Torches illuminated the wagon stage area in flickering light. Fergus and Utopia were just going up the steps off to the side. Frank stood in the first row among many other suitors. The music stopped when Utopia walked to center stage. The crowd cheered and whistled. Several suitors shouted, "Pick me. Pick me."

The sheriff managed to get through the crowd to the front row and right next to Frank. Henry detected that John's loud footfalls were no longer crunching turf behind him, and he turned to see where the Scot had run off to.

"Sheriff Mays, it's good to see you again," Frank greeted. "You've arrived in time for the announcement of the contest winner."

Henry locked eyes with the greasy politician who was giving him a lying smile.

"You're one of the fathers. Henry, isn't it? Your daughter's told me so much about you."

Henry applied a ton of reserved loathing into his crushing handshake and kept a hold of Frank's hand just to bug him. "I know a lot about you, too. Much of what I've heard ain't good."

"I would have gotten here sooner," Mays said. "But my horse came up lame."

Henry's brain took in the clue. The sheriff's arrival had been expected. He scanned the crowd for someone he could depend on if trouble erupted. Where was Lance?

That was when he spotted John. The Scotsman had a gun poked in his ribs. A second gunman stood behind Pearl with a lethal weapon at her waist. Henry's first instincts were to take off running, but when the sheriff's revolver cocked and the barrel went into his belly button he gave up that notion.

"I knew it," Henry growled. "Whatever it is you're up to, Frank, you and your store bought lawman won't get away with it." He spit on Mays boots. "And you call yourself a sheriff."

Mays raised a hand to bash Henry and stopped when Frank shook his head. "Be a good father, Henry, and maybe I'll let you live long enough to see your daughter's wedding."

Henry looked to the stage and his jaw clenched. There was nothing but sheer panic on

Fergus's face, and when his gaze met with Utopia's imploring green eyes, his vision blurred with his hot tears. Utopia silently mouthed, "I love you."

The pleading sadness on his daughter's lovely face said it all. She didn't want him to do anything foolish. He nodded and mouthed her loving words back to her.

"That's a good father-in-law." Frank turned his attention back to the stage.

Utopia saw the glimmering tears in Henry's eyes. Her heart felt so heavy she didn't think she could carry it around any longer. At this very moment, she and two of her three fathers shared a common thread of helplessness, as did her dear friends, Pearl and John. *Not anymore*. The thought of her loved ones being at the mercy of these scumbags sparked a resolve to damn well do something about turning the tables.

Jargus was proud of saying a shotgun was a good enforcer if the need be strong. Right now, Frank held all the guns aimed at everyone she loved. There could be no stronger need for this wedding than that.

Pushing the bad of the situation out of her thoughts, she reasoned the good of it. She'd have riches. She'd live in a big mansion. And she'd have that most puzzling thing of all, respectability.

It was a word Lance and Frank had both used. It was a word she now despised.

How could she expect to have respectability married to someone like Frank? Would she have respectability once her body had been repeatedly violated by the scumbag?

Likely the answer to these questions came down to one word. No.

There'd be a wedding, but first things first. This crowd would learn something about Frank. Utopia wiped her sweaty palms on the skirt of her Sunday dress. The cotton fabric gave her resolve to do something about her circumstances.

She took tentative steps to the edge of the stage. The crowd silenced. Utopia took a deep breath and prepared herself to address the throng. The hoot of an owl broke the crisp night air.

She willed a smile on her face and took hold of Fergus' hand and squeezed. He squeezed back. That was all the support she needed.

"I've come to a decision about who I will be choosing to marry up with."

Utopia turned loose of her father's hold. In as sultry a saloon girl sashay that she could muster in her muck boots, she strutted herself back and forth across the stage. "It's not been easy picking just one of you handsome fellas. You've all given me some fine gifts."

Her hands showed off Banniger's ring, the crown on her head, and lastly she twirled around to show off her Sunday dress.

"Picking one man to live my whole life with has been harder to do than mashing corn for all that whiskey you fellas are enjoying. Phew." Utopia wiped her forearm across her brow. "I'm plumb tuckered deciding."

The crowd burst into uproarious laughter at her quirky banter. Her eyes glanced to Frank, who only half-laughed with the crowd. She continued her stall, all the while searching the crowd hoping to spot Lance but fearing he'd not appear.

"Well, I finally decided choosing a man by his gift wouldn't be a fair way to go about picking my husband. I decided to pick my fella according to the one that proposed the best."

Utopia spotted her next humorous target. She pointed toward the left side of the stage. "And Melvin Tuttle, right off I ruled you out 'cause you fell asleep on the courtship log twice whilst you were on your courting time."

The crowd roared with laughter at her disqualifying of the eighty-year-old Melvin, who sat in slumber on one of the campfire logs. A shove from a nearby suitor startled the man awake. All the contestants wailed when Melvin fell off his sleeping perch.

Utopia looked again to her soon-to-be husband. Frank leaned over and whispered something in the sheriff's ear. In the next instant, she saw the sheriff wave another man over. This fellow forced a gun in Henry's ribs and they made their way through the crowd to the edge of the clearing.

Henry and his executioner disappeared into the woods. Frank's leather-gloved hand went up in silent command mode. Fear sank any bravado Utopia had planned for her performance, leaving her feeling weak and vanquished.

"Wait." She hoped her eyes sent Frank the message she'd now cooperate.

He crossed his arms and waited.

The crowd grew so quiet the only sounds she could hear were the cicadas and the popping embers of the campfire. Her eyes darted from one suitor to the next, men who were totally ignorant of what was actually going on here.

"There's one man that's proposed to me in a way I just can't refuse." She took a deep breath, not sure the deplorable words would even come out of her mouth. "I've chosen Frank Sharps to be my husband."

Suitors at the far back of the crowd booed and heckled her choice. Those contestants closest to the chosen man broke into acquiesced applause.

The proud winner clasped his hands above his head in a victory pumping motion.

On cue, one of his thugs cupped hands on the sides of his mouth. "Speech, speech."

The crowd fell into the speech, speech cadence. It only took seconds for Frank to work his way onto the wagon stage and take hold of Utopia's hand.

When she tried to pull free, his hold tightened, causing Banniger's ring to dig into the side of her pinky finger. She leaned to him and quietly growled, "You're hurting me."

"Then hold still, my dear." Frank smiled at her and then the crowd. "I must confess it wasn't my intention to enter this contest. But, when my eyes fell on this lovely creature yesterday, I knew I immediately needed to seek her hand in marriage. I'm sorry to have outdone all of you with my zealous courting, but I am thankful I've won this lovely prize."

Utopia felt numb and dreaded the next moments that would soon doom her to this man. She'd tuned his talk out so completely, it took her brain several minutes to notice his dialogue had changed to campaign promises.

"I have many things planned for Tin Cup's future." The crowd cheered. After a sufficient period of applause, Frank raised his hands for silence. "But tonight is about this lovely creature beside me. I would not care to delay my vows even one hour more. I've called upon Reverend Pardee to wed us right here, right now. I ask all of you faithful supporters be my witnesses to one of the happiest days of my life."

All of a sudden his words sank in her brain. She'd very soon become Mrs. Frank Sharps. A wave of lightheadedness washed through Utopia and she stumbled.

Frank pulled her against his side. "I've got you. Smile, my dear, it's your wedding night."

CHAPTER TWENTY-EIGHT

Lance knelt over a small puddle of water at the bottom of the wall and splashed his face. The water smelled metallic from the washed erosion of mineral deposits. He stood and continued to survey the mine littered with rocks, dust, crates and various mining tools, some in working order, and others pinned beneath debris and totally useless.

He didn't know if it was day or night. They were lucky to have the use of a torch and a match. Feeling despondent and depressed, Lance tuned his ears to the slow, methodic passage of time. Each minute highlighted by the echoing drips of water plunking in a puddle in some part of the mine. Lance never figured he'd end his existence dying of starvation in a mine.

Travin and Jargus spent their last hours sitting on their rears consuming hefty rations of whiskey. Broken pieces of empty jugs littered the cave. Lance could see that the more Travin sipped liquor, the more downtrodden the lad's spirits slipped. He tried to take the lad's drink away and repeatedly got slapped for it.

"I ever, never, ever got 'round to tellin' Lil I wanted to marry with her." Travin jabbed a thumb at his chest. "I'm a big-fat-no-good sssscoundrel."

"Aw, shut up." Jargus disgustedly waved at his drinking buddy. "I can't stand a man that blubbers. For crying out loud, let me drink in peace."

Lance preferred to spend his time searching for something to get them out of their predicament. He opened another keg labeled gunpowder and was disappointed yet again. Nothing but more of Jargus' home brewed rot gut. He dropped the wooden lid to the floor. "You old coot, you mind telling me what you did with all the dynamite and gunpowder that you had in these crates?"

Jargus did some beard scratching. "Hmm, I recollect I used some fishing."

"Fishing?" Lance and Travin asked in unison.

"Dynamite. One stick blows them fish clean out of the creek. *Kapow*." Jargus waved his arms in an explosive circle. "It's a hell of a lot faster than using a pole."

It would stand to reason the old man would use an unorthodox way of catching a meal due to the rheumatism in his knees. "Might it be too much for me to hope that one of these crates could still have dynamite or gunpowder left in it?"

"I'll look." Travin staggered to his feet and very carefully set his jug down. He failed miserably at inserting his hands into his pants pockets and gave up. "What was I doing?"

"Holding the walls up." Jargus chuckled.

"Right." Travin moseyed to the nearest wall and braced his palms flat on the slippery wet surface.

Jargus roared laughing. "Put more muscle into it. I think the wall's leaning."

The drunken lad put his shoulder into his task. The slippery damp flooring caused his feet to slowly skate away from the wall. "Hey . . . I think the wall's moving." The angle of Travin's body leaned far beyond upright and he slipped and fell.

Jargus laughed so hard he started coughing.

"Have you had enough fun, old man?" Lance asked. "Don't you think it's time we get ourselves out of here?"

"So you're looking for dynamite?" Jargus put his jug on the floor and got to his feet. "Only one of these kegs might have explosive left in it. Now which one did I put it all in?" He rubbed stiffness out of his backside and searched around the area to his left. "Ah, here she is. I put her waaaay back here." He pulled the lid off a box marked with an X. "Yep, there's one stick left." Jargus held up the red cylinder. "Say, you ain't planning to use this, are you?"

"How else do you think we're going to get out of here?" Lance reached for the stick and the old man jerked it away from him.

"No. Not on yer life, sonny. I just found my lucky vein of gold. If'n you go blowing yer way out of here, it will bury us and my gold." Jargus yanked the fuse out and tossed it through the space at the top of the rubble blocking the exit.

"*Unbelievable.*" Lance grabbed the now useless dynamite. "You crazy coot, why did you

THE COURTSHIP OF UTOPIA MINOR   293

throw the fuse away? You've ruined the one thing that could have freed us."

"Hah. If you used that explosive in here, you wouldn't live to tell about it."

"Have it your way. You always do." Lance crossed his arms over his chest and took a seat on Travin's crate. "At least I'm trying to think of a way out of here rather than sit on my ass getting smashed. Right now, Frank Sharps might be after your daughter. Have you thought any on that?"

Jargus fisted his hands tight. "Yer getting yerself all worked up over nothing."

"Nothing?" Lance shot to his feet. "It means a little more than nothing to me. There's a man who right this minute is planning to harm the woman I love. You call that nothing?"

Jargus hobbled over and picked up the axe that had nearly parted Lance's head. He took hold of the lantern. "You grab him." He nodded Travin's direction. "Follow me."

Lance helped the inebriated Travin to his feet, wrapping his arm around the limp man for support. "Mind telling me where we are going, old man?" Lance followed the crusty miner, dragging their comrade along.

"Out."

"You mean there's another way out of this cave, and you're just now mentioning it?"

Jargus turned with an aggrieved look on his face. "Now, it wouldn't have been too smart an idea to mention it when the bad men were around, would it?"

"Why did you wait so long to mention the way out to me?"

The old miner spit to the cave floor. "Testing ya."

"Testing me? What the hell for?"

"If you intend to marry my girl, I needed to know what kind of sand my future son-in-law is made of. You showed me something when you never once concerned yerself with getting a share of Utopia's gold after we found the vein."

The mention of her name brought a bundle of emotions rushing through Lance. He feared never seeing Utopia again. That fear drove him. Escape looked slim but at least now he had hope. Lance redistributed Travin's weight. "Your gold is of no matter to me."

"I needed to see fer myself," Jargus replied. "If you took the tools and went to digging, I'd know you were just a gold-fevered bastard using my girl to get yer hands on our claim."

"Your little test wasted valuable time when we could be saving Utopia."

Jargus scratched his beard. "I hope not."

They followed the passageway lined with kegs and crates, making several turns and twists, worming farther and farther into the cavern.

All Lance could think about was Utopia and if she was safe. "How much father do we have to go?"

Jargus made an abrupt stop, and Lance nearly dropped Travin.

The old man held the lantern toward the ceiling. "See those tree roots poking through?"

"That means we're close to dirt, right?" Lance had never been so happy to see roots.

THE COURTSHIP OF UTOPIA MINOR

Jargus took a seat on a crate. "Sit Travin down next to me then take this axe and get to chipping away at those loose rocks. I'll look after our buddy."

Lance sat his bundle on a keg seat beside the old miner.

"Thanks for bringing me with him." Drunken Travin patted Jargus' belly. "Know what?"

"What?" Jargus grumbled.

"I wike you."

"Sober up, you ninny." Jargus pushed the drooling Travin away from him.

Lance removed his shirt and grabbed the axe. "Somehow I knew if there was work involved that I'd be the one doing it."

"What was yer first clue?"

"When I saw you only brought one axe ~~with you~~." Lance wielded the tool above his head and gave one good whack at the ceiling. He shielded his head from the falling debris.

"Leastways, I'm not getting a dumb-ass like him for kin." Jargus pointed at Travin.

"Shhh." Travin put a hushing finger to his lips. "I think I hear sump-thin."

"That's it." Jargus pushed Travin upright. "He gets no more shine from here on out."

Lance kept whacking away at the rocky ceiling. He wouldn't quit even though his shoulders ached with the burn of swinging the axe above his head. Thoughts of what could be happening to Utopia drove him on. His next hit to rock ceiling made a thud sound. "I think I've broke through."

Jargus leaned Travin upright against the wall, stood and held the lantern up for a closer look. "You sure did."

Joy raced through Lance. He dropped the axe and jumped around so excited he wrapped his arms around Jargus in a big hug. He even kissed the old man's whiskered cheek. "We did it. We're free."

"You're getting friendlier than I care ta be with, sonny-in-law."

Lance backed off. "Sorry." He rolled a keg over and positioned it under the crack of daylight and climbed on the lid, keeping his balance on the wobbly keg as he stood upright. He pulled and yanked tufts of sod lose, dropping the clods on the floor, continuing to tear way grassy clumps until he'd made an adequate hole. "I think I've got the hole big enough for us to squeeze through."

Lance stacked one keg on top of the first and then a third keg until they'd be able to reach the exit. "All we have to do now is climb up there and we'll be out."

"What are we gonna do with our buddy, Travin?"

That was a problem. And so was the old man. Getting to Utopia would be faster if he went alone. "Dragging a drunk through the woods will only slow us down. We'll have to leave Travin here for now."

Travin stirred to attention. "I ha–heard that. Don't leave me in this awwwwful place. I'm too young to die." He belched.

"For crying out loud, pull yerself together." Jargus gave Lance a hopeless look. "You go. I'll stay with him. Besides, my crippled legs would slow you, too. Now, go on. Get my girl." He wiped a sleeve under his suddenly drippy nose.

"You can count on it, old man."

Jargus' emotional breakdown turned on a dime. "Who you calling old?"

Lance climbed up on the first barrel and turned back to Jargus. "It might not be the smartest thing I ever do, but I'll come back for you."

"If you leave me in here to die with him, I'll come haunt you forever, sonny-in-law."

He cringed at the thought of a pestering father-in-law ghost. "I just told you I'll be back. Although I know I'll regret it later." Lance climbed out of the mine and looked to the stars to gather his sense of direction. He looked down the hole one last time to check on the two characters below. "You two lay off the drinking while I'm gone."

"I want my Lil." Travin began to sob.

"Git off me, you slobbering sissy."

Lance chuckled. It'd do the old man good to spend some quality time with a drunk. For him, it was time to make some fast tracks.

A full moon above lighted his way. Lance thanked his lucky stars otherwise he'd never make it through the treacherous pass. By horseback, the distance to the camp was forty-five minutes. It'd take him two hours to do the trek by foot.

By the time Lance reached his cabin he could barely stand. Once inside, he went behind his makeshift desk and overturned the keg he used for a chair. He reached beneath the wooden storage space and grabbed his leather holster wrapped like a bandage around his Colt.

It had been three years since he'd last strapped on this gun. He'd been trying to convince himself that he could erode away the past by not wearing it. His plan had been to bury himself in the newspaper business, printing the news instead of being in the news. No doubt about it, his past clung to him like apples on a tree.

It was time he faced the fact that being a lawman ran thick through his blood. Maybe a life without a gun wasn't possible for him. The world always seemed to have another place, another time, another someone to bring to justice. No matter how hard he tried to change professions, his inner soul forced him to uphold and defend others when they wouldn't or couldn't do it themselves. Even here, he'd taken on keeping order amongst the suitors.

Lance buckled the holster around his waist, tied down the leather tight to his thigh. Taking the Colt in his hands, he clicked the cylinder around, checking his ammo. There were six bullets, one for each of Frank's men, and if it came to it, a spare for the governor himself. He settled the weapon in his holster then grabbed his saddlebags out from under his bed and tossed them on his cot.

No more running, and no more looking the other way. He had a job to do. He'd save his woman or die trying. He rooted through the pouch until he found what he was looking for. Lance pinned the marshal's star on his shirt, thankful he'd not gotten around to turning in his resignation papers to the court. He hadn't wanted to burn his bridges if things don't work out with his newspaper plans.

CHAPTER TWENTY-NINE

Utopia watched the preacher make his way toward the wagon stage. She had the eerie feeling a decade of preaching had trained this man of the cloth to spot good men from evil ones. She hoped he'd notice that she wasn't a willing bride and would refuse to do the wedding.

Reverend Pardee's boot heels thumped and spurs chinked with each tread he took up the stage steps. The lean, tall man dressed in a black shirt trimmed with a minister's white collar also wore a long black duster, outerwear more worn by gunslingers than a man of the cloth. "Hold this for me," he said in a gravelly voice, passing his flat-brimmed hat to Fergus.

Frank extended his hand to the Reverend. "I appreciate you marrying us on short notice."

The pastor narrowed his steely gray eyes on the groom. "I told the young lady that I would perform the ceremony for her no matter the choice of her husband." He turned his head and spit on the stage. "I'm sadly disappointed in her choice."

Utopia's chest pounded and her knees quaked. Her hands were shaking so badly one would think she suffered from sobering-up tremors.

The reverend took hold of her hand and place it on the Good Book, wrapping her jittering fingers in his reassuring fold. Reverend Pardee drilled Frank with a second hard stare then patted her hand. "Not to worry, pretty lady. Trust in the Lord and everything will make a turn for the better ... given time."

Frank's eyebrows drew together. "What do you mean by that, preacher?"

Utopia wondered the same thing. Personally, she'd not talked to the Lord much, but if the Almighty saved her and her loved ones from Frank, why, she'd pray every day from here on out.

"I'm just giving my blessings to the lovely bride and, of course, to you." Reverend Pardee opened his bible. "Shall we get started?"

Utopia's knees went weak, so weak she almost toppled, but the reverend reached out and once again took her hand. Any minute, her guts were going to spew all over the wagon stage. Her mind screamed *this can't be happening*. Her heart yearned for Lance to appear. Where was he? No, she shouldn't wish that. It was best Lance wasn't anywhere near here. Frank would have a gun on him, too.

The Reverend released Utopia's hand and ushered her to stand beside the groom. Frank took hold of her hand. The vile man's touch rushed a frigid chill through veins and freeze-dried her heart like deer meat hanging in a cave during winter. Reality set in. From here on out, each day married to Frank would be another day that part of her would die. Her dream and Lance would be gone. A tear rolled down her cheek, and she didn't even bother to remove it.

"Dearly beloved, we are gathered here this evening to wed this man and this woman in holy matrimony." The minister glared at Frank, looked to Fergus and then his eyes met the bride's teary eyes. "If there be any amongst you that objects to this union, state your reason now. Or forever hold your peace."

A long moment of silence followed.

Reverend Pardee nodded. "Very well. We'll continue. Frank Sharps, do you—?"

"I object," a voice yelled from far back in the crowd.

The crowd murmured. Most of the suitors turned to look upon the man brassy enough to intrude upon Frank Sharp's ceremony. A human wedge formed, widening from the back and spreading the throng open, parting the group like the Red Sea.

Utopia's heart skipped ten beats when she saw him. *"Lance."* She bolted for the steps.

Frank caught her by the wrist and pulled her close to him. "Stay here, my dear. Remember I hold your loved ones at my disposal."

"You're a bastard, Frank Sharps," Lance yelled. "If you're making threats to my woman, you better recount your gun support first."

Frank scanned where his men should be holding hostages at gunpoint. John and Pearl had turned the tables on two of his men. He looked to

Mays standing before the stage. "Sheriff, please remove this intruder from our midst so I can get on with my wedding."

Mays looked to Lance, then back to the man barking orders to him from the stage. "Sorry, Frank. This reporter's made me an offer I can't refuse. He says I'm to arrest you for embezzlement, assault, and other crimes, or face going to jail myself. I decided prison should be your fate, not mine."

Frank yanked Utopia in front of him and used her like a shield. He pointed a small gun at her temple and dragged her across the stage. When she tripped on the hem of her Sunday go-to-meeting dress, she heard a rip. Her dress wasn't the only thing torn. Her brain needed to make some decisions. And right now. Should she run? Could she run? What would happen if she did something? How many could get hurt because of her?

"Is it wise to challenge me when I have a gun pointed at this lovely woman's head?"

"Let her go. It's over, Frank. I'm a federal marshal." Lance pointed to the badge pinned on his shirt. "There's a jail cell waiting for you in Tin Cup. Drop your gun and let her go. Do it. Or I'll kill you dead where you're standing."

"Is that so?" Frank barked. "I think not. You wouldn't want to endanger your mistress. Come with me, my dear," he whispered in her ear. "We're taking our leave of this place."

Frank kept her pinned against him, protecting his black-hearted hide, sidestepping them both across the stage. Utopia had no intention of letting him get her off the stage, much less to his carriage and off to parts unknown. She made up her mind to do one thing to help Lance. She went totally limp like she'd fainted in Frank's arms, making her body a heavy piece of dead-weight to be dragged along.

"Get on your feet," Frank hissed at her.

She continued to be passed out, letting her head wobble to and fro, hanging as limp as she could under the tension of her nerves. Occasionally, she'd bob her head a slight tilt, enough to glimpse what was going on below the stage. She spotted someone at the edge of the crowd, and her heart hopped in big happy throbs.

It was Pa Henry. He was running out of the woods waving his arms high in the air. Thank goodness he'd escaped his captor, but wait. He seemed to be giving some kind of a warning and yelling, but she couldn't hear him from this distance.

The crowd then scrambled for cover, getting out of the line of fire of any impending gun battle. A man with a gun chased after Henry. Utopia panicked. This chaser didn't have his gun aimed at her father. It pointed at—

"Lance. Look out."

Lance spun to his body and ducked at the same time his hand flew to his Colt, and like lightning, she watched him draw the weapon and fire. The man that held her Pa Henry captive crumpled to the ground with a slug dead centered in his forehead.

The next minute became slow motion. Out the corner of her eye, Utopia registered Frank's gun arm shifting toward the crowd, aiming for her lover. *"Lan—"*

Frank cut off her warning by shoving her to the stage floor. Sheer panic forced her next move. When the trigger cocked, she reached up and yanked his arm down.

A shot rang out and Utopia's heart stopped. *Dear Lord Almighty*. She dreaded what she'd see if she dared to look out to the crowd. A flash of those empty pants floating in the water rushed through her head. She swallowed her fear and looked for … A huge smile surfaced.

Lance stood before the stage with a dead gunman sprawled on the ground several yards away. She jumped to her feet, totally overcome with happiness. It was over at last.

Then came a second shot. The crowd looked stunned, some pointing behind her, which sent new chills up her spine. A gurgled sound made Utopia look back. She gasped. Frank staggered toward her. His eyes stunned. A trickle of blood seeped from the corner of his mouth. He reached for her with an outstretched arm and stumbled one step. Then his gaze dulled, and Frank tumbled off the platform to the ground below.

Reverend Pardee dropped the barrel of his smoking gun into his holster, which had been hidden beneath his duster. "You live by the gun– you die by the gun."

Utopia couldn't be more surprised or relieved. "Thank you." She scampered down the steps, ran to Lance and leaped into his arms, wrapping her legs around his hips. She planted the biggest stage two kiss on him she could muster.

When they came up for air, she gazed into his eyes. "Where in the hell have you been?"

"I'll tell you later." Lance pecked her lips one more time before putting her back on the ground. He knelt down on one knee and took hold of her hand. "Utopia, I've had enough excitement for one day, but I could stand a little more. Will you marry me?"

Tears weld up in her eyes. The joy in her heart choked her voice completely off. A nod was the best she could answer.

Lance took her by the hand and led her to the stage and addressed the preacher. "Long time no see, Dan."

"Last I heard you'd given up the law." Pardee grinned.

"I thought so, too. Reverend, would you repeat that ceremony using a different groom?"

The pastor grinned. "If she's the reason you turned in your badge, you're a lucky man." The reverend glanced to Utopia. "Miss, if you don't mind me saying, he's a much better choice."

Utopia smiled. "I know he is." She'd pick Lance for a husband over any man in the whole wide world. But, she couldn't get married. Not even to Lance. Something she'd had her heart set on a long time was the little stopper. "Lance, I want to marry you. But . . ."

"But what?" His eyes blinked, stunned. "Didn't you tell me last night that you love me?"

"Yes. And I do love you. Only right now . . . uh . . . I got to get something out of my system before I consider getting married to anyone."

Utopia looked at the reverend's puzzled face then back to Lance.

Lance's jaw clenched. His face reddened, and he abruptly turned loose of her hand. "What's more important than getting married to me? And what's wrong with now?"

"I just can't. I need to finish up with my dream first. I have to be a saloon girl even if it's only for a short while."

"You're telling me you have to be a dancehall hussy before you'll say 'I do' with me? Forget I even asked." Lance turned his back on her and headed for his shack.

Utopia ran after him and grabbed his arm. He shrugged her off him and kept walking. "Lance. *Please understand*." Her plea fell on angry ears and a male's hurt pride.

She knew she'd wounded Lance far worse than any of Frank's bullets ever could.

CHAPTER THIRTY

Utopia raised her head from Pearl's cushiony bosom and whined, "I don't know what made me do it. Lance should know by now that being a saloon girl means more to me than just about anything except him." Her face went back in hiding in the large bosomed pillow, and she flew into another fit of crying.

Pearl placed her hands on each side of Utopia's face. "Honey, you can't just dump a thing like being a saloon girl on a man. Especially, after he just saved your life and proposed to you. That's like dumping a bucket of cold water on him, in the middle of winter in a blizzard. You done shriveled up the man's ego and likely a few other parts of him right fast."

Lil rotated her body on the keg she sat perched on. "I do believe you're the first female I've ever heard of that turned down a handsome, romantic, good-looking man like Lance to be a saloon girl. Did I mention that Lance is a fella that's pleasing on a woman's eyes?" Lil got to her feet. Her hands shot to her hips. "Utopia, damn you, girl.

You're just gonna have to make this right somehow. That's all there is to it."

A pale hand slowly lifted up in the air.

Pearl's mouth dropped open. She pointed toward the bed. "Look. She's moving."

Lil spun around to her friend.

"Quit. Holl-er-in' at my girl," Sadie whispered.

Utopia jumped to her feet. Pearl rolled off her bed. The girls formed a circle and hopped up and down, around and around, in joyous elation.

"Praise the Lord," Pearl wailed. She tossed her blonde hair in the air, letting big tears rolled down her face. "Sweet Sadie's come back to us."

"What . . . time . . . is it?" Sadie reached for her head. Her fingertips felt along the bandage.

Lil quickly took hold of Sadie's shaky fingers and folded them back on her friend's chest. "Sweetie, leave your head alone. You've had yerself a bad hurt."

"I'll go fetch Doc Cruthers." Utopia dashed from the tent. It'd be good to give the girls some privacy with their dear friend. Besides, she needed the fresh air and time alone, too.

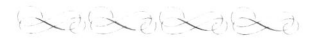

Lance worked off his anger and disappointment by going back to the mine to rescue his two pals. With a rope, his horse and some teamwork from John and Henry, they managed to get drunk Travin and crabby Jargus out of the hole.

His night of lawman business, mine rescue and proposal rejection had Lance worn out. He'd done all the recounting of the day's heroics that he cared to. He got up from his seat on the log by the campfire. "Well, gents. I'm turning in. Thanks for the good vittles. I'll see you all in the morning before I head out." He poured out the last of the coffee and handed the tin to Jargus.

"Y ... you're not leaving, are you?" Fergus asked. "Y . . . you gonna see Utopia first, ain't you?"

Lance scowled. "There's no reason to."

"What about marrying her now that you ruined her? Jargus growled. "Henry says you done asked my girl to marry you. So why ain't you?"

"Your girl turned me down. There's nothing more for me to say. Now leave me be."

Lance turned and angrily stormed away before Jargus could threatened him with a shotgun, not that the threat held much worry now. A bullet would put him out of his misery.

He headed for his shack to think his plans through. He'd decided it'd be best to head back to Tin Cup at first light. Staying around any longer would just be more torture for him. Nearly to his cabin, something made him look to his left. He stopped dead in his tracks. Utopia was headed his direction.

Thanks to her, he'd spent what should have been his honeymoon with a bunch of men, retelling events that had no relevance to his future. His thoughts warred with the multitude of emotions inside him. He'd risked his damn life for the frustrating woman. He'd even risked his life for that stubborn father of hers. And the bad thing about those brainless acts of his, he'd do them all over again if it came down to it.

THE COURTSHIP OF UTOPIA MINOR   311

Women. Why did men need them? And why on earth did he need this particular woman? Why couldn't he face the fact he loved Utopia, but she didn't love him. He would give his life for Utopia in a heartbeat. Heck, he'd even risk being haunted by Jargus, if that was what it took to have her as his wife. But there was no way he'd have any wife of his prancing, dancing and singing in some damn saloon.

She was now ten feet away. Seven feet. He couldn't help but feel glad to see her. What would he say when she got to him? Their eyes met. Then she turned and bolted a different direction. Seeing her run off like that, the agony of being rejected washed over him again. He watched her leave only because it maybe would be the last he'd ever see of her.

Then Utopia halted and turned back around and that made him totally ecstatic. He had another chance to make things right if he'd let go of his stubborn, stupid pride. By damn, she was headed back his direction with that determined look on her face that he so adored. *Shit.* What would he say to her? He needed to keep calm. He'd say it was not over and done. That he understood about her dream, even though he didn't. That he could accept her wishes to pursue that terrible career she wanted. Leastways, that was what his brain wanted him to say. The only trouble, his heart kept telling him something totally the opposite.

She stopped two feet from him. "I have something I need to get off my chest."

Lance stuck his hands in his jeans pockets. His gaze drifted to the mention of her bosom then back to her sleep-deprived eyes. Clearly, her evening hadn't been any better than his. She'd been crying, and bucketsful by the looks of it. "Where are you going?"

She pointed toward the shelters on the right of the camp. "I'm fetching Doc Cruthers."

His first thoughts were that something must have happened with Sadie. "Is she dead?"

Utopia shook her head. "No, no. She woke up." Her arms flapped out to her sides. "All of a sudden–poof. She opened her eyes and talked."

Lance kicked at the dirt with the toe of his boot. "That's good news."

"Yep, it sure is."

"So." Lance shoved his fingers through his hair. Their cordial conversation turned into unbearable silence. Then their eyes met again.

"I'm sorry—" they both blurted out in unison.

"It was all my—" Again, they uttered words simultaneously.

Lance held up his hand to stop the tongue-tied conversation. "Ladies first." His strategy would be to hear what was on her mind, and then maybe he'd know where to go with this crazy love affair of his. Hers. No. It was their love affair.

"I can't eat. I can't sleep. Dang-nabbit. I don't even want to breathe without you." Utopia swiped at a tear that slipped down her cheek.

"Me neither. I mean about the breathing. I did eat some. *But not much*," he quickly added in case she intended to hold that against him. A man never knew what one wrong word would hang him. Lance softly brushed that beautiful wayward curl behind her ear. "It's only about nine. The evening's young. I'm sure there's still some food over by the campfire if you—"

"No. I'm not hungry." Utopia fidgeted with the white lace collar of her dress. "I've decided on something."

His eyes focused on her mouth. When her tongue seductively licked at her bottom lip, all he could think about was kissing her. "Stop that."

"Stop what?"

"Stop licking your lips. I can't concentrate on what you're saying if you lick your lips."

"Oh." Utopia fidgeted more with her collar. She clasped her shaky hands at her waist.

Lance had no idea what she would say but he hoped. "Take yourself a deep breath and tell me, without the mouth licking, what you've decided." He watched her eyes close. She inhaled deeply. His gaze drifted to the rise and fall of her chest. *Have mercy.* If she didn't get to telling him about her decision, and quickly, his brain would lose all ability to discern her words.

"I don't want to be a saloon girl. I've thought on it . . . and . . . I'd rather marry you."

"That's it? You're giving up being a saloon girl?" Lance wouldn't let her off the hook so easy. She really did love him. He'd just been through hell the last few hours. Now she wanted to give it all up. "I did a lot of thinking, too." He looked into her tear-swollen eyes and his heart melted. "I . . . I've decided you should be a dancehall girl but only for one night. Can you accept that?"

Utopia's mouth dropped open. "You do? Why?"

Lance stepped a bit closer. "I want nothing unsettled between us when you marry me. And if you don't have your saloon girl performance, it will forever hang over our marriage like one big dark cloud of an unfulfilled dream. I know something about unfulfilled dreams." His gaze fell on her lips. "You're having your dream come true. I'm behind you one hundred percent."

She licked her lips. "Is that more or less than eighty-twenty?"

"Don't do it again. I'm warning you." He pointed at her mouth. "You do that lip licking once more time, and I'm going to have to kiss you."

Utopia's mouth curled in a slight smile. She licked.

Lance wrapped his arms around her waist and pulled her against him. He gazed into her eyes. "Now you're going to get what's coming to you, missy."

"Well, don't take all day. Are you gonna kiss me, or not?"

His mouth devoured hers. They were both equally needy in the kiss they shared. Her lips parted for him, and in that one embrace they sought to end the hurt of the night by reaching into the very depths of their souls. They pulled apart a minute. "We'd better take this inside," he suggested.

"No. I can't. I have to go fetch the doc for Sadie."

"Can't we have just a minute alone? After all, I did save your life . . . and your dad's life. And you know how hard that was for me to do." He waited and hoped she'd say yes to coming inside his cabin. He'd be on familiar territory then. A few kisses, a bed—"

"I'll come in for just a minute. For just a few kisses." She jumped up and wrapped her legs around him, making him carry her with his hands under her backside. "I've really missed your kisses."

Lance let out a guttural moan. His hands cupped under her bottom and hauled her to the door of his cabin. "You mind getting the latch? I seem to have my hands full."

Utopia did as he asked. Once inside, she kicked the door closed. Lance removed his hands and let her feet drop to the floor then he crushed her body against the door. They resumed their kiss and both urgently undressed so they could feel flesh upon flesh.

She worked at the tiny buttons on the front of her Sunday dress. Lance worked at getting his shirt off. When he glimpsed the swells of her breasts showing above her camisole, he pulled the bodice of her dress open, off her shoulders and pinned her arms and smothered kisses down her long slender neck. Lance hungrily pecked kisses on her cheek, her forehead, her mouth. "My sweet," he whispered. "I love you so much."

His body was hot and getting hotter and hotter. He couldn't wait to get her in his bed.

A heavy fist pounded the other side of door. "You in there, sonny-in-law?" There were more pounds. "Come out of there. Both of you."

Utopia gasped. "Oh, no. My pa knows I'm in here." She pushed Lance away and hurriedly went to buttoning her Sunday dress.

Lance's passions totally shut down, and he quickly tried to rush back into his clothes. He put a finger to his lips. "Shhh. You keep quiet. I'll go out and see what he wants." He stuffed his shirt back in his jeans, streaked his fingers through his mussed hair and stepped outside leaving the door open only enough to shed some lamplight outside. He stuffed his hands in his pants pockets and faced the pesky father with the really poor timing. "Jargus, what can I do for you?"

The old man gave Lance the usual once over mad look. He spit to the ground. "Yer hair's all mussed. I'll make me a wild guess that you've changed yer mind about leaving. You got her in there right now, practicing yer sonny-in-lawing with my girl before you've said the marrying words."

"Look, old man this is between me and your daughter."

"There ain't gonna be no more 'between my daughter's' anything. Not until she's married. Utopia, you git yerself out here."

The door opened and she stepped outside. "Hi, Pa. I was helping Lance look for his hat."

"Yeah." Jargus spit. "I can see just how hard you two were looking. What's this I hear you won't let this fella make you a proper married woman?"

"We were inside discussing things when you interrupted."

Jargus took his daughter by the arm and pulled her a good distance from Lance. "Then it's settled. We'll be having a wedding tomorrow."

Lance wanted to be sure he had time to purchase a ring, a nice suit and find a romantic place to honeymoon. "We need more than a day to plan a proper wedding. I suggest we have the ceremony in a week."

"No. I won't have a wedding until Sadie's better." Utopia put herself between Lance and her father. "Pa, I love Lance, and we plan on marrying. We don't need you doing no insisting on it. All I want is time for Sadie to heal so she can attend my wedding."

Her words set Lance's heart to soaring. Right now he was the happiest man in the world. "You do want to marry me? For real?"

"I just said so, didn't I? It's just I want to wait for Sadie to recover."

"I guess I can wait that long. Or at least, I'll try." Lance took her in his arms and planted a deep passionate kiss on her lips.

Jargus pulled the two apart. "That's enough with the samplin', sonny-in-law. You'll be saying 'I do' to get anymore." The testy father started to escort his daughter to her cabin, and she put a stop to his dragging by digging the heels of her boots in the ground.

"But Pa, I was fetching the doc to check on Sadie." Utopia gave Lance a departing look over her shoulder.

"I figure I know what you were fetching. You git on to yer cabin and stay there. I'll go git the doctor." The annoyed Jargus turned back to Lance and pointed a finger. "I'm putting the Scotsman outside her door as a guard. You come within two foot of her before the wedding, and I promise you one thing, sonny-in-law. You won't live to say any vows."

CHAPTER THIRTY-ONE

Two months later

Sadie had stayed on one month and recovered after the contest ended. Utopia missed all the girls but today was a happy day for they were back and visiting for the whole weekend.

"That spendthrift boss of ours," Lil complained. "He's got the entire back of the saloon ripped open. He's putting in a damn billiard room."

Pearl sat on her chase lounge eating out of a heart shaped box of chocolates. "We have the weekend off to visit with our little gal."

"I've missed all of—" Utopia ran from the girls' tent holding her mouth. Once she got around the corner she lost her morning meal. When she turned around, Lil, Pearl and Sadie were poised with their arms crisscrossed over their chests, giving each other knowing glances.

"What's wrong with all of you?"

"Honey," Pearl cajoled. "I know you and Lance agreed you'd wait until Sadie had herself recovered before having your wedding. But, sugar, she's been well for going on two months. And, I hope to tell you that you're stirred and the muffin's baking."

Utopia hands flew to her hips."What on earth are you talking about?"

Lil pushed herself ahead of Pearl. "She's tellin' you that yer having a baby."

"A baby?" Utopia gave a big wide grin. "You mean I'm pollinated?"

"I'll have you know that I'm recovered enough for a wedding, sweetie." Sadie wrapped her sheer robe about her, warding off the morning chill. "You best have that wedding soon, or you won't fit the dress we done bought for you."

Utopia thought on how often she'd gotten together with Lance. It must have been often enough. "When can I see my baby girl?"

"Honey, you have a fifty-fifty chance you'll be having a girl," Pearl stated.

"I like eighty-twenty odds better." Utopia rubbed her hand on her stomach. She couldn't feel anything moving inside. "Are you sure there's a baby in me?"

"You ain't tossing yer breakfast every morning for nothing," Lil stated. "We'll take you to Tin Cup to see Doc Cruthers after the wedding. He'll check you out."

"Can Doc Cruthers tell me if I'm having a girl?" Utopia bit on her nails wondering if she should tell Lance about the baby now or wait until after the ceremony.

"You best come inside and sit a spell, honey." Pearl walked over and wrapped her arm about Utopia's shoulders and escorted her inside their tent to a comfy sit on a keg. "Honey, the doc will be able to figure out when you'll drop that baby."

"Drop my baby?"

"You're not going to drop the kid," Sadie stated, giving her friend an angry scowl. "Pearl's talking out her fat ass. What she's saying is the doc can tell you when you'll be going into hard labor."

Utopia didn't know exactly what the girls were talking about. She had a feeling that no hard, no soft or any other kind of labor would help her know how to birth this infant. She'd labored plenty in the mines and around the camp all her life and never had a baby pop out.

Lil clapped her hands together. "Welp, we've got a wedding to prepare."

Utopia wanted to get more of her questions about babies answered. "But I—"

"No buts. No more stalling. Yer getting married. I figure Saturday's good," Lil stated.

"Imagine that, our little girl and a real wedding. This is going to be something. Umm, Umm." Pearl fanned her hands at her face in excited glee. "I hope my heart is up to all this."

"I'll bake a cake," Sadie declared.

"Make it chocolate. That's my favorite." Pearl's face lit up. "We'll have Lance run an invite in his newspaper for any old suitors that may want to come for the wedding."

Utopia watched the girls getting all fidgety fisted and giddy pick one, holding hands and hopping around. "Aren't you all in a bit of a hurry on your planning?"

"I'm telling you right now," Lil stated with a hand on her hip. "No adopted grandbaby of mine is gonna be a nameless bastard."

Pearl wrapped her arm around Utopia. "Honey, Lance is the father, isn't he?"

She knew Lance was the only person who could have planted the seed of a baby in her. "Yes, he's my babe's father."

"Then honey, once you have Lance's last name, folks won't be calling your baby boy a bastard," Pearl patronized.

Utopia stomped her foot. "No, I'm having me a girl."

"The baby deserves the father's respectable name," Sadie stated.

There was that respectability problem again. Would she ever get a hold on what the word really meant? "Fine. If the wedding's gonna be on Saturday, I best go let my fathers and Lance in on the news."

"You go do that," Lil declared.

The three women went into a wedding planning huddle.

Utopia left the tent. When she got outside, Pearl's words were on her mind. She immediately crossed her right leg over her left, keeping her thighs good and tightly together. By gosh, by golly, she'd not be dropping her baby on the ground. She successfully scissor-walked the entire distance to her cabin without a baby accident.

Utopia entered her cabin and immediately Lance's arms embraced her. He backed her against the door and worked at unbuttoning her red plaid shirt. His lips hungrily pecked kisses along her neck.

"I've been waiting for you," he whispered. "I bribed John to give us a half-hour. That's just enough time if we're quick."

"Lance, I'd like to talk to you about—"

He moved his lips to hers, cutting off her words. He scooped her up in his arms and carried her to the bed. "We don't have much time, my sweet." Lance hurriedly shed his pants.

Normally she never turned away a chance for pleasuring. But she wasn't so sure pleasuring would be a safe thing to do now that one seed had already been planted.

"Let me help you with these." Lance grabbed hold of the waistband of Utopia's pants.

How should she approach the touchy situation? He had her lower half nearly undressed. "Lance, stop. I need to ask you something." He gently pushed her down on the mattress and his magic kisses had her lying beneath him in two shakes. She forgot her purpose for a minute or two as his hand slipped inside her opened shirt and cupped one of her breasts. She had to do something fast, her lower half was beginning to sweat, and real quick, she'd not be able to stop herself from letting him go ahead and pleasure her.

"Can't it wait? I'm busy." He nibbled his lips down her neck.

She quickly turned her head aside to avoid having her words trapped in another kiss. "I need to talk . . . about babies."

"Umm hmm," he mumbled.

Lance positioned his leg between her thighs, wanting her to open for him. Her insides wanted that pleasuring part of him in her. But she fought the temptation of spreading her legs. First she needed to know if more lovemaking would hurt their babe.

It was hard but she managed to keep her darn legs closed.

"How about you relax, and enjoy the moment, and open those fine legs of yours?"

"No." Utopia put a firm hand on his shoulder and pushed him back. She wiggled out from under him. "Dang-nabbit, I need to know something."

Lance rolled onto his back and swiped his fingers through his hair. "Talk? You want to talk? Fine. Why not? My interest is shot all to hell now. So let's talk."

"You sound mad at me."

"Mad? Why would I be mad? I've only been waiting half the day to be with you. I bribed John with a month's pay to be with you. I had every intention of spending the little bit of our time making love with you. And what do you want to do? Talk." He crossed his ankles and braced his hands under his head. Lance stared at her. "*So talk.*"

"Shhh. Someone might hear you." Maybe she should talk about something else a moment, to kind sort of sneak up to the subject of telling him about his baby seed.

"Where's your law badge?"

"That's the important thing you want to talk about?"

She bit on her nail. "It's one of them. Why didn't you ever mention you were a lawman?"

Lance shrugged. "I don't know. I was scared. I guess now's as good a time as any to tell you about my past. You need to know what kind of man you're getting for your husband."

Utopia never saw Lance so serious. She leaned on her side and supported her head. She laid her hand on his chest. "I already know what kind of man you are."

"No, you don't." He took a deep breath. "Now let me tell this. I was a lawman in a town in Kansas. The townsfolk had been harassed by a gang of hired guns for several months. One night, a rowdy cowhand decided to start shooting up the saloon. He'd been drinking the majority of a day. The man fired his gun once too often. His bullet ricocheted off a wall and killed a man."

"What did you do?"

"I arrested the fellow. The townsfolk wanted to hang the man without a trial. An angry mob gathered. I stood my ground, insisting the man was entitled to his day in court."

"Good for you."

"You would think I'd done my duty. The next night while I made my rounds, someone shot me. During my incapacity, vigilantes took the man from his jail cell and hung him. So much for the theory you're innocent until proven guilty."

Utopia touched his ribcage. "That's how you got this scar?"

Lance glanced down at his memento. "Yes." He took a breath. "After that, I took off my badge, swore to give up being the law and moved on. I took a job as a guard on a gambling boat. Their pay was good, and I had little trouble keeping the games peaceable."

Utopia saw Lance's jaw tense. "Why don't we talk about something else?"

"No. You need to hear this." He took another breath and looked into her eyes. "One night me and this gal that worked on the boat, we had an argument."

"Was she a dancehall girl?"

"Rachel was in a similar line of work, yes."

"Was this Rachel your sweetheart?" Utopia held her breath, worried if Lance ever loved someone else. Now she guessed she knew the answer. A tinge of jealousy stung her heart. "How close were you two?"

He pulled Utopia to him and looked in her eyes. "We were close friends and shared a bed but that's all." He kissed Utopia's forehead. "Anyways, that night, I decided I'd let Rachel stew in her anger a bit. Trouble broke out when a fellow she'd been flirting with started to get rough with her. The man was drunk. Since her line of work was exactly what we'd fought about, I decided to let Rachel get out of her predicament on her own."

"What happened?" Seeing Lance's eyes water, Utopia feared the worst.

Lance swiped the show of emotion off his face. "The man pulled a pistol. I had searched all the passengers when they boarded the boat—I guess I didn't search them very well. I heard the shot and turned." His eyes closed and he took a deep breath to compose himself. Lance reopened his eyes and looked at Utopia. "Rachel was dead."

Utopia swallowed the knot in her own throat and put a hand on Lance's chest. She could feel how hard his heart labored. "What did you do?"

"I was furious. Without thinking, I drew my gun and didn't blink an eye." Lance made his hand into a pretend gun and aimed at the ceiling. "Pow. Pow. Pow."

Utopia startled at the loud shouts of his imaginary gunfire.

"I fired off three shots, right in his chest." Lance sifted his gaze back to Utopia.

She could see him battling to hold back the deep emotions. "You did the right thing."

"No. I didn't." His jaw clenched as he grew angry. "Don't you see? I handled the situation just like those vigilantes back in Kansas had done. I took away a man's right to a fair trial."

Utopia disagreed. "If you hadn't acted like you did others might have been hurt or killed. And the man in Kansas would have been found guilty and hanged."

"We'll never know that for sure, will we?" Lance ran his hand down his face as if wiping that thought from his mind. "When the boat docked, I gave Rachel a respectable funeral then headed west. I swore I'd never pick up a gun or that badge again. I met Barris Baines, he's my editor in Tin Cup. He gave me a chance at a new kind of job."

"And that's how you wound up here to do your newspaper writing, isn't it?"

He gave her a dimpled smile. "It's the best work I've ever had. It brought me to you."

Lance rolled over and pushed her back down on the mattress. He kissed her.

She knew he'd poured his soul out telling her about his past. "What happened to your friend Rachel is why you don't want me doing saloon work, isn't it?"

"That's a big part of it. It's not a safe job. If anything ever happened to you, I'd be lost."

Now she could understand why Lance wanted her to give up her dream, but it still didn't give her any comfort in giving up something she'd held onto most of her life. "The girls have picked this Saturday as the day we should get hitched. They've already started making plans."

Lance's head jerked back in surprise. "Saturday? Why so soon?"

Utopia didn't want to tell him about the baby seed. If he wasn't too keen on the idea of kids, she'd need time to soften him up to the notion of being a father. "I suppose the girls are in a hurry to see me in the dress they bought for me. But . . . " Her nail went to her mouth.

"But what?"

"I don't mean to sound like I'm not grateful, but the dress they got me is all white. I'm going to have to tell the girls I'm wearing my mother's saloon dress. I don't know how I'll break the news to them without hurting their feelings."

Lance sat up in bed. "Hold on. You said you were giving up that dream of yours."

She tried to remain calm even though Lance getting irritated. "And I will, but I was thinking that maybe I could do both things at once. I could get married and be a saloon girl all on the same day."

He sprung off the bed, grabbed his britches off the floor and stuffed his legs in his pants and pulled them up. "I said I'd give you a saloon day, but for Pete's sake." He shrugged on his shirt and angrily worked on the buttons. "I hoped that after I explained about Rachel you'd give up the notion all together. Now you tell me you want to be a saloon girl *on our wedding day?"*

Lance jammed his shirt into the waistband of his pants. "Our wedding is going to be a normal, respectable ceremony. My bride will wear white and not some flashy, revealing saloon dress. And the woman I marry will not sing and dance her way down the aisle. Some other time maybe, but not on our wedding day."

Utopia never felt more hurt and at the same time more riled than right now. But she'd be darned if she'd let those blasted waterworks start in again. She flew off the bed and jabbed her finger at his chest. "I thought you understood. I've dreamt about wearing my mama's dress and being like her my whole life. And you're trying to take that away from me." She grabbed her shirt and shrugged it on. Then she stepped into her buckskins. Utopia reached for one of her muck boots and reared it back over her shoulder ready to throw it at him. *"Get out."* She pointed to the door.

"Fine. I'm going. Boy, I'm running out of here as fast as I can." Lance stopped at the door and turned back to her. "Think about that dream of yours, sweetheart. Think about what you're asking me to let you do. And you tell the girls and your looney fathers that until you come to your senses, the wedding's off." He slammed the door on his way out.

Utopia dropped her boot to the floor, ran across the room and flopped on her bed.

She cried her eyes plumb dry of tears.

CHAPTER THIRTY TWO

Saturday, wedding day

"The man's busted his butt on a surprise for you," Jargus yelled. "He's worked all week at getting ready for your wedding. First yer agreeing not be singing, then you two are back to fightin'. It's been a week of fighting. My neck's got a crick watching you two running back and forth. We're having this wedding. You find Lance and say yer sorry, or I'll see to it yer hitched with my shotgun aimed on *you*."

"I want to find Lance. But I don't know where he's run off to."

Pearl shoved Jargus aside. "She can't go seeing the groom two hours before the ceremony. She'll jinx their marriage. Any fool knows that it's bad luck to see the bride before you get to the altar."

"Bad luck?" Utopia certainly didn't want to bring any more jinx on their marriage or her baby than she already had. "I shouldn't have brought up my saloon day again. Lance is right. Our wedding should be respectable."

Sadie turned Utopia so they were face-to-face. "Lance should be a little more understanding, what with you in the motherly way and all."

Utopia cringed.

"Honey, you did tell him about the baby, didn't you?" Pearl asked.

"Not exactly." Utopia bit her nail. "I want it to be a surprise."

"Surprise?" Jargus shouted, throwing his hands up in the air. "The man would have to be blind not to see the signs of you being pregnant."

Utopia's eyes watered, and for no reason she could rightly put her finger on, the flood gates opened.

Sadie patted Utopia's back and scowled at Jargus. "Now, look what you've done."

Lil escorted Jargus to the tent opening. "Don't fret. You go find Travin and send him to look for our poor groom. Lance is too crazy in love with the lass to even think about backing out over a silly little thing like singing. He'll show up, don't you worry."

Pearl escorted Utopia over to a seat in front of the mirrored dresser. "Now, now. Let me fix your hair up for you. Calm yourself down like a good little bride. We'll find Lance and everything will be fine. We got to get our little princess cheered up and prettied up for her wedding."

Utopia couldn't believe how quickly Saturday had come upon her. She looked in the mirror while Pearl put the finishing touches to her coiffure. Lance had avoided her all week. And that was probably for the best. It seemed all they did lately was argue and usually over something silly.

Nonetheless, Lance had been acting peculiar all week. He said he had work to do on his secret project. And darn if the man hadn't sworn everyone in camp to secrecy. No one would even give her a clue about this secret thing of his.

So she followed him every day her fathers and the girls weren't after her to do chores.

All week long Lance hauled things in a wagon up the hill to the area of the courtship log. Then he'd travel some distance farther by foot making it harder for her to stay out of sight. On Tuesday, Pa Henry caught her tailing Lance and dragged her back to camp.

Utopia glanced at the girls by way of the mirror. "Please won't one of you tell me what Lance has been up to?" The girls smiled at each other. "I can't stand not knowing this secret any longer. I'll die if you don't tell me."

"You deserve to stew a bit after what you've put that poor man through," Lil stated. "Baby or no baby, you pitched one too many fits about needing to be on a saloon stage singing."

"Our lips are sealed," Sadie replied.

All three women put their fingers to their lips and locked their rouged mouths shut.

Travin barged in the tent. "Buttercup, Lance sent me to fetch your dangly crystal lamp."

Utopia twisted on her keg seat. "What on earth does Lance need your lamp for?"

Pearl rotated Utopia back around to the mirror. "If you don't sit yourself still, young lady well, I ain't taking the blame for your hair looking like a bird's nest." Pearl added a few more pins. "There now. I'm done. Now let's get you in your dress."

Utopia got to her feet and went over to the cot where two dresses were displayed. She picked up her mother's ruby red. The satin gown was exquisitely trimmed with a large rose of black beads in the center of the bodice.

Lil's face frowned a bit. "I don't see why you won't wear the white dress we done bought you. You could always change into your mama's saloon dress after the ceremony."

"I don't want a plain white dress. I've always dreamed about wearing my mother's gown, and my marrying day is the only chance I have to do it. And I won't be talked out of it." Utopia's well of tears ran again, and no amount of wiping could stop the flow.

Pearl shook her blonde wigged head. "Umm, umm, umm, honey, you're as stubborn as your old coot of a father, Jargus." She picked up the ruby saloon gown and tossed it over the tearful bride's head. "Have it your way."

"My grandbaby better not be stubborn like you," Lil declared.

Sadie buttoned up the back of the dress. "It don't matter what color gown you're wearing, Sassie Lassie. You'll be the prettiest thing this side of the Mississippi. Turn around, let us get a gander at you."

Utopia slowly turned and held her arms out wide at her sides. She caught a glimpse of herself in the mirror. Her hands lightly rubbed the red silk of her gown and her fingers halted on the sparkly beads of the bodice. "How do I look?"

"You only need one more finishing touch," Sadie said, settling Hennessey's crown on Utopia's head. "There."

All three of the women's eyes watered. "Beautiful," they all murmured in unison.

Lil ran her forearm under her nose to catch the slip of a sniffle. "Enough sprucing, we need to get you to the whiskey barn. Folks are waiting on you."

The girls and bride left the tent. For the last day of September, Utopia was pleased the weather was bright and sunny. The temperature was a rare warm fall day of around seventy degrees. Not bad for Indian summer.

"You've got yourself a fine day for a wedding," Pearl acknowledged. "There's not a cloud in the sky."

When the girls got to the whiskey barn, they stopped on the porch of the newly renovated and improved saloon. Lil looked in the large window but was careful not to touch the red shutters just put up and painted this morning.

Sadie fluffed the ruffles on the bodice of the bride's gown. "Now, Sassie Lassie, you wait out here and don't come inside until you hear the music." She gave Utopia's cheek a light kiss. "This is your special day. Enjoy it."

The girls pushed through the swinging bi-fold doors that Fergus had constructed. The little change gave a true saloon feel to the old whiskey barn.

"Thank God they found him," Pearl yelled, spotting Lance at the end of the room.

Lil poked her red nails in her chignon. "Boy, I tell you. If I wasn't already smitten with Travin, I hate to tell ya what I'd like to do to that handsome Lance."

"Put your eyes back in your head," Sadie chided. She loudly clapped her hands. "Take your seats everyone. Let's get this wedding started." There were many former suitors in attendance. Sadie's announcement sent one and all scampering for their chairs.

Upon hearing the scraping sound of chairs scooting across the flooring, Utopia looked through the window. The changes inside were absolutely astounding.

Travin and John had constructed a two-foot high stage across the far end of the room. A real bar now existed along the left side. The same familiar round poker tables and chairs were available for the guests, all arranged so an aisle ran down the middle of the room, a lane wide enough for her to make her way to her groom.

Sadie took her place between Henry and Fergus at the table on the right side, closest to the stage. Jargus sat and stretched out his bad leg.

At a second table on the left, Pearl and Lil joined Travin and John. Both girls pulled handkerchiefs from their bodices, ready for what would be a tearful and happy moment.

Banniger Raspberry walked up the steps of the stage. He spaced his feet comfortably apart, rested his fiddle on his shoulder. He placed his chin on the curve of the instrument. His bow stroked the first notes of a soft, waltzing melody.

THE COURTSHIP OF UTOPIA MINOR 337

Utopia heard the music, but her feet wouldn't move toward the doorway. Her hands crushed the stems of the daisies and baby's breath bouquet the girls had made her. She fought back her emotions, and stemmed off, as best she could, the tears associated with her fear of the unknown. Her life on the mountain had been a simple until Lance came along.

Now nothing seemed simple.

She was having a hard time deciding on where she wanted to raise their baby. Lance said he'd live anywhere she wanted.

Her life had changed so much since the day he claimed her heart with that starter kiss.

Today would be the first of many happy days. But would it be the last of her life on this mountain? And she had plenty of terrifying worries about becoming a mother, not had no confidence whatsoever that she'd know how to care for her baby once it arrived.

Utopia pushed the saloon doors open, stepped in the saloon and paused. All eyes in the room were on her, but her gaze went directly to Lance. He stood at the end of the aisle, right in front of the stage waiting for her. And my, what a sight for her sore eyes he was.

His soft brown eyes gazed at her with that lusty look. He mouthed, "You're beautiful."

Her insides suddenly felt like she'd swallowed a swarm of butterflies. How could one man be so handsome? His fine tailored suit accentuated every manly part of him to perfection. His dark hair teased the collar of his white shirt.

He gave her that wonderful, dimpled smile of his, and she knew he'd forgiven her for her temper fit over singing a song. And with that forgiveness, she accepted the fact that he would be beside forever more. Beside her as they raised their child, helping her with whatever things she needed to know in order to take care of their baby.

In her heart of hearts, Utopia knew that wherever Lance wanted to go for a job, well she'd be right beside him for now, always and until they met their maker. Her only hope was that their love lingered on for a very long time.

Banniger's fiddle went into the second rendition of the bridal song before her feet somehow made a step or two.

"*Oh, no.*" Utopia covered her mouth. "I'm going to be sick."

Pearl, Lil and Sadie immediately left their chairs. Lance made a move toward his bride, and Sadie put a hand to his chest and stopped him. "You wait here, handsome. Your girl needs a minute to get her jitters out."

Utopia ran out the swinging doors with a hand over her mouth and a hand on her stomach.

CHAPTER THIRTY-THREE

"You may now kiss the bride." Solemn Reverend Pardee added one last word with a smirk, "Finally."

Lance wrapped his arms around his lovely bride and pulled her up close to him. Her green eyes sparkled with emerald clarity. Her face had a soft pink glow. Her dress was a sparkling, vibrant, ruby red. No dull white for his girl. Her gown matched everything he loved about Utopia. The woman before him never looked more beautiful than at this very moment.

He'd struggled all week with his past memories of Rachel, with the problem of letting Utopia have her one saloon girl day. They'd reached a compromise of wearing her mother's dress last night. But seeing how happy she was, he now had second thoughts about denying her the rest of her dream. The crowd gathered in this room weren't drunks wanting to bed her as a prostitute. They were Utopia's friends, some of them his friends, too. She was still his innocent sweet girl wishing and waiting for a chance to fulfill a childhood dream.

Lance waited all week without bedding her for this moment to finally call her his wife. And now that they were married his love-starved body craved their honeymoon. He wanted her to the point of insanity, but the cheering, clapping crowd meant he'd have to restrain himself several more hours.

"That's my girl," Pearl cheered, blowing her nose loudly into her handkerchief. She leaned toward John. "Weddings always get me weepy."

"Travin, open that bar. I need me a drink," Jargus ordered.

The newlyweds made the rounds of the room. Lance felt jealous when several of her past suitors thought they had every right to overdo their kiss of the bride.

Lance turned Utopia toward him. "Have I told you how beautiful you look?"

"I need to say I'm sorry," Utopia stated.

"No, you don't. I was wrong. I'm the one that's sorry." He took her hand and walked her toward the steps of the stage.

"What are you doing?"

"You're going to get up on that stage and give everyone a terrific saloon girl song."

"But, you said that you didn't want me to sing saloon stuff on our wedding day."

"I did say that. But I changed my mind. I hope you've practiced." He gave her cheek a light peck. "Now get up on that stage and show us what you got, missy."

Henry banged a hammer on the newly built bar, drawing the crowd's attention. "Everyone take your seats. It's time for my daughter's saloon girl performance."

Pearl straightened Utopia's crown. "Honey, don't forget to smile."

"And give a few winks to the fellas," Sadie reminded.

"I don't know if I can do this." Utopia held her hand over those swirling butterflies in her stomach.

"Honey, you ain't gonna be sick again are you?" Pearl asked.

Utopia shook her head. "No. I don't think I can remember the words."

Lil pushed her up the first couple steps. "It'll all come to ya once the music starts."

Now that her big moment was at hand, Utopia wasn't so sure she wanted it. What if the words to the song wouldn't come to her brain? What if her voice wouldn't work or she sang off key? What if the audience threw tomatoes at her? Lil had told her it happened to her once.

She looked out at her audience. Lance sat the first table with Jargus, Fergus and Henry. John, Pearl, Travin, Lil and Sadie sat at the next table over.

Utopia was mesmerized by her handsome husband, looking at her with adoring eyes, and gleaming with encouragement. He put two fingers to the corners of his mouth and gave a shrill whistle. He clapped his hands and started a chant, "Sing. Sing. We want you to sing."

The audience chanted, "Sing. Sing. We want you to sing."

"Are you ready?" Banniger asked.

Utopia nodded and took a deep breath.

Banniger raised his fiddle to his chin.

The crowd silenced, so quiet a person could hear the fizz on beer or the pop of a cork on a whiskey keg. The fiddle player struck the first cord.

"Buf–faaa–lo gaaaal–won't you come out to–" Utopia stopped singing. A couple extra notes were played before Banniger stopped his tune. "I was a bit off key. Would you mind starting over?"

The musician nodded, raised his fiddle and strummed the song a second time.

"Won't you come out to–" Utopia stopped again. Time after time she started the medley over, wanting to get the pitch and tempo just right. Now on her umpteenth restart, only the folks not half-asleep knew the exact count of her retries. Those still attentive in the audience probably had fingers, toes and all their hairs crossed, hoping she'd get through the song this time. She started again and got all the way to, *". . . and danced by the light of the mooonnn."* Utopia curtsied to let the crowd know she'd finally finished.

All the guests got to their feet, some shaking out the stiffness from such a long performance. Lance gave Utopia an enthusiastic handclapping. Others in the room joined in. She'd never felt so happy in her entire life, or so loved.

"If anyone of you asks her to sing another song I'll get my shotgun," Jargus warned.

Lance walked up on stage and took her by the hand. He wanted to get her to himself as soon as possible. "You were great, my sweet, but now it's time for us to go." He gently led her down the steps and over to her fathers and the girls. "Thank you all for a lovely wedding. My lovely bride and I are departing."

"Sonny-in-law, you take care with my girl, you hear? Don't let her go fallin' off the—"

Pearl elbowed Jargus in his ribs. "Hush, you dang fool. You want to spoil his surprise?"

Big John got to his feet. "Lance, I'd like you and Utopia to stay a minute. I've something I want to get off me chest. I'd like the two of ye to be witnesses."

"Certainly, John. What is it?"

John got down on his knee. "I need to speak what's in me heart. From the day I first laid me eyes on ye, I—" John took his woman's hand. "Will ye marry me, Pearl?"

"I wondered when you'd get around to asking."

John got to his feet. "Would that be a yes yer giving me?"

"Well, hell yes." Pearl gave her big Scotsman a kiss then straightened her fake red hair.

Lil gave Travin a punch on his shoulder. "Why can't you be romantic like that?"

"Well, I just might." Travin stood and took a small box from his pants pocket. He opened the lid and showed Lil the sparkly ring inside.

Lance smiled at Lil. "The man was a bucket of tears over regretting he'd not proposed to you. It was all Jargus and I could do to keep ourselves from drowning in a flood of his sorrow."

"I was upset," Travin agreed. He took Lil's left hand in his and slipped a ring on her finger. "Buttercup, I swore that if I ever got out of that mine I would ask you to marry me."

"You've been out of the mine two months," Lil chided. "What took you so long to ask?"

Travin scowled. "Can't you be agreeable for one minute? I'm proposing now. Is it a yes or a no?"

Lil put a hand to her hip. "You want to marry me? You're sure of that?"

"Well, yeah. Ain't that what I've been trying to say if you'd let me?" Travin pulled Lil to him. "What do you say, Buttercup? Will you tie the knot with me?"

"All right. I'll marry you." Lil planted red kisses all over Travin's face.

Now that everyone's proposing was over with, Lance wanted to sneak his lovely bride away. He leaned near Utopia's ear. "It's time for your surprise."

Her face broke into a happy smile and her eyes lit up. "Where is it? I want to see it."

"You'll have to come with me." He bid everyone good afternoon, took Utopia's hand and ushered her out of the saloon.

Outside it was late afternoon with just enough sun left to traverse the woods and trail, to get to the place where his bride's honeymoon awaited.

"Where are we going?"

"You'll soon see."

At last, they reached the place where they first shared apple butter sandwiches. Utopia stopped near the log.

"Don't stop here." Lance snatched her hand and kept walking. "We've got farther to go."

They continued up the gravely hill.

"Lance, you best tell me your secret before my curiosity kills me."

He laughed but said nothing.

"Fine," she huffed. "You won't talk then I won't either."

He laughed at all the contrived ploys she used to try and loosen his tongue. His mirth at her expense riled her enough to chuck a few good-sized rocks at him. Finally, they were close enough to hear the waterfall. His heart's tempo increased with the anticipation of how his bride would react. "We're here."

Lance led her to the large pine tree and tugged on the rope. Down came the familiar ladder. "Ladies first."

Utopia looked up to the platform above, then back to Lance. "I'm wearing a dress. The whole time I'm climbing the ladder, you'll be looking up my skirt."

Lance gave her a big dimpled grin. "I know."

"Okay," she grumbled and hitched up the front of her skirt. "I swear, Lancelot Jones, your hands grab me whilst I'm climbing, I'll knock you plumb off the ladder."

"Don't worry," he chuckled. "I wouldn't want to give my ornery father-in-law an excuse to make me into a whiskey sieve."

Utopia started to climb. Lance gave her a four rung lead then he climbed. His eyes watched her stocking-covered legs move from one rung to the next. He couldn't resist a touch of the nearest silky calf.

"Lance, dang-nabbit." She kicked at him with no intention of really connecting. "Wait until we get up this dang ladder. Now, I mean it. Keep your hands to yourself."

"Okay, okay. Just be careful, would you?"

She smiled, expecting that he'd probably have himself one or two more feels on the way up. "You want me being careful then you best keep your dang hands off my legs."

She reached the top and stepped onto the tree floor and gasped. "*Oh. My. Stars.* This is the grandest tree any girl could ever want to have one of them honeymoon things in."

Amidst the branches and needles of the tall pine, the last bit of sunrays passed through. In the center of the tree floor was a keg, with a square board on top, covered with a white lacy table cloth. The red crystal lamp sat in the center of the small table. Lance lit a match to the wick and turned the flame up just enough to set a soft glow about the treed canopy.

Utopia recognized the table's draped covering as big Pearl's lacy robe. A single red rose in a Mason jar sat beside the lamp on the keg table. A place setting for two rounded out the romantic promise of dinner to come. To the right, he'd made a pallet and in the near corner—if there was a corner in a tree—the folding screen from the girls' tent stood at an angle to the bed. "Why on earth did you bring that up here?" She pointed to the short divider.

"I have my reasons. I had to saw part of the screen off at the bottom to make it fit our space. Guess I'll have to buy the girls another one." Lance popped the cork on some champagne and poured two glasses. Setting the bottle down, he walked behind the screen, picked up a large rectangular box with a big red bow on it. He handed Utopia the present.

"What's this?"

"That's for me to know and you to find out. Go behind that screen and put the gift on."

"You're being so secretive. Is this my present or not? And why can't I open it here?"

"Yes. And no. When I get to see you in it, I believe the present will be more for me."

"Hmm." She suspiciously narrowed her eyes. "So far this gift you've given me has your name plastered all over it."

Lance smirked. "It does seem so, doesn't it?"

Utopia went behind the shortened screen, which stood only tall enough to cover her up to her chest. She opened the box. "What the heck? You expect me to wear this?" She came out from behind the screen holding up the scanty outfit.

"Oui, oui, mademoiselle, I wish to have my dinner served by a French maid." Lance waggled his eyebrows.

"There you go again. So far, everything you've planned seems to be about you tonight."

"Your supper awaits you, madam. Get changed so we can eat."

Several minutes passed. Utopia emerged wearing the very short, black French maid uniform, complete with garters holding up mid-thigh smoky black stockings. The tiny skirt flared over her hips, showing a white underskirt with lacy ruffled panties on her bottom. The push-up bodice topped off the erotic outfit.

Utopia adjusted the tight bodice of her enhanced bosom. "I hope you're pleased with yourself." This was the first time in her life she'd felt every bit like a hussy. And she knew he'd planned it that way.

His eyes lustily gazed on her plumped up bosom. "Hum, maybe we could wait to eat?"

"Hell, no. I'm near starved. You best feed this French maid of yours or she's leaving."

Lance pulled out one of the two chairs he'd carried over from the whiskey barn earlier in the day. "Well, I certainly don't want to run off the help."

She took her seat. "Where's this fabulous meal you've been promising me?"

"I'll get it." Lance went to the area cattycorner from the screen. A pulley hung on an upper branch with a rope hanging over the top. He pulled on the rope and the rusted pulley squeaked loudly until at last his pulls produced a basket. Lance grabbed the familiar wicker picnic basket off the hook and carried it over to the table.

"You seem to have thought of everything, wine and dinner and ..." Utopia's eyes darted to the pallet on the floor. "A bed. I'll wager you have more than eating on your mind."

"You'd have a winning wager," he retorted with a dimpled smile. Flashes of her first poker lesson came to mind. He'd forfeiting the entire game because of those luscious lips. A lesson

THE COURTSHIP OF UTOPIA MINOR 349

learned. Never bet against his charming wife. She'd get the pants right off you real quick.

"It sure smells good. What are we having?"

"Fergus delivered the food during our wedding toasts. I hope it's not too cold."

She sniffed the air. "I'm so hungry if there's a horse in that basket I could eat it."

Lance filled their plates with roast beef, mashed potatoes, gravy, green beans and fresh baked bread. They dined. For dessert, they enjoyed two pieces of Sadie's chocolate wedding cake.

Utopia sipped on a glass of the sparkly wine. Lance wiped his mouth with his napkin and tossed it on the table. He got to his feet. "Now my sweet French maid you must get to work."

"Work?" She huffed. "Doing what? Where are you going?"

Lance walked over to the pallet on the floor, pulled off his boots then turned back to her. "It's time for bed, and I need my pretty French maid to undress me."

Utopia gave a big grin and jumped up from her chair. "Now you're talking. I've missed our getting together something terrible." She yanked off Lance's jacket and undid the buttons of his white shirt and pulled the shirt open. She rubbed her hands over his chest. "I love how furry you are."

Lance quickly stopped her hands. He hadn't gone through all this preparation just to hurry. He wanted slow, exquisite ecstasy with his bride and that would take a great amount of control on his part. "Easy, my sweet, you'll ruin my fun."

She teasingly scowled. "This isn't all about you, I'll have you know." Two could play this game of his. She gave her lips a slow, teasing lick.

His gaze locked on her mouth. "I dare you to do that again."

Utopia gave him a sweet smile, and teased her tongue across her bottom lip.

Lance shook his head. "Okay. You asked for it." He tore the rest of his clothing off his body. Once naked, he dropped to the pallet and gave the bed a pat. "Come to me, my sweet."

Utopia slowly stretched out beside him. He gently pulled her to him, close enough she could gaze into his soft brown eyes. She focused on his lips. "Kiss me, my wonderful husband."

The minute his lips touched hers, she knew she'd just gone to heaven, in an earthly sort of way.

Lance looked into her eyes. He held her close and let the cool night breeze softly float across their bodies. "My sweet, you've made me so complete."

The crystals on the lamp gently tinkled when the wind blew, sending shimmering rainbow stars amongst the canopy of branches and needles.

"Complete? What do you mean?"

He rolled up on his side and supported his head. He brushed some of her flowing red hair behind her ear. "From the moment you entered my life, I've been a changed man."

This was the perfect time to tell him about their soon-to-be little bundle. "Umm . . . my life's changed quite a bit too. In fact–"

Lance gave her lips a peck. "Since our first kiss in this tree, you've possessed my heart, my very soul. Each day since—"

"That's nice but I have something to tell—"

"Can I finish, please?"

Utopia scowled and bit her tongue. "Sure, go ahead."

"Where was I? Oh yeah, I've want nothing more than to spend all my days in your arms. For the rest of my life, I'll repay my debt to you with total love and devotion."

A tear rolled down Utopia's cheek. The man was getting her all mushy and she didn't want to open the dam of tears. "I know you love me, if that's what you're saying."

He smirked. "I'm trying to tell you I will treasure you all the days of our lives, in sickness and in health until death do we have to part."

His hand swiped away a couple of her tears.

"I heard that in our vows. Now since you're talking about treasuring things, I have–"

He put his fingertips on her lips. "Shhh. I have one more surprise for you first."

Oh, boy. She loved presents. Maybe she could wait until after she opened his gift. "Another surprise? What is it?"

"I won't tell you until you close your eyes."

Utopia covered her eyes, but left a teensy space to see through her fingers.

"If you peek, I won't give it to you."

"All right." Her husband sure did know her well. She blew a dangly curl off her brow and closed up the gap in her fingers.

"You can open your eyes now."

Lance held his fist out and slowly unfurled his fingers. Utopia gasped and took the shiny nugget from his hand and pressed it to her bosom, holding it tight, cherishing this moment. "Where on earth did you find this?"

"There's plenty of time to explain later. Let's just say it's on loan from Jargus. Right now, I think it's time we get to making us a baby." Lance reached above his head and tugged on a rope. A bucket tipped, raining rose petals and confetti over their bed.

Utopia giggled. "Where'd you get all these flower petals?"

"I'll have you know I bought every long stem rose this side of the Rockies. Except for the one on our dinner table, I plucked every darn petal by hand. I even got a thorn in my finger."

"Poor baby, let me see." She put his wounded digit in her mouth and sucked. "Does that make it feel better?"

"No, but you've put my mind on other things." Lance kissed her luscious lips and lowered her to the pallet.

Before they got to the fun part of this honeymoon, Utopia needed to tell him about the baby. "Lance, I have to tell you something." He tried to kiss her again, and she turned her head. "Are you gonna listen to me or not?"

"Yes, my sweet," he half answered, diverting his nibbling to her neck.

"Darn it, Lance." She thrust her hand between his mouth and her neck. "Stop. Dang-nabbit. It's my turn to give you a surprise."

"All right." Lance rested his chin on her shoulder. "What is it you're so anxious to surprise me with?"

"We-l-l-l-l . . . " Utopia twirled her hair around her finger. "I reckon we don't have to make a baby if you don't want to."

Lance sat up some. "But I've planned this fancy honeymoon with the intention of doing my very best to pollinate you tonight."

Utopia moved him aside and sprang up, sitting on her knees. She splayed her arms wide open and couldn't hold her joy any longer. *"Surprise!"*

Lance looked totally baffled and lifted the covers looking for a gift. "What surprise?"

Utopia rubbed on her belly. "You're gonna be a daddy."

EPILOGUE

The early spring thaw and a sunny day had spurred a picnic. Utopia struggled to get up from the courtship log. Her eight month pregnant belly hindered her ability at packing up the basket. She hated to end the day but her back was killing her. "Can you come help me?"

Lance collected up the wash pans and fishing poles from their afternoon activities. He put two fingers to the corners of his mouth and gave a shrill whistle. "Come on, Shorty, we got to head home. Let's go help mommy with the packing."

Utopia watched her little redheaded girl with pink ribbons on the ends her braids go running up to her father.

"Daddy, daddy, look what I found."

Their little girl's miniature pink saloon dress fell just past her knees and rustled with the petticoats underneath. She had a hard time running in the muck boots on her small feet.

Utopia chuckled when Lance knelt down and examined the rock in their daughter's hand. His mouth dropped open. His hand slapped to his cheek in an act of surprise.

"Holy cow, you've found gold. Let's go show mommy."

"Crystal Lil Sadie Pearl Jones, don't you jump up on your da—" Before the last syllable could escape Utopia's mouth, Lance hoisted their rambunctious three-year-old, muddy boots and all, up on his shoulders.

"Mommy, look." Crystal showed the discovery held in her tiny fist.

Utopia mimicked Lance's surprised look. "Well, we'll just have to put this one with the others and soon you'll be a very rich little girl."

"Mommy?"

"What, pumpkin?"

"After I get rich, and I'm all grown up, do you know what I want to be?"

"No, what do you want to be?"

Crystal flipped her braid over her shoulder. "I want to be a princess like Aunt Pearl."

Utopia chuckled, but silently hoped that her daughter didn't follow in her footsteps of chasing after childhood dreams.

Lance gave Utopia a cross look. "There aren't any princesses in Scotland."

"Uncle John says there are princesses in Scotland," Crystal argued. "So I can, too, be a princess if I want to. *And I want to.*"

"I'll have a talk with your Aunt Pearl and Uncle John about telling you such tall tales." Lance smiled at Utopia. "We wouldn't want you to get your princess hopes up too high."

The three enjoyed their walk down the path back to their new-cabin. Only the camp's number of occupants had changed in the short couple years since she and Lance had married. The landscape remained the same, beautiful and unspoiled.

Lance had built them a larger house, so Sadie now lived in Utopia's former cabin. Henry and Fergus shared turns bunking with their favorite harlot. Lil was gone.

Cyrus would be done with his jail time in the spring, then Lil and Travin could stop running the Palace Oak saloon in Tin Cup and come back to the mountain. She and Travin finally got around to saying their vows on Christmas Day. Utopia planned to have a big welcome home party for them when they returned.

Thinking back on the past three years, Utopia kept her promise and thanked the Lord each night for first off bringing Lance to her door that wash day long ago. And even more, she counted her blessings that she'd been spared a miserable life with Frank.

Lance ran a huge story about Colorado finally becoming a state in his newspaper. She didn't rightly understand all the politicking stuff. She kind of got the gist of how the election turned out. With Frank dead and buried, that opponent person he'd been running against, he won the election in something called a landslide. Utopia feared her husband misprinted the information or fudged a bit. There couldn't have been a landslide. Not around here. It hadn't rained in this part of the country for over a month.

Lately, her spirits were kind of low. She couldn't help thinking on how her time was getting short with Pearl. Her big friend would be heading across an ocean called the Atlantic with the Scotsman. They planned to be married in his homeland. She'd miss Pearl so much. Who knew? Someday Lance, she and the kids might take one of them big steamships across that ocean to see Pearl and John.

The one thing that hadn't changed on the mountain was Jargus. Lance enjoyed teasing her father each and every day. In the evenings once she had Crystal bedded down, they'd entertain themselves with a friendly poker game. Lance would swear to her fathers that he'd never played very much cards before. Utopia didn't let on that Lance was honeyfuggling.

"I don't know. I think you got me beat this time, old man." Lance studied his cards.

"Who you calling old, sonny-in-law? So, I got you beat this time. You swear?"

She watched Lance put his arm behind his back and cross his fingers. "I swear."

Utopia smiled. No wonder she was so madly in love with her handsome husband.

They had so much in common.

THE END

HISTORICAL FACTS HINTED AT IN
"THE COURTSHIP OF UTOPIA MINER"

Historical authors do a ton of research for the time period that they choose to set their story in.

Hopefully, these details and facts of a particular era and lifestyle are sprinkled into stories in unobtrusive bits and pieces.

For this book here are a few tidbit facts you may or may not have known prior to reading:

There's actually a ghost town in Colorado called Tin Cup. The gold mining town was founded in 1859. It got its name from a prospector named Jim Taylor that carried his gold dust around in what else, a tin cup. For a time, the town called itself Virginia City, but was constantly confused with the more well-known Virginia Cities in Montana and Nevada. This cause the residents to revert to using its earlier name of Tin Cup. Only a few old buildings remain of this place that once had a thriving population of 1,495 in its hay day in 1880.

It was a dangerous town with a corrupt underworld element controlling the residents. Members of this underworld murdered many an honest sheriff if they dared to implement a rule of law. Town marshals, Harry Rivers and Andy Jameson, were shot to death trying to enforce the peace in this wild mining camp. Like many western towns, Tin Cup had a Boothill Cemetery.

My heroine, Utopia, uses some colorful western slang in several places in my story. Some of her comments are: "little end of the horn" a reference to getting the short end of the stick, to come out of a situation disadvantaged. Utopia gets insulted when she thinks Lance calls her a honeyfuggler, which of course insinuates she's a liar. Insulted, she fires back that she's mad enough to sockdologer him right in his smeller. In more citified terms, that means she'll punch him in the snout.

I shifted historical fact a bit with regards to the newspaper that Lance works for and wants to own. His articles were for a newspaper called the *Rocky Mountain Gazette*. The actual newspaper with this name, and in this time period, was located in Helena, Montana. It printed valuable news for lonely, homesick prospectors from 1866 to 1868. I liked the name of the newspaper but wanted my story to be set in a little known ghost town in Colorado.

The Colt Frontier Six-shooter became known as the "Peacemaker" and "the gun that won the West". It is a single-action revolver meaning it has a revolving cylinder that holds six cartridges. It was manufactured by Colt's Fire Arms Manufacturing Company in Hartford, Connecticut in 1873. At the time it sold for $17.00. Many lawmen and outlaws preferred this weapon. During the year 1875, the setting of my story, this "Model P" would have used a .44-.40 Winchester caliber cartridge. The ability to use a bullet that could service this six-shooter and also be used in a Winchester rifle made this weapon very convenient and cost effective.

My hero, Lance, uses a Colt Peacemaker to kill the villain and save Utopia.

ABOUT THE AUTHOR

Hello Readers,

I'm Linda Gilman, a historical western romance author. My zodiac sign is Gemini which means I'm always busy doing something. A relaxing day for me isn't sitting in front of the TV eating myself into the next size in jeans. I have a husband, three grown sons, two daughter-in-laws and *four 'n a half grandchildren*. The other half's due in the spring.

I live with a crazy Golden Doodle named, Dory. She's an hour-long people greeter, that's a warning for those that come to visit my home.

My hobby is barns. I'm crazy about barns. When I want a break from writing, I like to go on what I call "Barn Storming" trips. My husband chauffer's me around the countryside while I skillfully shoot pictures of barns from the car going about 60 or 70 miles per hour. Needless to say, some of my photographs are blurry. Occasionally, he'll pull over so I can get a few clear shots.

I couldn't be a western writer if I didn't drool over men wearing cowboy hats, with no shirts on and great muscles *(That's really why I like to write westerns)*.

Laughter is the potion that heals misery, and l love 'Wild West' quotes. They are witty and funny with more than a ring of truth to them.

Such as:
- Life is short and full of blisters.
- A lasso is not a dating tool.
- Never let your yearnin's' get ahead of your earnin's.
- It don't take a very big person to carry a grudge.

Happy Read to you, and many, many laughs.

If you are interested in receiving emails when I have new book releases, please sign up for my email distribution list by visiting my website and clicking the "contact" tab: www.lindagilman.com. Be sure to join my online Facebook community where you will find contests, quizzes and special sneak peeks of new books.

Find me Online: www.lindagilman.com
and on
www.facebook.com/lindagilman.com

Made in the USA
San Bernardino, CA
08 November 2015